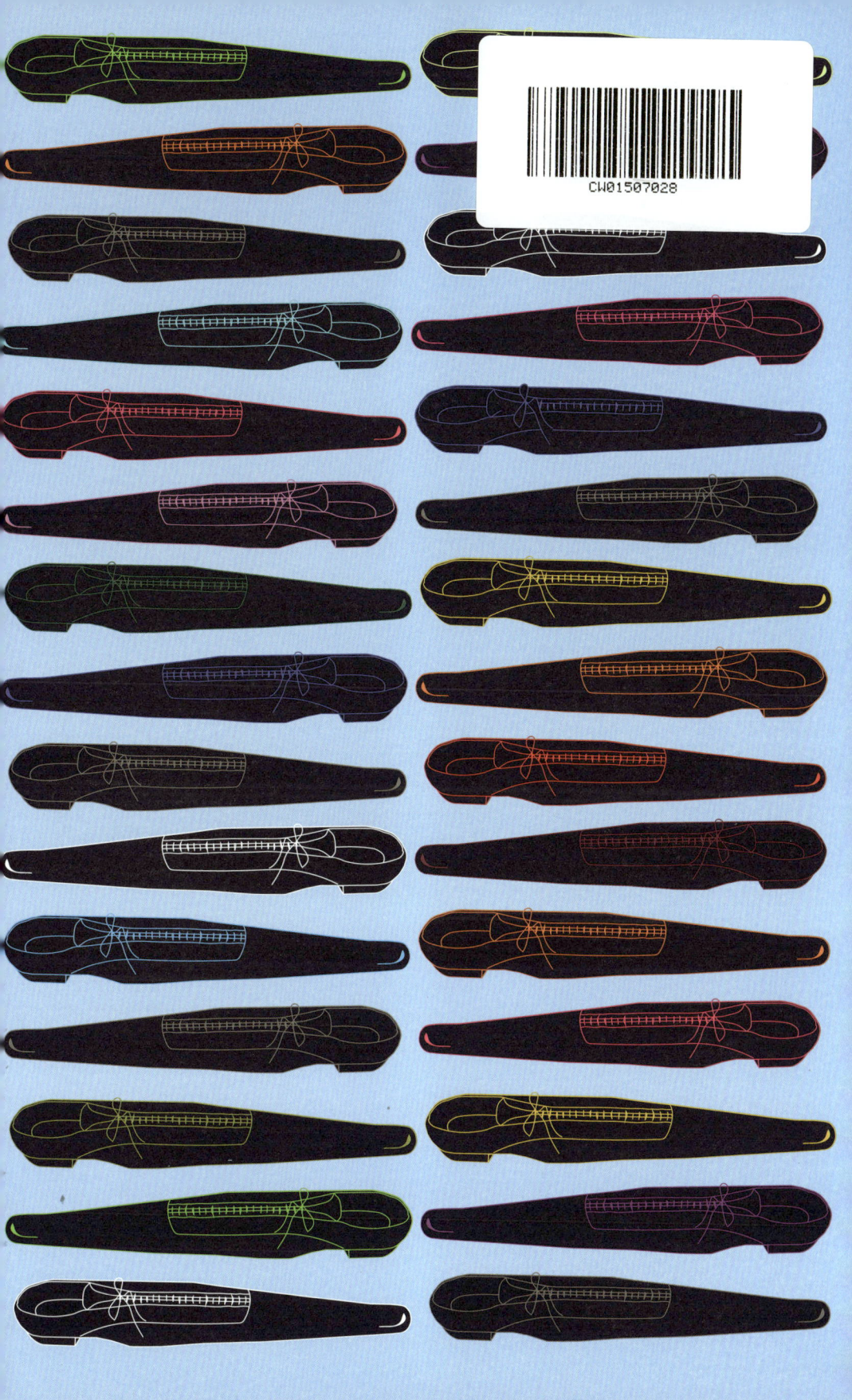

BOB MORTIMER

THE LONG SHOE

GALLERY BOOKS UK

London · New York · Amsterdam/Antwerp · Sydney/Melbourne · Toronto · New Delhi

First published in Great Britain by Gallery Books,
an imprint of Simon & Schuster UK Ltd, 2025

1 3 5 7 9 10 8 6 4 2

Simon & Schuster UK Ltd
1st Floor
222 Gray's Inn Road
London WC1X 8HB

www.simonandschuster.co.uk
www.simonandschuster.com.au
www.simonandschuster.co.in

Simon & Schuster Australia, Sydney
Simon & Schuster India, New Delhi

The authorised representative in the EEA is Simon & Schuster Netherlands BV,
Herculesplein 96, 3584 AA Utrecht, Netherlands. info@simonandschuster.nl

A CIP catalogue record for this book is available from the British Library

Hardback ISBN: 978-1-3985-4804-6
Trade Paperback ISBN: 978-1-3985-4805-3
eBook ISBN: 978-1-3985-4806-0

Typeset in Bembo Std by Palimpsest Book Production Ltd, Falkirk, Stirlingshire

Printed and Bound in the UK using 100% Renewable Electricity
at CPI Group (UK) Ltd

MIX
Paper | Supporting
responsible forestry
FSC
www.fsc.org
FSC® C013604

For Harry, Tom and my hairdresser Goodmonson

1

EGG DAY

The moment I woke up, it hit me.

I really fancied a soft-boiled egg.

I put on a T-shirt and my cheap, loose-fitting supermarket jeans, walked through to the kitchen and opened the box of eggs sitting beside Harriet's fancy American toaster.

It was empty. I was eggless.

It wasn't the end of the world, but an egg craving only comes along once in a while and it's quite a powerful pull. I paused and stared inside the empty egg box. It was very and brazenly empty. I could have sworn there was one, perhaps even two eggs in there just yesterday.

Harriet doesn't eat eggs, so she couldn't be to blame. My cat Goodmonson had never shown any interest in eggs, so he was out of the picture, too. I thought maybe I'd cooked a forgotten omelette, as they can be very fleeting in the memory – like weeds are once they've been placed in the wheel-barrow. I doubted it though, as I always use three eggs for an omelette and there is no way I'd had as many as three eggs left. I resigned myself to an egg-free breakfast, took a slice of white bread from the bread bin and popped it in the toaster. I made a mental note to buy some eggs that afternoon, although, chances are, the egg craving would be gone by then.

My name is Matt Giles. I don't have any quirks in my hairstyle or clothing and the songs I sing would all work well in a lift or a dentist's surgery. Don't bother me and I won't bother you, that's my motto. I'm thirty-eight years old and three months unemployed after losing my job as a sales executive at a large retail bathroom company. I was told it was due to cutbacks and restructuring but it may have had more to do with my falling sales record. I had lost my passion for sanitaryware and, to be honest, was happy to take six months' salary by way of severance. I missed my work colleagues for a week or two but soon settled into my new life. At the end of the day I'm very self-contained, and happy with that approach. I'm enjoying these lazy, ordinary days without worries or commitments and with nobody to please except my partner, Harriet.

I met Harriet three years ago at a house party hosted by an acquaintance of mine. I had helped with the refurbishment of his bathroom a year or so earlier, and he had insisted on keeping in touch. He was a good contact work-wise, so I had felt obliged to put in a brief appearance. It was a warm evening and I was stood outside in the back garden admiring a swathe of purple alliums in full bloom, their big spherical heads balancing miraculously on long, thin, overburdened stems.

Harriet appeared by my side.

'My favourite plant, no doubt about it,' I offered, barely turning my gaze towards her.

'Bit corny if you ask me. Bit like those plastic windmills parents stick in the ground when their kids have got bored with them.'

At this, I turned to face the allium hater. She was petite and slightly pissed, with a bottle of wine held precariously by two fingers around its neck. She wore her bleached blonde hair in what I believe is called a pixie cut, a hairstyle that suited her thin face. Her large brown eyes were playful and in a word kind. She was dressed in baggy jeans and her T-shirt was emblazoned with the words: 'I BOUGHT THIS T-SHIRT'.

'Fair point,' I replied, 'but I like to think of them as big purple lollipops, and that's a striking look in an outdoor environment.'

'Who are you? Willy fucking Wonka?'

I liked her very much. Straight away. No hesitation. Fast forward three years and she is the rock in my life that makes it easy to enjoy these ordinary days of nothing to do until she returns home.

My phone rang on the kitchen table and I took a quick glance at the screen. I didn't recognize the number so ignored it and let it go to voicemail. I had briefly hoped it was Harriet phoning to check in on me, as I could have asked her about the eggs. She had left for work well before I'd even got out of bed and hadn't left the usual cup of tea for me on the bedside table. I assumed she must have been running late for her train.

Harriet works for the Crown Prosecution Service in London

and takes the 7:39 from Hither Green station every morning. She arrives home around 6:35 p.m., unless she telephones to say she'll be late. That's happened quite a few times recently, as she's currently working on a very big case – a fraud and money-laundering prosecution that will be 'career-defining', she keeps telling me.

As far as Harriet is concerned, I spend my days looking for a new job and a new flat for us to live in (our tenancy expires in six weeks), but the truth is I have made very little progress on either of these fronts. I must get my arse into gear.

We had a brief chat about it the other evening. She was sat on the sofa engrossed in her laptop, her forehead wearing a deep frown of concentration.

'Fancy popping down the pub later?' I asked.

'I can't,' she replied, without looking up from the screen.

'You should take a break. It's no life working every minute of the day. We've hardly seen each other these last weeks.'

'This case *is* my life at the moment. You go to the pub if you must.'

'I thought *I* was your life,' I said, hoping to ease her away from her work.

She looked up towards me, the frown still etched on her face.

'No, you're the life that supports *this* life,' she said, pointing at her laptop screen.

'And which of those lives is most important to you?' I asked.

'Don't ask me that,' she replied. 'It's not fair. Let's just say they are symbiotic.'

'Makes me sound like a growth.'

'It does, doesn't it?'

'You ever going to tell me what this big case you're neglecting me for is about?' I asked.

'I've told you a million times, I'm not allowed to discuss my work with anyone outside the office – not even you. It's a huge fraud case and it's been a nightmare. Let's just leave it at that.'

'I won't tell anyone.'

'I know you would never intend to, but what if you accidentally let something slip to the wrong person? I could lose my job, which has actually happened to two people in the office. It's not worth it.'

'Official Secrets Act, is it?'

'Yeah, something like that.'

'Does it involve a footballer? Or one of the cast of *The Fast and The Furious: Tokyo Drift*?'

'No. Shut up, Matt.'

She returned to her work, but the frown had gone.

The toaster ejected my slice of toast. I left it where it was, with its head poking out of the toasting slit for a few minutes to let it cool and increase its crispness. (I don't like the butter to melt into the surface of the toast as I find it slightens the crunch.) I buttered the toast and took my first bite. It needed egg – or rather I did. The craving was still strong. I decided I would set off for the park and maybe buy a box of eggs on the way home.

We rent a furnished two-up, two-down terraced house in

Hither Green, south London. It has a bright red front door, a small front garden with a low wall and a little wrought-iron gate leading to a path to the front-door steps. The door is the only one on the street painted bright Post Office red. Most mornings I go for a walk in my local park, which is a peaceful, manicured pleasantness with a large ornamental lake, café and acres of landscaped lawns and meadows. I finish my walks at the café, where I treat myself to a coffee and sometimes a cake before returning home. In the afternoon, I might read a book, go to the cinema, or simply sit in front of the TV. If I have a nap, I make sure I set my alarm for 5 p.m. so that I can clean and tidy the house before Harriet gets home from work.

I chucked what remained of the toast in the bin, checked the egg box was still empty, put on my green puffa jacket, and headed outside. It was a beautiful day: sunny and cloudless, but bitterly cold. As I entered the park through its wrought-iron gates, a jogger overtook me and disappeared into the distance.

It reminded me that a man of my age really should be committed to some sort of proper exercise regime. I hate the occasional guilt I feel at the absence of such a thing. My one problem, apart from the lack of motivation, is that I don't have the self-confidence to display my flouncy running technique in public spaces. My backside is quite high and bulky and my legs splay outwards from below the knee. I tend to run with my head stooped towards the floor and my hands in my jeans pockets to stop them falling down. Imagine a six-foot duck running towards you at full quack and that's something akin to my technique.

I do occasionally break into a short run every hundred metres or so, trying to look like a man in a hurry rather than a man on the jog, though if I see someone approaching me up ahead, I slow down immediately. It's usually a very stop-start process, as there are always lots of dog walkers and mothers with baby strollers smothering the park. On blustery days, my baggy morning jeans also cause severe wind flap around my legs, only adding to my lack of jog confidence.

Having said that, I wouldn't be seen dead in public, let alone a park café, wearing running shorts or sweat-laden sports gear. The main reason I go to the park is for my coffee and cake, and it's a rule of blood for me that men in Lycra shorts should never, ever be in the vicinity of food or its preparation.

I took a seat at one of the café tables on the outdoor decking overlooking the lake. A few brave souls had hired rowing boats, and dotted along the lakeside path were mums and toddlers throwing bread for the ducks. It's a good job ducks can't buy their own bread, or else I reckon a lot of these parent–child trips would lose their focus. I always enjoy it when a toddler eats the bread for themselves, or shouts at a particular duck for being too greedy. Better still is their confusion when they throw a chunk and it falls behind them into the hood of their little jackets. They must think they have powers their parents can only dream of.

After a few peaceful moments watching the boats and sucking the froth off the top of my cappuccino, my next-door neighbour but one, Carol Thompson, joined me at the table.

We are often at the café at the same time and I enjoy

having a chat with her. It's not a definite arrangement, but certainly an unspoken one. Carol's ten years older than me, posh and divorced with two children. Both her kids have left home to study something or other at university, so she has a lot of time on her hands and a lot of chat to deliver. I liked her from the very first day we moved into what turned out to be *her* street.

'Morning, Matthew darling. Nice-looking bit of cake. Date and walnut? Am I right?' she asked.

'Yeah, would you like a piece?' I replied, knowing full well what the answer will be.

'I really shouldn't but then again I don't mind if I do.'

I broke off a little chunk of cake and handed it to her on a folded serviette. She put the whole piece straight into her mouth and began to chomp down on it as she gazed over towards the lake.

Carol has a pleasing profile, neat, with high cheekbones and no hint of a double chin. Today, her auburn hair was tied tightly back from her forehead into a short ponytail and she was wearing even more makeup than she usually did for her morning jog. She looked youthful in her running pants and fluorescent orange zipped running top. She is fierce but lovely, and although she doesn't listen to your every word, she always catches enough to make the conversation flow. I'm not surprised her marriage failed but suspect that, from time to time, her ex-husband misses her terribly.

She finished chewing and then removed a hard morsel of walnut from her mouth before flicking it onto the decking.

'Nice bit of cake, that. Why are you not eating your piece?' she asked.

'I'm beginning to think it was a mistake.'

'Partaking of the cake is never a mistake, darling.'

'I know, but you see, when I woke up this morning I really fancied a couple of soft-boiled eggs, and I reckon that if I have that cake, I'll lose the yearning, and that would disappoint me.'

'Well, give it to me, then. Problem solved.'

'Maybe I will because, the truth is, an egg craving doesn't come along that often for me, and if I can sustain it, I'll get a massive egg hit when I eventually pop that first piece of soft-boiler down my neck. I think they call it delayed gratification.'

'Why didn't you have eggs for breakfast and put an end to it then?'

'Because I don't have any eggs in the house.'

'Oh, darling, you poor thing. An eggless house is a fool's palace.'

I laughed. She was a funny lady.

At that moment a waitress passed by carrying a tray of soiled cups and plates. She'd been working at the café for a month or so and I would often catch her staring at the punters with a sort of curious indifference. She had a slightly miserable, 'put-upon' look about her face, suggesting she didn't really want to be there.

Carol intercepted her.

'Excuse me, sweetheart, have you got any eggs back there in your kitchen that I could buy?' she asked.

The waitress's face turned instantly defensive. 'What do you mean?'

'You know,' Carol continued, 'eggs – the things hens lay. They're egg-shaped and often brown-coloured, tend to come in boxes of six. Humpty Dumpty was one before he turned to booze.'

'Yeah, I know what an egg is, but this isn't a shop, it's a café.'

'Oh, but sweetheart, look here at the menu. It says the cakes and sandwiches are all baked on the premises, so surely there must be some eggs in the vicinity.'

'We have some hard-boiled eggs for the salads and the sandwiches.'

'No, I just want an uncooked egg in the same condition it was when the hen laid it.'

'I'll go and ask Dennis.'

'Who is Dennis?' said Carol.

'You would have to ask him that,' said the waitress, throwing Carol an insincere smile before sallying off back into the café.

I would say that the encounter had been a score draw.

'If she has no joy with Dennis, whatever he is, you can pop into my place on your way back and take a couple of eggs.'

'Thanks. You might as well finish the cake then. I've made my decision: I'm going to hold out for the eggs.'

'Such a brave boy. Now, tell me, what's happening with your flat search?' she asked as she grabbed the remaining cake from my plate like a heron plucking a minnow from a pool. 'Have you managed to get your act together, darling?'

'Haven't done any viewings for a couple of weeks. I can't find anything that we can afford at the moment. I think Harriet is getting pissed off with me but we need to find out what salary I'll be earning in my next job before we can commit to somewhere.'

'What about that place I recommended to you, with the hot floorboards and the concierge?'

'Oh, Satsuma Heights, next to London Bridge?'

'Yes, that's the one.'

'They wanted two thousand pounds a month rent. We offered them fifteen hundred and they told us to fuck off.'

'Good for them. I would have done the same. How *is* Harriet, by the way? I was at my window seat this morning and I didn't see her pass by on her way to the station.'

'She's fine, I think. Working hard, bringing home the bacon.'

'Maybe she took a different route.'

'Maybe you turned your back when she passed your check-point.'

'Hmm, I doubt it. I noticed your shitty car was gone, too. Maybe she's given up on the trains.'

'I don't know anything about that.'

'You should pay more attention to her – if you think she's worth it, that is. Oh, darling, this cake really is shit hot. It looked a bit dreary on the plate – you know, like a dead mouse or a brown dustbin – but it's magnificent.'

'Shouldn't judge a book by its cover. I mean, you present as pleasant and approachable, but you're actually a cold hard assassin.'

'Thank you for noticing, darling.'

The waitress returned to our table.

'Dennis says he doesn't have any raw eggs and even if he did, he's not allowed to sell them to the public.'

She remained standing next to us, clearly expecting Carol to respond to her announcement.

Carol, in return, just stared at her blankly for five or six seconds and then broke into a forced smile.

'Tell Dennis I'm sure he will find true love one day and a big thank you to you for all your efforts.'

The waitress shrugged her shoulders. 'Anything else you want?'

'Like what?' asked Carol.

'I dunno.'

'Did you have something in mind?'

'No, not really.'

'Fascinating,' said Carol with a shake of her head. 'Come on, darling, let's go and get those eggs.'

I smiled apologetically towards the waitress as we left the table. She stared back at me as if I was a dog dirt on a luggage carousel.

When we arrived at Carol's house, she led me straight through to her kitchen and proudly opened a full half-dozen box of eggs in front of my face.

'Look at those beauties!' she exclaimed. 'Do you want me to put them on to boil now or later?'

'What do you mean? I just want a couple of eggs to take home – I don't need you to cook them for me. But, hey, thanks for the offer.'

'I just thought that maybe we could go upstairs and then we could have the eggs once we'd worked up an appetite.'

'Are you serious?'

'Yes, of course I am, but if you haven't got the balls then that's your problem.'

'Where's this come from?'

'Boredom, mainly. So, shall we go upstairs or not?'

'I'm going to say not. I don't think it's a good idea.'

'Well, out you get then. And I've changed my mind about the eggs.'

'Oh come on, Carol, I sacrificed good cake for those eggs.'

'No, fuck off,' she said, as she gestured for me to scarper with her elegant, moisturized right arm.

I left her house, still eggless. I think she was joking about going upstairs, or maybe it was just one of her power plays that she likes to unfurl every now and then. A tiny part of me hoped it wasn't a joke – I don't know, an ego thing or some such indulgence.

With thoughts of egg still lingering in the back of my mind, I watched TV until 4 p.m., leaving me a couple of hours to shower and clean and tidy the place. I find housework a useful distraction from focusing on my lazy man guilt and an easy way to show Harriet that I'm actually a worthwhile addition to the household. She hates ironing, but I find it very calming, especially if I listen to my old records while flattening the cloth. A nice plump pile of ironed clothes on the table never fails to put a smile on her face when she walks in the door (and I always leave it on the table until she comes home so that she can't fail to see my good work).

Just as I was finishing the last piece of ironing – a pair of underpants (yes, I do that) – I remembered I hadn't checked to see if there was any post today. We have a little cage on the inside of the letterbox that the mail falls into, which Harriet insisted I install after the cat pissed on a flyer from a dog charity that had been lying innocently on the doormat. I grabbed the contents and settled down at the kitchen table to inspect them. All of the letters were addressed to Harriet, so I popped them on top of the ironing pile (another chance for Harriet to appreciate my good work). The only other item was an A4 piece of white paper neatly folded in two that had evidently been placed through the letterbox by hand, rather than delivered by the postman. I unfolded the sheet. There were four sentences typed dead centre of the page.

> I won't be back tonight. Not sure when I will
> be. Please don't try and get in touch. Take
> care of Sergeant Walnuts . . . Harriet x

A wave of dread rushed through my stomach and my mouth filled with saliva. I read the note again and my mind was overcome with panic at the likelihood of my life being turned upside down and fear at the prospect of losing the first person I had ever loved.

I read the note again. Was it Harriet's attempt at a joke? Was it a hoax placed in the letterbox by a cruel neighbour? No, it must have been written by Harriet. It was a habit of hers to always type out messages or notes that she wanted to be treated with great importance. What's more, I don't think any other living person knew that her nickname for the cat was Sergeant Walnuts. I remembered what Carol had said about Harriet taking the car that morning. I rushed out onto the street to check and, sure enough, the car was nowhere to be seen.

I wanted to phone her immediately. I needed to hear her voice. The note told me not to get in touch, but how could she expect me to do that? Surely I deserved an explanation or some details of her intentions? At the very least, I needed to know where she was. I had to be able to picture her – be it sat at her work desk, travelling on the train, drinking in a pub or booking into a hotel. Maybe she was at her mum's or her brother's? Either way, I wanted an answer. Who was she with? Who did she *intend* to be with? Had she found someone else? How could I possibly live without her by my side? Why do I only feel any real emotions when things turn towards the shit?

2

CROISSANTS

Ignoring her request not to get in touch, I rang the main number for Harriet's office. I would ask to be put through to her extension number and then, if she answered, I could put the phone down without her knowing that it was me calling.

When the main reception put me through to her desk, it rang exactly ten times before switching to answerphone. I ended the call. Then I remembered I had the mobile number of a colleague of Harriet's called Will who worked in the same section of the office as her. I dialled his number.

'Hello, Will speaking,' he answered.

'Oh, hi, Will, this is Matt, Harriet's boyfriend. I don't seem to be able to get hold of her. Just wondered if I could leave her a message?'

'Is she not at home with you?'

'No, well, actually, I can't be sure, because I'm not at home at the moment,' I lied, embarrassed at being out of the loop. 'She's not there in the office, then?'

'No, she sent us a message saying she wouldn't be in for a

few days. We just assumed she wasn't feeling well. She's been working herself into the ground recently.'

'Yeah, she is a bit under the weather . . .' – this could be true? – 'I hadn't realized she didn't go into work. She's probably just asleep in bed. My mistake. Don't worry about it. Thanks a lot, Will. Cheerio.'

That phone call sent my mind into a spiral again. I re-read the letter and focused on the 'X' she had handwritten after her name. It was something she always did, but nevertheless it gave me a glimmer of hope.

I wondered what it was about today that had triggered her exit. The last conversation we'd had before going to bed the previous night hadn't felt particularly ominous. She was sat on the sofa reading through a work file on her laptop, her forehead taut with concentration, and I was sat in the easy chair opposite her, watching TV. I was rubbing my fingernails together absentmindedly to the tune of 'Take On Me' by A-ha.

'Can you stop with the finger noise please?' she said.

'Sorry,' I replied cheerfully.

'It's just I'm trying to concentrate here.'

'Yeah, I know, won't happen again.'

'It will.'

There was an audible silence that I felt the need to fill.

'Could you tell what tune it was I was doing?'

'Shut up, Matt, I need to concentrate.'

She sounded pissed off. I couldn't cope with the silence. I needed to check the extent of her anger.

'It was "Take On Me",' I blurted. 'By A-ha. The Norwegian lads.'

'I didn't realize that song was so tuneless and irritating,' she replied, then raised her hand above the keyboard and executed a flouncy, dramatic press of the 'send' button. 'Thank fuck for that. Case prepared, reviewed and approved. Nothing more I can do.'

She tossed the laptop onto the sofa, let out a huge sigh of relief, and leant back into the sofa cushions.

'Well done, mate,' I said, offering her a little round of applause. I got up from my chair, walked over to her and gave her a hug and a kiss on the top of her head. I was proud of her. This case had obviously been a bastard.

'Hey, I bought some fancy croissants from the deli today. Do you want one by way of a celebration?' I asked.

Harriet took off her spectacles. This usually meant she had something with a slight barb to announce.

'Why would you do that? You know I don't like them.'

'Really? I thought you liked the occasional croissant.'

'You must be thinking of your ex.'

'Maybe,' I replied.

'Definitely,' she responded with her middle finger raised towards me.

'Why don't you like them? I thought everyone loved a croissant?'

'The croissant is a calorific shit storm. You'd be better off having a bacon sandwich for breakfast than a croissant – nice bit of protein, and a hell of a lot more flavour for the same three hundred and fifty calories.'

'I didn't know you knew so much about breakfast calories,' I said.

'Yeah, well, I do. How do you think I look so good?' replied Harriet.

'I'll give them to Carol, then. She loves croissants. Stops them going to waste.'

At that, she picked up her laptop and got up off the sofa.

'I'm off to bed. I'm shattered. Don't forget to put the cat out and don't make any noise when you come up.'

So, that was it: our last conversation. A little chat about croissants. She didn't say goodnight, but that wasn't unusual. When I eventually joined her upstairs, she was fast asleep. It had just felt like a normal evening. Harriet seemed her normal self. I was happy, and even Goodmonson had a spring in his step when I booted him out for the night.

I decided to take a punt and make passive contact with Harriet by texting an emoji of a waving hand. I regretted it instantly. My thoughts shifted to the possible (mostly negative) consequences of sending the emoji when she had instructed me not to get in touch with her. Goodmonson joined me on the sofa.

'Don't think Mum will be home this evening,' I informed him, keeping my voice cheery so as not to indicate anything untoward might be going on.

'So can I stay inside tonight?' he asked, his face full of pleading.

'Yeah, I suppose. You can sleep upstairs with me, keep me company.'

'So it's just you and me again, like old times,' he said as he laid on his back and thrust his two back paws up towards the ceiling.

Harriet wasn't a big lover of cats, but Monson came with me as part of the deal. We had been together for nearly ten years and he had seen a couple of girlfriends come and go before Harriet arrived on the scene. The two of them had grown to accept each other and become friends, which had pleased me greatly. It even crossed my mind that Harriet would probably be missing Monson more than me.

I went into the kitchen and poured some biscuits into Monson's dish. He sniffed the contents and turned his head to me.

'Fucking dry shit. No deal – you're on your own tonight.'

He shook his paw at the food, jumped up onto the sofa and dug himself a nook in the cushions. I checked my phone (for the hundredth time since finding the note) and there was a text from Harriet: a waving hand emoji.

A small pulse of reassurance swept through my body, and when I got to bed, sleep came sooner than I could have dared anticipate.

That night, I had a dream I owned the world's biggest oar and was being interviewed by a local news channel.

'It's not as big as I thought it would be,' said the presenter.

3

VANILLA AND POTATO

When I woke up the following morning, I checked my phone for any further messages from Harriet. Nothing.

I needed to talk to someone about the situation, and Carol seemed the best option. Truth is, she was the *only* option. Hopefully I would bump into her at the café in the park.

When I grabbed my puffa jacket from its peg, I noticed what looked like a coffee stain on the front. It was the classic coffee-stain shape – thinner at the top, then a bulbous flourish below. It reminded me of the outline of a country but I couldn't think which one. I showed it to Goodmonson.

'Do you know what country this coffee stain resembles?' I asked him.

He looked up at me, then blinked and yawned. 'Norway.'

'That's it! Norway! Thanks, Monson, that would have bugged me.'

'I've been thinking,' he said. 'Could I have a motorcycle?'

'No chance,' I replied.

'Well, could I go to a motorcycle event, then?'

'I'll think about it,' I said as I left the house.

'No, you won't! I know you!' he shouted after me.

I half jogged, half walked to the café and took up my usual seat on the outdoor decking. I nearly bought a croissant to accompany my coffee but at the last minute decided to switch to a jam doughnut.

Just along from me, tucked around the corner, I could see the waitress from yesterday puffing away on her vape. She was around my height (five foot seven and a half) and I guessed around twenty-two years old. She was wearing a black roll-neck sweater with a black skirt and black boots. Her jet-black, shoulder-length hair was worn beneath a baseball cap. Her skin was pale and her face was round and rural. I noticed a large tattoo on the calf of her right leg. It was a circular, solid block of ink, about the size of a saucer, and its darker and lighter patches gave the initial impression of a moonscape.

I felt a bit rotten about how curt Carol had been with her during the egg conversation yesterday, so took the few steps over to her to say hello and thank her for her help.

'Hi there. What flavour is your vape? It smells unusual,' I asked.

'Oh, I suppose you're going to complain about me using it out here, are you?'

'No, not at all. To be honest, I'm a big fan of nicotine, but I packed in smoking to try and reinstate some crispness into my brain.'

I took a deliberate whiff of the vape trail as she exhaled another cloud of gas. 'Is it vanilla and potato?'

'No, it's raspberry and coconut,' she replied, looking at me as

22

if I were an advert for a donkey sanctuary – i.e. with part pity, part disgust.

'Of course it is! Very nice combo.'

I regretted the use of 'combo' immediately and glanced down to the floor as if I had been emotionally affected by the plight of the donkeys.

'Why are you pretending to be interested in my vape?' she asked. 'Is there something you want?'

'Yes, I suppose there is. I just wanted to apologize for my friend yesterday. She came over a bit aggressive and I don't think that was her intention. I don't think she realizes how rude she can sound.'

'The woman who wanted the eggs?'

'Yeah, that's her.'

'So you want to distance yourself from her, do you? Is that your game?'

'No, I just didn't want you to think it was anything personal. It's just the way she is.'

'So, you're the good guy, are you? Listen, she didn't bother me at all. We get loads of her type in here.'

'Must bother you a bit.'

'Maybe it does, but not enough to get me down.'

'Well, thanks for trying to help out with the eggs. Much appreciated.'

'If you think it must bother me, then why doesn't it bother you? I bet she treats you just the same, and she's your friend, isn't she?'

'Yeah, she is. I just take it with a pinch of salt – you know, water off a duck's back.'

'Seems that we are quite similar, then. People like her search us out. You should be more choosy. She's not your girlfriend, is she?'

That question took me by surprise. Why would anyone think that Carol and I were romantically involved? I just couldn't see how that mistake would arise.

'No, not at all. Just friends,' I replied.

'But would you like to be?' she asked with a playful smile on her face.

'I've never even given it a second's thought.'

She took a big old suck on her vape and blew the gas in the direction of the lake. She was still smiling.

'I like your puffa jacket, by the way,' she said as she turned back towards me.

'Thank you,' I replied. 'You don't have to be cold to be cool.'

She made her way past me and back into the café. I got another glimpse of the tattoo on her calf and concluded that it was probably a small pizza. Either that, or a two-egg omelette.

I sat back down and gazed over the lake. Not long into my stare, Carol came into view. She was jogging at quite a stride over the bridge at the far end of the lake. She was wearing a bright yellow running top and black leggings. Her white and orange training shoes looked massive on the end of her long, skinny legs. As she approached, I expected her to divert onto the cinder path that led up to the café, but instead she carried on along the side of the lake and off into the distance, out of my sight. It was the first time I had ever seen her reject the café as a pit stop. Maybe she was doing a second circuit of the lake, I thought. Maybe she was upset with me after yesterday. I waited to see if she would come around again but she didn't. I finished my coffee and made my way home.

The road I live on is made up of dirty yellow-brick Victorian terraces with tiny walled front gardens, each one with a large bay window on the ground floor overlooking the street. Carol's house, by far the grandest on the street, is two down from ours, at the end of the terrace. I saw her trainers on the front step, so went through the gate and knocked on her high-gloss lime green door. Her face appeared at the bay window and stared straight through me. I gave her a wave to break the moment, but she just continued to stare before disappearing out of sight.

I waited on the step, thinking she might be coming to answer the door, but it didn't open. It was only once I'd walked back down the steps and opened the gate to leave that I heard the front door behind me. When I turned round, the door was wide open, but Carol wasn't in the doorway. I took it as an invitation nevertheless, and stepped inside.

I found Carol on her sofa drinking a glass of what looked like thin mud.

'What do you want?' she asked. 'Still after my eggs?'

'No, I just came round for a chat and to apologize for yesterday.'

'What is there to apologize about?'

'Well, it felt a bit awkward, you know, with you throwing me out.'

'Wasn't awkward for me, darling. Have you changed your mind yet?'

'No, I haven't. Listen, I'm really fond of you, Carol, but—'

'Oh, save it, darling. So, is there anything else you want?' she asked, staring me full between the eyes.

She wasn't wearing any makeup, and I could see that the faint mark I'd noticed on her cheek the previous day had bloomed into a real shiner.

'What have you done to your face?' I asked.

'Fell over on my jog the other day.'

'It looks nasty. You should put an ice patch on it or something.'

'I won't be doing that, darling. I've got this Moroccan sea gunge that will do exactly the same job. So, come on, I can see it in your eyes: you've got something on your mind.'

'I was after some advice.'

'How about this: don't do hurtful things to people who have only ever shown you kindness. That's good advice, don't you think, darling?'

'It's to do with Harriet.'

'Oh, I noticed she didn't go into work again this morning. Is she sick or something?'

'No. I think she may have left me.'

'Good girl. About time.'

'No, I'm serious, Carol. She left me this note. Would you read it and see what you make of it?'

I gave her the piece of paper and sat beside her as she put on her reading specs and took in its contents. When she finished, she removed her glasses and let out a theatrical sigh.

'She's got another man, darling. Seems obvious to me.'

It was the very last thing I wanted to hear. My stomach took a large wallowing gulp of panic.

'Why do you say that?'

'Because she doesn't want you to get in touch. She's full of guilt, darling. She doesn't say how long she'll be gone because she's hedging her bets. This new fella might not turn out to be all she's hoping for. You haven't tried to contact her, have you?'

'I sent her a wavy hand emoji.'

'Oh, you fucking idiot. That's just giving her permission to frolic and feel less guilty about it. Did she respond?'

'Yeah, she sent me a wavy hand emoji back.'

'What are you, a couple of kids in a playground?'

'I couldn't help myself.'

'Promise me you won't do that again. It will just remind her of you and whatever it is she's trying to escape.'

'I'll try not to. So, that's your first thought? That she's with someone else?'

'That's my instinct, and I'm a woman. I'm good at this shit, darling. Don't tell me you weren't thinking the same?'

'I was trying not to.'

'My advice is just to sit it out, start thinking about what life on your own might look like, and get comfortable with it. You're not a child, darling. Am I right?'

She fixed her gaze on my nose and put her spectacles back on without shifting her focus. I began to feel uncomfortable, and it crossed my mind that she might be about to pounce on me. Her stare continued and seemed to increase in intensity.

'What are you looking at me like that for, Carol?'

'Can I get it?' she asked.

27

'Get what?'

'That blackhead on the side of your nose,' she answered, still not taking her eyes off me. 'It's perfectly ripe.'

'No chance. I was saving it for myself.'

'Please, I beg you,' she responded as she slowly lifted her hands in the direction of my face.

I jumped up off the sofa and took a few steps towards the front door. She remained seated with her hands still outstretched, making pincer movements with her fingers.

'Come on, Matt, give it to me.'

'No, I won't. Why would you want to steal it off me? Especially on the day that Harriet might have left me.'

She put her arms down, crossed her legs and removed her glasses.

'So, you accept that she might have left you?'

'Maybe, but perhaps she just needs a break. That's something that happens with couples. It's perfectly possible, isn't it?'

'It's possible, but not very likely, especially if you treat her the way you treat me.'

For my only available friend, Carol hadn't been as helpful as I had hoped. She almost seemed happy at my distress. She was just being Carol, I suppose: unflappable, matter-of-fact and honest – all the things that I found so difficult to pull off myself.

I refused to believe her regarding Harriet, but she had managed to sow a seed of doubt in my mind.

Where was she?

4

RICE CAKES

A couple of hours after the chat with Carol, I was sat at my kitchen table having a cup of tea when my phone rang. It wasn't Harriet. I let it go to voicemail. The caller left a short message.

'Hi, this is Kiara from Lansdowne Estates in London Bridge. I would like you to contact me concerning your search for an apartment. My number is—'

I deleted the message without waiting for the exciting contact details. My mind wandered again to the very first time Harriet and I met at that house party. When I told her what I did for a living, she seemed to think I was joking, like she thought that selling bathroom fittings was a job that couldn't possibly exist. Her attitude put me slightly on the defensive and I fell into the not-unfamiliar trap of trying to big myself up.

'The bathrooms I sell are really high-end stuff. We get people visiting from miles around just to see the furniture first-hand. No intention of buying.'

'Did you just call it "furniture"?' she asked.

'Yeah, you should come and have a look round.'

'I don't want to visit a furniture shop. I don't have any furniture in my bathroom and I don't expect I will ever want to.'

'You have a bath and a sink, don't you?'

'Yeah, but no furniture.'

'A bath and a sink *are* furniture.'

'Only if I buy them from you. Anywhere else and they would just be a bath and a sink. I suppose you charge hundreds of pounds more just because you call it furniture?'

'We are quite pricey, but we offer a much better experience than your bog-standard shop or discount warehouse.'

'I wouldn't go to a bathroom shop looking for an experience. I would just want it to be functional and forgettable.'

'Well, maybe I'm not the bathroom supplier you're looking for,' I said with a certain amount of clout.

'Maybe you're right. Listen, I'd better go and mingle. Catch you later.'

Before I left the party, I gave her my business card and told her she should come and visit the showroom, maybe I would be able to change her mind. She took the card without comment, took a swig from her bottle of wine and walked away.

I remember having the feeling that we would probably never speak again, and that that would be a shame.

My phone rang again. I picked it up without thinking. It wasn't Harriet.

'Hi, this is Kiara from Lansdowne Estates. So glad to be able to speak to you.'

'Sorry, but this is not a good time,' I replied.

'I think that it is, and could I just say how sorry I am about your change of circumstances.'

'What do you mean?' I asked with a hint of attitude.

'That you are no longer in employment,' she replied in a soft, precise tone that indicated she was confident of her information.

'How do you know that? How have you even got my number?'

'I'm Kiara from Lansdowne Estates.'

'Is that meant to mean something to me?' I asked with a slice of irritation.

'Yes, I would hope so.'

'I'm sorry, but it means nothing to me at all.'

'We showed you an apartment back in November – Satsuma Heights. I think you should remember that.'

'Yes, I remember, and you rejected our offer, so why are you phoning?'

'We think that you liked the apartment very much.'

'Yes, I did . . . But, hold on, you haven't told me how you know I lost my job.'

'I telephoned the work number that you gave us when you registered with us, and they told me you no longer worked there. I put two and two together and guessed that you are currently between jobs.'

'Oh, I see. Sorry, but, like I said, this really isn't a good time.'

'It *would* be best for you if you made time for my call. We have a very generous offer to make you that could send your life in a totally different direction. I think maybe that's what you need right now.'

'Listen, I don't mean to be rude, but can I call you back tomorrow?'

'I'm afraid tomorrow may be too late. I strongly recommend that—'

'Look, I'm really sorry,' I interrupted, 'but I can't talk right now.'

I ended the call, which was a bit rude of me, but I really was too agitated to have a sensible conversation. I didn't want to speak to Kiara from Lansdowne Estates. I wanted to speak to Harriet. For the first time in ages, I felt a pressing desire to tell her that I loved her. A lot.

I needed to get busy, so decided to mop the kitchen floor and clean the living-room windows outside and in. Once that was done, and feeling slightly more in control, I made another cup of tea and sat on the sofa listening to Steely Dan through Harriet's smart speaker.

There was a knock on my door that I ignored in the hope that it would go away. It didn't. I knew it wasn't Harriet, as she always used the doorbell if she didn't have a key. After the third or fourth bout of knocking, I got up and answered.

It was a young lady; slim, maybe thirty years old, with short, boyish blonde hair. She wore a dark grey business suit, and there was an orange and grey bag slung over her shoulder and white training shoes with orange detailing on her feet. Her skin was flawless and pale, in stark contrast to the vibrant red lipstick she had on. Her heavily painted eyebrows gave her a quizzical demeanour. I suspected this was a deliberate ploy on her part.

It was a face that was hard to pin down, like trying to find a mouse's handbag in a builder's skip. There was something familiar about her, but I couldn't pinpoint what it was.

'Hello, how can I help you?'

It was a strange thing for me to say, given that unless she required bathroom input or a television show recommendation, I had little to offer.

'My name is Kiara from Lansdowne Estates. We have just spoken on the phone but now we are meeting in person.'

'So, you were phoning from outside my house?'

'Not far away. I think you will find this matter is urgent and my employer is not someone who allows time to be wasted. May I come in?'

'Sorry, but could you maybe explain what this is about first?'

'Like I say, I'm Kiara from Lansdowne Estates, and this concerns a property we manage called Satsuma Heights.'

'Yes, I know the place. As I said on the phone, we viewed an apartment there and put in an offer but it was rejected.'

'It was me that showed you around the apartment, and I think you liked the flat very much.'

Then it clicked – that was where I had seen Kiara before. She'd had dark brown hair when we'd done the viewing with her, so that had thrown me off the memory.

'Yes, but unless you've reduced the rent by around half, then I'm afraid we just can't afford it.'

'How about we do exactly that in return for you carrying out some minimal administrative duties?'

I laughed. Kiara didn't. In fact, she seemed absolutely serious.

I decided to invite her in and offered her a cup of tea. She requested a glass of water. As soon as we were seated at the kitchen table, she removed a packet of rice cakes from her handbag and placed two of them on a napkin that she took out from her pocket. She opened her laptop on the table and took a bite from a rice cake as she scrolled through her files. When she had found what she was looking for, she looked up from her screen briefly and gave me a smile that could only be described as ambiguous.

'I think the arrangement we are proposing would be beneficial to both parties. We have looked into your background and think you are a good fit.'

'What do you mean, "looked into my background"? That sounds a bit ominous. A bit irregular.'

'We have simply followed up on the information you gave us when you registered with Lansdowne Estates – made a few phone calls, followed a few leads. I think any responsible potential employer would do the same,' she answered, her gaze still fixed on the laptop screen.

'Well, maybe *after* they've offered someone a job. I'll be honest, it sounds a bit creepy.'

'You shouldn't feel that way. Like I've said, we don't want to waste a person's time. There is nothing creepy about being thorough and professional. I think you would agree with that.'

'What do you mean by "administrative duties"?'

'It's not for me to be specific, but essentially my client would want you to ensure that the property is running smoothly and that he has a reliable on-site presence.'

'Like a caretaker?'

'That would not be your formal title, but you are in the right space. I would think that the reduced rental would far outweigh any obligations placed upon you.'

'So, would I still be able to have a full-time job away from the building?'

'Oh, I would think so, but you would need to discuss the details with my client. All I require today is to establish a general interest from you regarding the opportunity and, if that is forthcoming, arrange for you to meet with my client.'

'Why me?'

'We think that you have the profile we are looking for and the attributes that would make the arrangement a success for both parties.'

'But you don't know me. How can you say that?'

'We met at Satsuma Heights and I was impressed by you. My client is always on the lookout for people who would fit seamlessly into his operation. If you are uncertain or hesitant, I can assure you that there are a number of other suitable individuals we can approach. I think it is time that you commit to meeting my client, or for us to look elsewhere.'

'Then I will say that I am happy to meet him, but I won't commit to anything until I have all the details.'

'That is all I require from you,' she confirmed, closing her laptop and putting it back in her bag whilst chewing the last piece of her rice cake. After wiping a few crumbs off the table into her napkin and placing it in her pocket, she proceeded to stand up, sling her bag over her shoulder and pick up the glass of water.

'I will contact you with details of your appointment with my client. I think it will be sooner rather than later. My client is most anxious to conclude this arrangement.'

She handed me the glass of water.

'And I think that maybe you should get a filter for your tap. That water tasted like death.'

And with that, she left, leaving behind a dense waft of perfume that hit me hard with its fleeting intensity: lemons, cinnamon and eucalyptus coated in a blanket of marzipan. I watched her from the window as she walked away. She was reassuringly classy and trustworthy – a serious person that you could definitely take a punt on.

Carol suddenly appeared beside her on the pavement and struck up a conversation. She would have been watching the street from her window sentry post and wouldn't have been able to resist the temptation to do a quick interrogation. Kiara must have proved a worthy adversary, however, because she escaped Carol's clutches within thirty seconds.

5

HEAVY BATH

After Kiara from Lansdowne Estates had left, I settled down on the sofa and turned on the TV. Every twenty minutes or so, I considered sending Harriet another wavy hand emoji, but managed to resist. I tried to eat one of the fancy croissants I'd bought for her but my appetite was shot to shit. I could maybe have stomached a couple of soft-boiled eggs, but I remained emphatically eggless. I made a note to go to the local shop later.

I searched the website of Lansdowne Estates. It seemed a very flashy operation. From what I could see, they were primarily a property development company, and the site was full of glossy pictures of past and future projects situated all over the south-east of England – the portfolio composed exclusively of luxury blocks of flats in prime locations. Some of them offered facilities such as gyms and swimming pools, and many of them came with tiny, pointless balconies. I clicked on the link to Satsuma Heights.

It was just as I remembered: absolutely beautiful – the sort of place that would be used in movies and on TV to suggest wealth and success. Lots of floor-to-ceiling glass, designer kitchens with bar stools around a central island and luxury bathrooms clad in faux marble and fitted up to the nines. I had always known that the flats would be well beyond our reach financially, but had arranged the viewing just for the fantasy of it all.

As I expanded the photo of one of the bathrooms, Monson jumped onto the sofa beside me to claim a sun-drenched spot for himself. His tabby coat glistened in the sunshine by way of tribute to his diet of tinned salmon, tinned tuna and fresh ham.

'See those polished brass taps and shower fittings?' I said, pointing at the screen.

'Yeah, what about them?' he replied.

'They're Italian. We used to sell them in the showroom. Must be about five grand's worth of fittings in just that room.'

'Waste of money, boss.'

'You've got no taste. See that double-ended bath? It's by Ransom and Hilliard. Made of bonded powdered marble – weighs about as much as me.'

'That's a heavy bath.'

'The manufacturing process means there are no air bubbles in the structure, so the chances of blistering or cracking are zero.'

Monson yawned, then, on hearing a motorcycle engine approaching in the street outside, jumped off the sofa and onto the front windowsill to get a better view.

The bath looked magnificent in the perfectly framed brochure photograph. I'd only ever sold one of these beauties in my three years as a salesman, and I'd never dreamt that one day I might actually be able to bathe in one whenever it took my fancy. Harriet would love it even more. I'm an eater, whereas she's definitely a bather.

I found the website menu and clicked the 'Vacancies' link.

There are currently no employment opportunities at Lansdowne Estates. Please submit a CV and we will place it on file for consideration should any opportunities arise.

On the 'Properties To Rent' page, it read:

We do not currently have any apartments available for rental. From time to time our clients will offer short- and long-term lets. Please check back or register your interest using the link below.

I was beginning to get excited at the prospect of living at Satsuma Heights. Imagine the victory I would achieve when I told Harriet that I had found a new place for us to live – and, wow, what a place. Surely that would cleanse her of any doubts she might be having about my viability as a partner?

The last time we had spoken about our housing 'situation' had been a couple of weeks ago, and it hadn't gone well. She knew I hated being questioned about it and she would always leave a decent time-gap before raising the topic.

We were sat at either end of the sofa; I was watching the

football on TV while she was on her laptop working on her 'big case'.

'Can you turn that off, please?' she asked out of the blue.

'Why? This is the most important match of the season,' I replied with passion and pleading. (It was Fleetwood v Port Vale.)

'We need to talk about where we're going to live when our tenancy expires.'

My heart sank and I turned off the TV.

'Have you got any viewings lined up?' she asked. 'It's been two weeks since we went to see anything.' I sensed a bit of a tone.

'I'm trying my best,' I replied earnestly. 'There just isn't much on the market – not in our price range, anyway. It's the same old flats that we've already considered and rejected. I spend half the day on the phone with agents. I'm beginning to get on their tits.'

'You're beginning to get on *my* tits,' she said. 'Do you resent having to find somewhere for us to live? Is that what's going on here?'

I did resent it ever so slightly, but wasn't going to stir any pots.

'No, absolutely not,' I replied. 'I'm happy to do the graft.'

'Well, you need to up your game, Matt. The biggest prosecution of my career is coming up and my mind can't be elsewhere worrying about if I'm going to be homeless.'

'That's not going to happen,' I said, reassuringly. 'I mean, if nothing comes up, we can always renew the tenancy on this place. I've spoken to the agent, and as long as we take up the option within a month of the end of our agreement, we can have it on the same terms.'

Harriet tossed the laptop down and sat up on the sofa with anger in her eyes. I had said the wrong thing.

'I knew that was your plan: just stay here and rot in your smog because it suits you fine.'

'That's not fair. This place suited *you* fine when we moved in.'

'Matt, I've told you till I'm blue in the face: I need to be nearer to work, and I need some certainty around my living arrangements. Hey – and here's a fresh one for you: I need to be away from that woman.'

'What woman?'

'Carol. She's a fucking nightmare – watching our every move, gossiping with everyone in the street. I can't stand the sight of her any more. So get your act together. I'm going to bed.'

She went upstairs at quite a pace, and once I heard the bedroom door close, I turned the football back on. I can't remember anything about the match apart from liking the Port Vale kit.

That conversation with Harriet had jolted me into action and I had arranged viewings for the following two weekends. Four of them were cancelled on the Friday before and the only one we actually viewed was a semi-basement flat that Harriet immediately rejected due to the smell of damp and the Alsatian dog roaming and dirting freely in the neighbour's back garden.

6

I DON'T HAVE ANY CHILDREN

I looked up from the laptop as Monson leapt off the window sill and ran upstairs. There was a knock on the door. Not Harriet. (Like I say, she's a ringer.) I took a quick glance through the side of the bay window to see the estate agent who looked after our house. I'd forgotten that an appointment had been arranged for someone to view it. What a pain. The estate agent in question was Hugh Cavendish, a posh bloke in his early thirties, dressed, as always, in a tight, light blue suit with a pink shirt/white collar combo and pointy black shoes. His thick sandy hair was combed into a severe side parting and his complexion was as pasty as a pig's undercarriage.

A short, skinny man wearing jeans and a green Barbour jacket accompanied him. He was older, mid-fifties, and wore his thinning hair in a desperate side parting. His facial features were small and crowded, and his fixed expression reminded me of a stoat experiencing its very first vinegar crisp. I didn't want him to like the house. I wanted to keep my accommodation options open for as long as possible. Problem was, with all my cleaning and Harriet's good taste, it looked really quite appealing, especially for the price. I had to try to make the house seem less desirable.

I let them in with hardly a word, then made my way upstairs, where I closed the curtains, tossed the bed sheets into a heap and scattered whatever clothing came to hand onto the floor. In the bathroom, I half-filled the sink and mixed a large clump of shaving foam in with the water. I grabbed a bath towel and dipped it in the sink before tossing it theatrically onto the floor. I scooped up a handful of the sink milk and splashed it around the base of the pedestal to give the impression it might be leaking.

I stood at the top of the stairs and listened to Hugh give his spiel. He was as thick as two short planks but beautifully spoken. He knew next to nothing about the house but nevertheless spouted forth with absolute confidence.

'As you can see, the ground floor is open-plan – a seamless continuum if you like, which means there are no barriers to movement or sight lines. The walls are all vertical, which contrasts nicely with the horizontality of the work surfaces.'

'Is there any on-street parking?' asked Mr Barbour.

'I don't know,' replied Cavendish dismissively, as if parking was not really a matter that should be spoken of in polite company. 'The majority of the lighting comes from above, which excludes shadowing and glare, for example on your TV or laptop. It's an incredible and well-tested system. I love it.'

'Have you any idea what the internet speed is?' Barbour enquired.

'I don't know, but I would imagine it's bloody fast. A professional couple are living here at the moment and I'm sure they
have maxed out internet-wise . . . The sink is in the butler
style, which gives good depth and an increase in versatility due
to its extra capacity. They say that in the olden days they would
be used for bathing small children.'

'I don't have any children,' Barbour replied, deadpan. 'Have
any major repairs been carried out recently?'

'I don't know. If you look through this rear window, you
can actually see right through to the outside. It's a small,
manageable garden laid to lawn. Ideal for socializing in the
summer, and I'm told the grass is super soft under the foot.'

'Have there ever been any flooding or dampness issues?' asked
Barbour.

'I don't know but both fresh and waste water are received
and evacuated from the property by a system of concealed pipes
of various thicknesses, such a neat solution.'

'Do you allow pets?' asked Barbour.

'No, I'm afraid not.'

Shit. I had forgotten about Monson. I grabbed him off the
landing window where he was having a sunbathe and waited
for them to go out the back door. As soon as I heard it open,
I ran down the stairs and threw him out of the front door.

'Don't show your face until these two have cleared off,' I
instructed him through gritted teeth.

'You ashamed of me or something?' he replied.

I shut the door and casually sat back down at the kitchen table. I
gave Barbour a lifeless smile as he walked past me and disappeared

up the stairs with Cavendish. Moments later, they were on their way back down, Cavendish continuing to spout his shite.

'Yeah, the stairs provide a vital link between the two floors – really useful addition and great fun for the kids to slide down on, say, a tea tray or a cot mattress.'

'I don't have any kids.'

'Ah, Mr Giles, there you are – the upstairs could do with a bit of a tidy.'

I didn't want to reply, but then I had a thought.

'Yeah,' I said, apologetically, 'but it's so hard to keep on top of it, you know, with the rooms being so small, and the lack of storage . . .'

'Oh, I disagree,' interrupted Barbour. 'The bedroom is above-average size for this price range. You just have to be organized.'

His voice was nasal and piercing. I noticed that his teeth were pointy, stained and crooked. A closer examination of his jacket revealed a level of staining that is rarely displayed in a social environment. There was a particularly dense mark just beside his collar. It was somewhere between the shape of Cornwall and Italy.

'Thank you. I'll get onto that straightaway,' I replied as I got up from the table to make my way back upstairs. Unfortunately, at that moment, Monson jumped onto the front windowsill and pressed his face against the glass. I manoeuvred myself so that I was between Monson and Cavendish and stood my ground.

'Why are you giving up the tenancy?' asked Barbour.

'My girlfriend wants to be nearer her work. Commuting

into London can be exhausting from here. I mean really exhausting. The trains are a nightmare.'

'Yes, I know. Luckily for me I'm starting a job just round the corner, so that won't be a problem.'

Monson started to meow and scratch on the window. It was impossible to ignore.

'That's just a local stray,' I blurted. 'He's a right nuisance – always staring through the windows and doing his business in the garden. He even gets inside sometimes if you leave a door or window open.'

'Is that why you leave bowls of cat food in the kitchen and have a litter tray under the stairs?' enquired Cavendish, with plenty of smugness in his tone.

'Yeah, exactly that,' I replied, whilst staring down at a stain on the floor that had the shape of a snowman with an enormous penis.

'I love cats,' exclaimed Barbour. 'Maybe he doesn't have a home and I could adopt him. This is a sign. I love this place.'

'Right then,' said Cavendish. 'We'll leave you in peace. Thank you for having us visit, Mr Giles.'

When I shut the door behind them, I could smell a lingering odour that was both acrid and slightly savoury. I guessed it must be some cheap aftershave or perhaps a hangover from Monson's morning movements in the litter tray. I could hear Cavendish droning on outside about deposits and references and Barbour declaring that all his stuff was in storage and he was ready to move in immediately. It began to feel like all my eggs might be arranging themselves into the Satsuma Heights basket.

7

COBBLERS

The next morning, I woke and checked my phone. Still nothing from Harriet. There was, however, an email from Kiara at Lansdowne Estates.

Hi Mr Giles,

I have arranged for a car to pick you up from your home at midday today to take you for a meeting with my client at Satsuma Heights.

Please confirm this arrangement is acceptable.

Kiara (Lansdowne Estates)

I replied immediately, accepting the appointment. It was 8:40 a.m. so I still had time for a run/walk in the park and a cup of coffee. It would be good preparation for the meeting – get the blood flowing and clear my mind. I took the fact that they were sending a car as a good sign. It added to the bona fides of the whole thing, providing yet more proof that they were a serious outfit. I took a chance and left my puffa jacket on its peg. It was a bright, sunny day and I reckoned jeans and a sweatshirt would suffice.

When I took my seat on the café decking, I spotted the young waitress staring at me as she enjoyed a vaping session just around the corner at the end of the tables. She averted her gaze when our eyes met. There was an air of anxiety around her as she typed something into her phone and sucked greedily on her vape. When she'd had her fill of vanilla and coconut she approached my table, sat down beside me and let out an audible and genuine sigh.

'What's up?' I asked her.

'I think I should say sorry for yesterday. I was a bit rude to you and you were only apologizing for someone being rude to me. It kind of bothered me for the rest of the day.'

'That's okay, no need to apologize. But, like I say, what's up? I can tell you're a bit distracted, a bit on edge.'

She stared at a little sparrow that was listening in from its perch on the top rail of the decking balustrade, took another sneaky draw on her vape and then turned to face me.

'Do you really want to know?' she asked, as if expecting me to decline.

'Yeah, I mean, it's good to get things off your chest, especially to a stranger who's got no meat in the game.'

'I think you mean "skin in the game",' she suggested.

'But where there's skin, there's usually meat in the vicinity, so I wasn't far off.'

'Fair.'

She took another tug on her vape, then reached over and

broke a chunk off the slice of lemon drizzle cake that was on my plate.

'You've got a girlfriend, haven't you?' she asked.

'Yes, she's called Harriet. Why do you ask?'

'Because up until ten days ago, I had a boyfriend, and now I don't and I can't handle it.'

She went on to tell me that her boyfriend – Rupert, I think was his name – had gone off to university in north London and, she suspected, found himself a new girlfriend. Rupert (Roger?) was the love of her life, she declared. They had been inseparable these past couple of years and as a result she had lost touch with her friends, most of whom, like Rupert (Ronan?), had now left to go to university. In a nutshell, her world had collapsed and she was feeling isolated and very lonely. She didn't cry, though her words would definitely have justified it.

'It happens to the best of us,' I responded, well aware that I might be in exactly the same situation. 'You just need time to adjust. I've had my heart broken a good few times and it's never as bad looking back.' I pushed the plate of cake towards her. 'You just need time. It heals everything, just like Timpsons.'

'What are Timpsons? I think I might need some.'

'It's a cobbler's shop. You know, shoe repairers.'

She looked at me like I was from an era she didn't under-stand, and she was right to do so.

'I do mean it,' I said. 'You just need some time to pass so that you can adjust and distance yourself from the shock of it all.'

'That's what everyone says, but it doesn't feel like that to me. I'm getting worse every day.'

'Do you honestly think that Rupert (Russell?) was the love of your life?'

'Yes, I do. If I didn't, I would have left him. Is Harriet the love of your life?'

'Yes, I believe so.'

'You don't sound very certain. Should Harriet be worried?'

I was about to rephrase my reply to offer more certainty when Carol arrived at the table and plonked herself into the seat opposite me. She demanded the waitress fetch her an oat milk latte and a banana. The waitress immediately got up and left the table without giving me the chance to flash the reassuring smile I wanted to deliver.

'You trying to chat up the waitress?' said Carol. 'You should be after someone more your own age. What could she possibly see in an old suitcase like you, darling?'

'No, of course not. I was just trying to give her some relationship advice.'

'Lucky girl,' she said as she leaned over, broke off a chunk of my lemon drizzle and popped it into her mouth. 'Talking of which,' she continued, 'any news from Harriet and her adventures?'

'Nothing, and before you ask, I haven't tried to contact her.'

'Good boy – really good boy. My advice: expect the worst, prepare for the worst, and embrace the worst when it inevitably happens. Can't go wrong with that approach, darling. It's tried and tested by yours truly and take a look at me: I'm nothing short of fantastic. Am I right?'

'The waitress has just split up with her boyfriend,' I informed her.

'So you've got something in common.'

'Excellent humour, Carol,' I replied, 'but why do you always have to veer towards the cruel when it comes to my personal life?'

'I'm not being cruel. Like I say, expect the worst. It's the only sane approach.'

'She's feeling really lonely, which I suppose is to be expected.'

'Are you feeling lonely without Harriet?'

'No, not really. I don't think I've had the time to feel lonely,' I replied.

'That's because you still believe she's coming back. The loneliness will hit you like a hammer when you accept the truth. Am I right?'

'You're being nasty again.'

'No, I'm being a good friend helping you prepare for what's ahead. And remember, I'll still be here to help you pick up the pieces.'

I knew Carol could be cruel, but she was also incredibly honest, and so my heart sank at her interpretation of the Harriet situation because she was usually correct in her advice. For example, she had been the one to tell me I would lose my job if I didn't make more effort to socialize with my work colleagues. She had also introduced me to the versatility of the puffa jacket and the incredible benefits of magnesium supplements.

'Hey, I might have some good news,' I said by way of changing the topic. 'I've got an interview for a job that comes with accommodation later today.'

I told her about Kiara and the offer of an apartment in

Satsuma Heights. Unlike me, she wasn't at all suspicious of the arrangement.

'Sounds like good news, and it's turned you all perky,' she said. 'You think that if you get this place it will be enough to get Harriet back, don't you?'

'Well, it won't do any harm.'

'Tell me, darling, are you *certain* that Harriet is the one for you? I mean, do you actually *enjoy* being with her?'

'The waitress asked me much the same thing and I'll give you the same answer: yes, I am, and yes I do. And if I didn't, I would have left her.'

Carol stifled a laugh and spat out a blob of latte onto the table.

'Liar,' she said.

8

JELLY BABIES

The car, a large black Mercedes in pristine condition, arrived outside my house at exactly 11:55 a.m. As it pulled up, I received a text from Kiara informing me of its arrival.

I had decided that my old blue work suit would be the best bet for the meeting. Shoe selection was more difficult. I owned four pairs of potential footwear:

- My brown suede comfort-lined slip-ons (suitable for light outdoor use)
- A pair of green unisex rubber Wellingtons (in the garden shed, could be suffering from rot)
- My training shoes (originally white, now looking like I'd washed them with the contents of an ash tray)
- My brown suede desert boots

The desert boots would have been the obvious choice, but sadly the soles at the front of each shoe had separated from the uppers and clucked like a juvenile goose with every step. I plumped for the comfort slip-ons. I gave them a once-over with a dry toothbrush and they looked passable. Hopefully I would spend my time at the interview behind a desk, so they shouldn't be in sharp focus.

As I walked down the steps to the front garden, Monson was sat on the low front wall cleaning his whiskers.

'Look at you,' he said, 'all dressed up like a bloke that matters.'

'Oh, hi, Monson,' I enthused sarcastically. 'Oh dear, I seem to have shut the door behind me – you'll have to spend the day outside.'

'Not bothered, it still stinks in there from that bloke who came round. And I can keep a watch out for passing motor-cycles. You got an interview with the circus or something?'

'Maybe.'

'Why you wearing those clown shoes on your feet?'

'You don't have to be formal to be formidable. And I was just kidding, I've taken the tape off the cat flap in the back door so you can come and go as you please. See you later.'

'You wouldn't have taken the tape off if *she* was still here.'

I ignored him.

The driver of the Mercedes got out and rushed round to open the rear passenger door for me, and I prayed that Carol was watching this upmarket scenario. He was about fifty years old, well built with a sharp side-parted and slightly gelled buzz cut. I suspected the gym was his natural home.

I plopped myself down on the luxurious leather seat and the driver shut the soft-close door behind me. The magazine pocket on the back of the front passenger seat contained a bottle of spring water that claimed to be able to hint at the idea of raspberry, a copy of a magazine called *Business Insider* and an unopened packet of Jelly Babies. On the seat next to me was a box of tissues and a small telescopic umbrella.

'Good morning, Mr Giles' was all that the driver said to me before we set off. He was wearing a grey suit, white shirt and royal blue tie. I'm not great with silence in vehicles, so once we were under way I attempted to start a conversation.

'I like your suit. It's a nice shade of grey,' I said as my opener.

'It's okay,' he replied.

'Are you not convinced by it?'

'Never given it much thought,' he said as he turned the car radio on.

'Does your boss like blue suits?' I asked.

'Everyone likes blue suits,' he answered.

'What's your boss like? Is he a decent type?'

'He's whatever he wants you to think he is and that suits me fine.'

I assumed he was being cryptic by way of discretion, so changed the subject.

'Is it okay if I open the Jelly Babies?'

'It is.'

I opened the packet and searched out a green one. I offered the packet to the driver but he declined.

'I like the green ones best, then orange, then black. Not so bothered about the rest – especially the yellow,' I said, speaking directly to the roll of skin on the back of the driver's head.

He didn't make any comment, though I noticed one of the

fat rolls on his neck twitch slightly at the mention of the yellow Jelly Baby. I caught his eye in the rear-view mirror and smiled at him in the style of a Texan beauty queen. He immediately averted his gaze.

We drove through Catford, Lewisham, the Old Kent Road and on to Elephant and Castle before arriving at London Bridge. A few people in other cars glanced over at me through their windows on the way. I kidded myself they were thinking, *Why, if I'm not mistaken, that man is on his way to a meeting of such import, the outcome could affect every single one of us.* Or perhaps even, *That's the life I always wanted for myself; what with the car, the driver, the versatile slippers and the back-seat sweets.* Truth is, they probably didn't notice me at all.

Satsuma Heights was a new grey-brick building tucked behind London Bridge railway station on a road called Snowsfields. The rear of the block faced a small community garden bounded by iron railings, and beyond that, the old Home Office Immigration Centre. The Immigration Centre was around twenty storeys high and significantly dwarfed Satsuma Heights, which stood at around half that. To the east side of the apartment block was a small pub called the Horseshoe Inn, and to the west there was a row of shops that included two cafés, a laundrette and an agent that sold the news.

Seeing the Horseshoe Inn brought my mind back to Harriet with a jolt. When we viewed the apartment in Satsuma Heights, we went there straight afterwards to discuss the viewing and have a bite to eat. It was Saturday lunchtime and the place was only half full. It wasn't one of those pubs that had gone all in as a gastropub/restaurant and it only offered a simple all-day bar menu. You would describe it as a drinkers' pub – traditional, with no frills or tortured theme.

We both ordered toasted sandwiches: Harriet, ham and cheese; corned beef and onion for me. She was pumped up by the viewing, but my enthusiasm was dampened by the almost certain knowledge that we couldn't afford the rent. Harriet seemed happy to ignore that dilemma for the time being.

'I love it, love it, love it,' gushed Harriet. 'The decor, the hot flooring, the wine cooler . . . and did you see that fridge? Two doors . . . *Two doors!*'

I hadn't spotted the wine cooler.

'The location is just perfect,' she continued, 'right next to the station. I could be in work in less than ten minutes. And that view of the Shard from the roof terrace was stunning. Oh, and did you see the bath? What about the size of the kitchen island? Come on, say something!'

I realized that I had shot myself in the foot by arranging the viewing. What had I been thinking? All it had done was bring into sharp focus how unequal our financial partnership was at the moment and how different our priorities were.

'It's beautiful,' I said, 'but we can't afford it.'

She replied with the question I feared most at that moment in time:

'Well, then, why did you arrange to view it?'

'I just thought it was somewhere that you would like to see, maybe something to aspire to. More than that, though, I thought it would be a fun little trip out together.'

'Maybe, just maybe, you should have told me that before we came.'

'I'm sorry, I should have. Listen, we could put in an offer,' I suggested, with a hopeful bent to my face. 'You never know.'

'We must. I mean, you never know,' she replied.

'Definitely,' I said. 'And I did really like the bath and the taps.'

'That's it? That was your highlight?'

'Yeah, though the wine cooler was quite something as well.'

We put in our offer later that day, based on me earning the same salary as I had at the bathroom shop. It was rejected within fifteen minutes via email.

The Mercedes arrived at Satsuma Heights and the driver parked up in one of only two reserved parking spaces outside the front lobby. I stepped out of the car leaving the Jelly Babies behind. (There were only yellow ones left in the packet.)

Kiara stood at the entrance, ready for our arrival.

'Hello, Mr Giles. Nice slippers. They are clearly suitable for light outdoor use. That's quite unusual.'

We shook hands and entered Satsuma Heights.

9

LOW HANDSHAKE

The lift to the fifth floor had a brushed steel interior with a mirrored back wall. The lighting inside was perfect for inspecting blackheads on the face, but with Kiara in tow I didn't think it appropriate.

'Nice day outside,' I said.

'I think it could be a *great* day for you, Mr Giles – maybe life-changing,' she replied.

The fifth floor of the building housed four apartments. The carpeted corridor was generously wide and each of the four front doors was made from highly polished bird's eye maple panels. The wallpaper had a Japanese vibe to it and the concealed lighting was crisp and bright. The only sound I could hear was daytime television coming from inside one of the other three flats on the corridor. With the combination of my wool-lined slip-ons and the thick carpet, it really did feel as if I was walking on air. We stopped outside door 5A. Kiara opened it using a key card.

'This would be your apartment. Please go inside and make

yourself at home. My client will join you shortly. Can I get you anything to drink?'

'Yeah, could I get a water please?'

'There is water in the tap – a free and endless supply. Knock yourself out,' she replied as she gestured for me to step across the threshold.

Once I was in, Kiara shut the door behind me and I was alone in the apartment. The floors, I noticed, were matt sealed oak and pleasantly warm underfoot. The wall opposite me was fully glazed from floor to ceiling, giving a spectacular view of the immigration offices and community gardens below. The main space was open-plan with quality furnishings. To my right, an L-shaped dark brown sofa dominated the lounge area, and the kitchen area to my left was a bank of gloss-white units with integrated oven and fridge. The large kitchen island featured a hob and a sink with a spectacular mixer tap that hovered above it in the form of a swan about to dive for a river nugget. There were two brown hen's eggs on the surface of the island, and nothing else. They reminded me of my egg craving, which had by now long disappeared, to lie dormant until another day. They also reminded me that I needed to eat a proper meal sooner rather than later. Unfortunately, my appetite was still non-existent.

I took in the view and then moved through to the bedroom, where I was greeted by white fitted wardrobes, a queen-size bed with a dark brown suede headboard, and more hot oak under the foot. I entered the en-suite bathroom, and there it was: the Ransom and Hilliard, free-standing, double-ended, matt finish, powdered marble bath. It looked magnificent set atop the slate-grey floor and green-grey tiled walls. I lowered myself into its magnificence, fully dressed and totally in awe. I was able to lie full length inside its bowl without even a kink at the knee. I had found my happy place, so closed my eyes to drink up the feeling. When I opened them, a man was stood in the doorway looking down on me with what looked like sympathy on his face.

'You couldn't resist, huh?' he said, taking a further step into the bathroom and sitting himself on the rim of the bath.

'Sorry, yeah. I used to sell these baths, but I never dreamt that I would ever actually be entitled to bathe in one. It would be a bit of a dream come true.'

'That's what I'm all about,' he replied, 'making dreams come true for those who deserve it. You must be Mr Giles.' His voice was rich, educated and creamy.

'Yes, that's me,' I replied.

He held out his hand for me to shake and I adjusted myself to exit the bath.

'No, you stay in there a while longer. I like how happy it makes your face.'

I shook his hand, probably the lowest handshake I had ever executed. His grip was firm and dominant, and his smiling face reassuringly friendly.

'I'm Laurence, the owner of this building,' he said. 'Pleasure to meet you.'

Laurence was in his early sixties, slim and quite tall so far as I could tell from my sunken vantage point. His hair was cut close to his scalp, revealing his head to have a pleasantly smooth shape. There was stubble on his face and his brown, almond-shaped eyes had a trustful ring to them. He was wearing a black woollen coat and a black turtleneck top. It could have come off a bit gangster but, on him, it looked sharp as shit. He presented as rich and effortlessly important. Laid in the bath, I couldn't help but feel subservient and poverty-stricken, especially with those daft slippers on the ends of my feet and my occasional double chin pressing against my lower jaw.

'I know my assistant Kiara has explained my offer in outline – and by the way isn't she marvellous? Do you agree? Did you find her excellent? I know I do.'

'To be honest, she didn't really tell me much detail about your offer but, yeah, she's great.'

'Isn't she though? She's a superstar, that's what I say, and I mean it. You must have plenty of questions for me and I can't wait to hear them.' His voice was a tad patronizing, but not so much that he could be directly accused.

'Yes, first up, could I get out of the bath?'

'Of course. Come on, let's get down to business and see if we can get you on our team and under our embrace.'

He marched out of the bathroom and I joined him on the sofa in the lounge.

'I built this place,' he said, 'and it has made me a lot of money. I live in the penthouse and Kiara lives a couple of floors below. This and the sixth floor are the only rental properties; the rest of the units were all pre-sold off-plan well before completion. My developments never stay on the market for long. I have personally handpicked the residents that live on this floor. They think of me as a friend, but that is not necessarily the case. I'm just keeping them in my influence and under something of an obligation to me. Sounds fun, doesn't it? Do you agree? I do.'

'Is that what you intend for me, that I become obliged to you and under—'

'No no no no no,' he interrupted. 'I had a pre-existing relationship with the other fifth-floor tenants. You are a stranger to me and I have no interest in your life other than as an employee, a confidant, a tenant, and perhaps even a future friend.'

'When you say "employee", what exactly do you mean?'

'You will be taking care of things for me in a very limited but important way. You will be my on-site contact for any complaints or disputes or emergencies relating to the rental apartments. You will keep an eye on the cleaning of all communal areas and ensure fire regulations and tenancy conditions are all properly observed, noise nuisances and the like. That's some word, isn't it? "Communal." Suggests so much more than it delivers, do you agree? I think so for sure. Shouldn't rob you of more than a couple of hours a week.'

'And in return I get to live here for a grand a month?'

'Absolutely, sounds like a great deal, don't you think? I certainly do.'

It seemed too good to be true, so I tried to dig a bit deeper.

'You said you knew all the tenants on this floor before they moved in?'

'Yes, correct, and I want to get to know them better. And that, Mr Giles, is where you come in.'

'How do you mean?' I asked.

'I want you to be my sergeant at arms on the battlefield, as it were – to make sure everything is running smoothly, report anything untoward and provide me with peace of mind. I'm rarely here at the moment, so I'm hiring your eyes and your ears. Any responsible landlord would want such a service: a conduit for information and, if need be, speculation.'

'You want me to be a spy?'

I laughed. He didn't. I had a swell of disappointment inside me and for a fleeting moment wondered if I should just get up and leave. I didn't; it would have been rude and I had never learnt the rudeness skills.

'I don't like to call it spying. Think of it as residential intelligence gathering. It won't be much of a burden for a man of your qualities.'

'What qualities are those? This all seems very unlikely.'

'Do you not think you are a good choice? Are you not an excellent choice? Have I made a mistake? I don't think so, and I have an exquisite nose for these things. You are not, perhaps, a *complete* stranger to me after all, Mr Giles. I know you better than you might think. Kiara recommended you to me and, as I'm sure you are aware, she has done her research and followed up certain leads. There is information everywhere these days, and Kiara knows where to find it. Would you prefer I had advertised the job and interviewed a bunch of actual strangers? For that is what they would be. You gave enough information when you registered to view an apartment to make you something more valued than a stranger.'

'What exactly was it Kiara found out about me that appealed to you?'

'You have a good employment record; you are honest and loyal; you have very few people to whom you feel obliged; and no social media presence whatsoever. In a nutshell, you're a shadow. Someone who possesses the skill, if required, to pass amongst us unnoticed.'

'That all sounds about right,' I replied with a hint of despondency. He had made me sound deeply dull and irrelevant and the truth, even partial, can sometimes kick you in the teeth.

'I'm asking you to make new and possibly rewarding connections,' he continued. 'It will change your life for the better and you will thrive. I'm sure of it. Are you not? I certainly am.'

I was confused by the flightiness of the conversation. It was vague and playful rather than a serious proposal. What kept me interested, though, was my burning desire to live in this flat and take my first dip in the Ransom and Hilliard.

'So, what do you think?' he asked. 'What are you thinking? Your thoughts right now are the key to this discussion.'

'Can I go back to what you were saying about collecting information on the other tenants? What exactly do you mean by that?'

'Watch them, listen to them. Do they have lovers? Do they have visitors? Can you discover any of their secrets? We all have secrets, don't we? I certainly do. Do you have secrets? I expect so. Very hard to avoid them accruing even if you live the life of a saint. With that in mind, I'd like you to get to know your new neighbours, their habits and their needs. The smallest thing might be of great interest to me. All you need to do is inform me of your findings whenever something piques your interest. You'll soon get the hang of it.'

'Why are you so interested in them? Are they business rivals? Employees? Enemies of some sort?'

'It is best that you know nothing about my relationship with them. That would only taint your judgement. Let's just say I have every right to know what's going on in my own building.'

'To be perfectly honest, I don't have a great track record of making connections. I'm not the most appealing person in the world.'

'Don't do yourself down. Kiara has assured me you have all the tools I require; you just need the motivation. This apartment will be your motivation. *I* will be your motivation. You will be transformed. At your age, you still have the potential for change. No need for you to hide under a rock waiting for the final taxi to arrive.'

By 'final taxi' I assumed he meant funeral hearse, and that imagery hit home. I was certainly waiting for something; I just hadn't ever discovered what it was.

He got up off the sofa, clearly signalling the end of the meeting.

'I would like your decision by tomorrow morning. If you have any further questions, please direct them to Kiara. She really is ever so good – outstanding, in fact. I hope you will accept. You are in the loop now, as it were, so if you chose to decline then that would be a significant inconvenience to me. Let's not go there; let's build a connection.'

He held out his hand and I shook it. We took the lift down to the reception in silence and he walked out of the building without offering a goodbye.

There was no Kiara and no Mercedes to take me home. I suspected that Laurence wanted me to feel the difference between life under his wing and life without him. I walked over to the Horseshoe Inn for a pint and a think and the opportunity to stare at strangers and assess their levels of happiness.

I had to admit to myself that I was somewhat in awe of Laurence. He was the most engaging person I had met for some time. I felt energized and important just from being in his presence – a very unfamiliar feeling for me as someone who is naturally cynical and suspicious of strangers, especially male ones, who have made a success of their lives.

I really didn't want this to be the last time I ever saw him. I wanted to be part of his scheming; I wanted to be part of his plans. Most of all, I wanted to secure the apartment and bring Harriet home. She would never agree to the 'residential intelligence' aspect of the deal, but there were only three other flats on my corridor and it should be simple enough to make friendly contact with them and strike up a relationship without having to let Harriet in on the arrangement.

It was against everything I believed in to nose about in other people's business but, then again, the older I got, the less effort I was making to meet people and make connections with them. 'Don't get involved' had become my motto. As a consequence, my world had shrunk until it extended no further than Harriet,

Carol and Goodmonson. If Harriet didn't return, I was going to be very lonely indeed. Perhaps fate had brought me this opportunity to expand my world and force me to make some new connections.

My mind was made up, so I went out on a limb and texted Harriet.

I have some amazing news! Please contact me asap.

I added a smiley emoji for good luck and as a hint of contrition for my as yet unspecified failings. I ordered a sausage sandwich and it went down very well indeed. I have no idea if they were pork- or beef-based or a combination of both. I simply judged them by their taste.

10

PILCHARDS (ON TOAST)

There was no reply from Harriet to my 'amazing news' text by the time I got home. At around 6 p.m., my phone rang. It wasn't Harriet.

'Hello, Mr Giles, this is Kiara from Lansdowne Estates. So nice to speak with you again.'

'Hi, Kiara, I was about to ring you myself.'

'I should hope so. I think it is time you made a decision on my client's generous offer. Are there any questions you have that are causing you hesitation?'

'Yes, there are.'

'It would be best if you asked them to me, I think.'

'Of course. Can I ask if I will be getting a proper tenancy agreement?'

'Yes, you will be asked to sign a very standard one-year agreement that can be renewed at the end of its term.'

'What happens if Laurence isn't happy with the work I carry out for him?'

'I think he will be very happy.'

There was a silence as I contemplated her misguided confidence.

'Yes, maybe, but what if he isn't?' I asked.

'Your employment duties are in no way linked to your tenancy. They are mutually exclusive. You should understand, Mr Giles, that my client is very anxious to have you under his roof, and would feel the same even if your work, as you say, didn't make him happy. Any other questions?'

'No,' I replied. 'I would like to take up the offer.'

'I think you have made the correct decision. My client would like you to start at your very earliest convenience. Tomorrow would work well for him?'

I explained that I was happy to start within the next few days, but I needed to sort out my current tenancy. Truth is, I was nervous about leaving without having spoken to Harriet, but this was not a subject I wanted to discuss with Kiara.

'Do whatever you need to do regarding your present tenancy and let's give you another twenty-four hours. The day after tomorrow would be acceptable.'

'Well, I'll try, but no promises.'

She said she would arrange a removal van and ensure the move was stress-free. I agreed provisionally and promised to keep her updated. Better to accept now and pull out later if need be, was my thinking.

'Thank you very much, Mr Giles,' she said. 'Just one final thing. May I ask what you are wearing on your feet this evening?'

'My slippers.'

'Ah, the ones that can tolerate light outdoor usage.'

'That's the ones.'

'A very shrewd purchase. Goodbye.'

That evening I cooked myself a supper of tinned pilchards on toast and tried to relax by watching TV. It was hard to concentrate. What I had agreed to do felt flaky, even though I couldn't put a finger on an indisputable reason to decline. More worrying was the fact that I hadn't heard from Harriet. I went over the same old scenarios again and again, but my mind was becoming resistant to giving them its full attention. The thought of her being with another man was the one that troubled me most.

Could she be with another man? She had never spoken of anyone at work that she had made a particular connection with, and while I knew that a previous boyfriend of hers called Nick occasionally tried to get in touch with her, I was pretty sure he was in a new and happy relationship with a woman called Gemma. I recalled a conversation I'd had with Harriet about three months ago, when Nick's new life had been discussed.

'I got a text from Nick today,' Harriet announced.

'Oh yeah, does he want you back?' I replied with a friendly hue on my face.

'No, quite the opposite. He's moved in with a new woman called Gemma. She lives in Sevenoaks and plays the bongos.'

'Is that all he wanted you to know?' I asked.

'No, he wanted me to know that Gemma really loves cats. I think it's meant as a dig at me. He needs to move on.'

'Gemma sounds nice,' I said.

71

'Why don't you go and live with her then? she replied with her eyes crossed and a smile as wide as a KitKat.

'Because I hate bongos. They're too insistent, too relentless – the Morse code of percussion.'

'Nick loves a girl with a quirk,' said Harriet. 'He's easily drawn in. Sees the quirk before he sees the person. I bet she was playing the bongos when he met her.'

'Oh yeah, so what was your quirk when he met you?' I asked, genuinely interested in her response.

'I don't know, maybe my cropped hair? Is that what attracted you to me?'

'No. I mean, I love it, but it was the fact that you called me "Willy fucking Wonka" within thirty seconds of meeting me. Not a quirk – more of an attitude. A very appealing one, if you ask me.'

'You know what,' she said, having a sudden remember. 'I think I was going through a phase of wearing huge pink sunglasses all the time when I met Nick. Maybe that was my quirk.'

'I don't think I've ever seen you in sunglasses, apart from on holiday.'

'I know, it was just a quirk I was trying out at the time.'

'It's a decent quirk – understated. Unlike slapping bongos when they are not welcome, which is every minute of every day. Fucking bongos. So is that why you split up, because you stopped wearing sunglasses?'

'No, as you very well know, it was because he was an alcoholic who started stealing money from me.'

'Fair enough. I'm thinking maybe it's time I got *myself* a quirk. It might freshen up my outlook.'

'No need, you've already got one.'

'Oh yeah, what's that?'

'You're a short arse who talks to cats.'

I smiled at the memory. No, I thought, there was no way she was with Nick, and I couldn't think of any other potential suitor that featured in her life. In any event, Harriet wasn't a behind-your-back sort of person. If anything, she was too upfront. If there was another fella, she would have told me. At least, I think she would.

Goodmonson joined me on the sofa.

'She's still not back then, I see,' he said with a yawn of indifference.

'Yep, and she hasn't responded to the last text and smiley face I sent her.'

'Why do you do that?' he asked.

'Do what?'

'Send cartoons to adults.'

'Because it's endearing and a bit playful. It's meant to be fun.'

'Fun is overrated, boss.'

'Don't be so miserable, Monson. I need you to cheer me up, not bring me further down.'

'Oh, you want some "fun", do you?'

'Yeah, why don't you climb up on that cupboard and fall off into your water bowl or run around like a blue-arsed fly chasing mouse ghosts?'

'And why would that be "fun" for you?' he asked with attitude.

'Because, obviously, you would look like a prick and I would laugh at you and it would be archived as a "fun moment",' I replied truthfully.

'And what would I get from it?' he asked.

'The pleasure of knowing that you have made me happy.'

'Do you ever jump off cupboards or chase ghost mice around the room for Harriet?' he asked.

'No,' I replied.

'Exactly,' he stated as he jumped off the sofa and disappeared upstairs.

'I could throw you out, you know!' I shouted after him.

'Yeah, but you won't, because you can't stand being on your own. Goodnight, boss, try and be quiet when you come up. That would be fun.'

He was right. I was beginning to hate being alone.

11

THE SHED

I wasn't surprised to find out that Mr Barbour was over the moon at the chance to move in much earlier than he had anticipated. The estate agents were of course happy as long as they got their rent. They had arranged for him to visit again so that I could take him over how everything worked. I was happy to do this and it gave me the chance to mention to Barbour the remote possibility that Harriet might turn up thinking she still lived there.

The previous evening, I had emailed her.

Dear H,

Hope you are well. I miss you.

I know you asked me not to get in touch but I have to pass on some great news. In a nutshell, I have found us a new place to live! . . . SATSUMA HEIGHTS . . . Yes, SATSUMA HEIGHTS! . . . I'm moving our stuff there tomorrow. I'll explain more when I see you. Hope you understand that I had to let you know in case you went

75

back home and found a stranger living there (the new tenant is moving in the day after tomorrow). Don't worry, I won't leave anything behind.

Be great to hear from you, but no worries if you're not ready.

Matt x

P.S. Sergeant Walnuts sends his love.

She had not responded.

I had begun packing everything in boxes and Kiara had arranged a removal van for the following day, as promised. Carol had agreed to help me. Mr Barbour turned up at 11 a.m., dressed as previously with the addition of a pair of black leather gloves, which he declined to remove during the visit.

I gave him a quick guide to operating the central heating system, the washing machine and the dishwasher. I showed him where to find the stopcock and the fuse box and how to operate the loft ladder. He followed me around very closely and, unfortunately for both of us, his breath was severely tainted. It came at me in waves of invisible spears that exploded and released their poison the moment they arrived under my nose. The odour was indescribable – something akin to a gas leak from an infected pug or a recently flooded pet-food factory. I found myself turning my head away from him as I spoke and feigning an itchy nose so at least I could get temporary relief from the fabric conditioner on the cuff of my jumper. Strange that such a small, meek frame could emit such a severe punishment.

When the little tour was over, we had a brief, awkward chat.

'So can I assume you will give the place a thorough cleaning today?' he asked.

He obviously hadn't noticed that I had spent the previous evening and that morning cleaning the house, top to bottom, using quality products and buckets of elbow grease. I felt slightly bruised, as I considered myself one of the UK's foremost home cleaners and sprucers.

'I've already given the place a thorough once-over,' I replied. 'Is there something in particular you need doing?'

'Everything, really,' he continued. 'The windows need a good clean inside and out, the skirting boards are filthy and the sinks and bath need a good bleaching. The shed outside needs a good sweep, the light fittings need dusting and the grout in the bathroom needs scrubbing with a toothbrush. It all needs a deep clean. I shouldn't really have to tell you what needs doing. It's pretty damn obvious.'

That was probably his longest speech of the morning, and it released thousands of noxious particles of stench. I had to get myself out of range of this assault, so I rushed to the window overlooking the rear garden.

'Do you mean windows such as this one?' I asked.

'Yes, that is one of the windows that needs to be cleaned,' he replied sarcastically.

He was walking towards me and was clearly about to speak again, so I swiftly strode past him to the front window over-looking the road and placed my pointing forefinger up against the centre of the pane.

'And this one – is this a window that you need to be cleaned?' I asked.

'What's the matter with you? Like I say, I need *all* the windows cleaned.'

He was making his way towards me again. I didn't think I could survive another blast, so I opened the front door and stepped outside. I took a big gulp of fresh air and walked to the front gate, hoping that he would follow me. He didn't, so I was forced to return inside. I found him on all fours in front of the cupboard under the sink. He was removing various cleaning products and placing them on the floor by his knees.

'I don't want any of this stuff left here . . . Oh my word! Come here and have a look at this.'

As I walked over, he thrust his head further into the cupboard and then popped it out again just as I arrived beside him.

'Take a look at the state of that U-bend and all the filth on the back of the cupboard,' he demanded.

'No, it's okay, I know what you mean and I'll get it cleaned.' This didn't fend him off.

'Come down and take a look at the back of the U-bend,' he insisted. 'I need to know that you've seen it so you can't come back and say that you didn't know what I meant.'

I took a deep breath of the semi-fresh air and got onto my knees before slowly placing my head inside the cupboard. I immediately sensed his head entering the cupboard beside me.

'Can you see all that gunge on the back of the pipe?' he asked.

'Yes,' I said with my mouth almost shut. I could feel the air under the sink beginning to thicken.

'And what are those stains on the back? It looks like ketchup, or maybe blood even,' he blasted.

'Maybe,' I replied, forcing the word out through my nose to avoid breathing in.

His face was right beside mine as we crouched shoulder to shoulder inside the small cupboard. He reached forward and started to scratch at the ketchup/blood stain. I turned my head to the rear and chanced a small breath in through my nose. The lingerings hit me like a donkey kick. I fell backwards onto the kitchen floor, sprang to my feet and moved to the bottom of the stairs, where I took a tentative suck of air in through the sleeve of my jumper. He was back upon me within a moment.

'So you'll get that sink cupboard sorted, will you?'

'Of course. Is there anything else?'

'Come outside to the back garden,' he demanded as he made his way to the back door. I followed obediently, glad of the opportunity for some fresh air. He walked me straight into the small wooden shed. It was no more than four foot by four foot. Just a tool shed really.

'Don't hover around outside. Come in so that I can show you what needs doing.'

I stepped inside, hoping that the creosote and paints and general shed smells might provide some sort of shield.

'I would like all these hooks taken off the wall, and all these pots of paint and varnish and the like taken away. The floor could do with a sweep, and why would you think that I would want you to leave this pair of mouldy Wellingtons on the premises?'

I was holding my breath, so just nodded my agreement.

At this moment, Carol appeared in the doorway of the shed. 'I saw your front door was wide open so just thought I'd come in and check everything was okay.'

She took a step inside the shed, curious to see who was in there with me. 'Jesus fuck! What is that stench? Have you just opened a rat's coffin?' She reeled back out of the shed, covering her nose with the sleeve of her tracksuit top. 'Seriously, Matt, what have you got in there?'

'Like you say, smells like there might be something rotting under the boards,' I replied.

Barbour remained in the shed, sniffing the air like mice often do. 'I can't smell a thing,' he said. 'But whatever it is, I want it gone before tomorrow.'

'It will be, don't worry, and that is a guarantee,' I replied with one hundred per cent confidence. 'So, Carol, this is your new neighbour. He's moving in tomorrow. Say hello, why don't you.'

'Hello, darling. Moving home can be such a chore. How are you coping?' asked Carol, holding out her hand for a shake, which was declined by Barbour.

'Why do you ask? Are you a doctor or something? I haven't got time for this,' he replied, not making eye contact with Carol and still sniffing at the air. 'Right, I'm going. Don't forget to do everything I've asked or I'll be asking for a chunk of your deposit.'

'Lovely to meet you too,' shouted Carol as Barbour walked away and left via the back door.

Barbour had made a big mistake in making an enemy of Carol. She would want payback. I started wafting the shed door open and shut to get rid of the heavy air.

'Come here, Carol, try it out. See if the smell's gone.'

Carol took a step into the shed and declared: 'Yep, it's gone. Can't smell a thing. I wonder what it was.'

'It was his breath, Carol.'

'Fucking hell. That's not breath, darling, that's a weapon.'

We went inside and had a cup of tea. She told me she would miss having me as a neighbour and made me promise to keep in touch. As part of her divorce settlement, she owned a small flat not so far from London Bridge, and she said she hoped I would let her visit me whenever she was staying there. She showed little interest in talking about Harriet but did mention that, if possible, I should check if she had withdrawn any money from her bank account in the past few days or perhaps any large sums before she disappeared. It was a sound idea that I should have thought of myself.

Whilst chatting, it dawned on me that I had forgotten to tell Barbour of the small chance that Harriet might turn up believing that this was still her house. Carol assured me that she would pass this information on to him and I was sure that she would. Carol loved to be involved in other people's affairs and she would enjoy giving him the potentially inconvenient news.

After Carol returned home, I went up to the bedroom where Harriet kept a little Post-it note on the back of the dressing table with her important passwords written on it. Sadly, it did not include her banking login details. I opened the wardrobe and had a rifle through her coat and jacket pockets. I found a receipt for £24.99 from the Horseshoe Inn dated four days before she left. She had paid in cash.

12

HARRIET

I'm Harriet Matthews. I'm in a strange room with a man sat opposite me. The room is pitch black. I glanced at the man's face when he placed me into the chair. I have no idea who he is. I think I may have been unconscious prior to that. I remember receiving a blow to the back of the head. Since I've been here, I've been drifting in and out of sleep. My wrist is tied to a radiator. I'm too scared to open my eyes. My body is trembling. I feel sick. I'm desperate for a drink.

I keep my eyes shut tight, think about anything other than this man and his intentions. Disassociate. That's what defence barristers tell their clients when a trial is underway or they're facing their first night in prison.

I need to calm down before my brain explodes with fear. I can't look at him. I don't dare contemplate my immediate future. Maybe someone will come?

I need to take my mind elsewhere, away from this room. Keep my eyes shut.

Deep breaths. Stay still. Disassociate.

About me. I'm a senior case officer with the Crown Prosecution Service in central London. I have a team of ten working under me, and after six years in the job I haven't received a single complaint about the quality or quantity of my work. 'Dependable' is what my bosses would say. I love what I do and the people I do it with.

Sometimes I worry my life revolves too much around my career, but then, what's the alternative? Sit at home with Matt watching TV and talking to the cat? Matt doesn't give a fuck about work, but I wouldn't actually know who the hell I was without it. Shoot me if you want, but please do it when I'm on holiday.

Is it sad that my first port of call is to speak about my job? If you had asked me that a week ago, I would have answered with a resounding *no*, but in my current predicament, I'm not so sure.

Some basics. I'm thirty-four years old. I was born in Bolton in the north-west of England and lived there until I left to study Law at Leeds University. My mam was a housewife and my dad was the deputy headmaster of the comprehensive school I attended. I have one brother, Samuel. He's three years older than me and I'm not fond of him. As a kid, I was always an irritation in his eyes, and we were never close.

One summer's day, when I was eleven, he shot me in the shin with an air rifle he was playing with in the garden. The pellet broke the skin and it bled. He panicked, begged me not to tell our dad, and for a week or so after, played with me willingly and acted how I thought a proper brother should.

Then my parents found out about the air rifle incident. He was punished – Dad whacked him with a football boot – and he went back to the bullying and the teasing. He's married now with two large-headed children and a dog that Matt says smells like a freshly boiled saveloy. He works for a company that manufactures plinths and lecterns in an industrial park just outside Norwich. We don't really keep in touch. Matt has met him on a couple of occasions. They didn't get on. They are complete opposites. Matt describes him as 'relentlessly odious' and I agree with him.

I hear the man let out an exaggerated sigh. I'm hit by another wave of dread. My breathing is rushed and irregular. My lungs feel restricted and out of sync. He settles again. I take longer, deeper breaths through my mouth. How the hell am I meant to cope with this horror? I can't run, and blind fear has blocked my throat, stopping me from screaming or even speaking.

What do you care, anyway? I bet Matt has told you I'm the villain here. Careful, though, he rarely gets things right or includes information that might put him in a bad light. Has he told you that I like croissants, or that he often asks me if I'm happy? Probably, but neither's true. Has he told you about that woman, Carol, who lives next door but one? Even if he has, I bet he's left out the stuff that really matters and only given you the fairy-tale version. I'm a lot more reliable.

Back to my safe place, my little story.

More basics:

I'm five foot six, slim build, short cropped blonde hair and brown eyes.

I hate wearing high-heeled shoes, and leggings, and tight trousers. I never wear jewellery. My wardrobe consists of a dark grey suit for work, sweatshirt and tracksuit bottoms at home.

I like to cook, but Matt usually gets there first. I like to walk, but never find the time, and I read most nights before sleeping (biographies only).

I like hot baths and a warm bedroom.

I'm a good dancer (rarely get the chance, though, as Matt hates to dance).

I live in a two-bedroom rented terraced house in south London. It's not much, but Jesus wept I wish I was there now.

Mainly I work.

I attempt to grow vegetables every year, and have had some success with parsnips and courgettes. I usually make them into a soup, which I freeze then throw in the bin six months later.

I like walking in the Lake District, or better still the North York Moors. My walking boots are tan leather with red laces.

I learnt to play the cello at school and regret giving it up. I was happy at school. That's where I met my first boyfriend, Graham.

We were both fifteen and lasted until the summer holidays before I went to university. His hair was dark brown and mop-like. He was tall, had tattoos on his arms, and had a very kissable mouth. Matt would describe him as quirky. He was out of my league and, when he approached me one day as I walked home after school, I shit myself.

'Can I carry that bag for you, Harriet?'

'I haven't got a bag,' I blurted.

'So what's that over your shoulder?'

'Oh that! Yeah, that's my bag. No, it's okay, it's not heavy.'

'You live on Roman Road, don't you?'

'Yeah, just by the bus stop.'

'I live near there, on Claude Avenue.'

'Yeah, I know. I mean, I know you live somewhere around there. I've seen you walking about.'

'Is you hurting, Harriet?'

'Sorry?'

'I've seen you about. You always look a bit blue.'

'Yeah, sometimes I get a bit down. Don't you?' I asked.

'Nah, you've got to pick yourself up, get happy. Do you like bushcraft?' he asked.

'Don't know much about it,' I replied.

'Would you like to learn?'

'Yeah, why not.'

At which point he shoved me into a large bush leaning over a low front garden wall.

'That's your first lesson.'

We laughed. I felt electric. He invited me over to his house that evening. We spent an hour listening to Bob Dylan records. He loved his parents' music. He played along to some of the songs on his guitar, and I was dumbstruck and giddy. He kissed me on my forehead when I left. I wrote 'I love Graham' on my wrist that night as I struggled with my maths homework in bed.

From that day on, Graham was the centre of my life. He tried to teach me to play guitar, let me cut his hair into a council fringe, bought me a silver bracelet from Argos and took me for my first evening in a pub and got me drunk. He even wrote a song for me.

> *I am yours*
> *And you are mine*
> *We're bonded together*
> *Like garden twine*
> *Nothing can break us*
> *Or weaken our ties*
> *We'll be together*
> *Until one of us dies*

Something like that. I was so chuffed at the time.

He rarely came to my house unless my parents were away or out and about. When Dad found out about him, I was given a long interrogation. When I told him Graham was just a friend, I felt like Judas. Even so, Dad demanded that Graham come round for Sunday lunch.

It was a disaster.

'So, Graham, what are your plans for the future? Do you actually have any? What are your ambitions?' asked Dad as we sat eating pork chops, mashed potato and peas. No gravy. My dad thought gravy was common.

'Nothing concrete,' replied Graham. 'I know I want to travel and I'm really keen on learning bushcraft – you know, building shelters, foraging, trapping, that sort of thing.'

Dad didn't pick up on the fact that Graham was being a joker.

'And what exactly are you going to hunt for in Bolton? Pigeons?'

'Well, I don't intend to stay in Bolton for the rest of my life.'

'Are there many work opportunities for bushcraftsmen? I've never seen a "Bushcraftsmen required" advert. Maybe in the *Guardian*, I suppose.'

'I wouldn't be doing it as a career, more just to develop as a person, make a connection with nature and expand my horizons.'

'Oh wow,' interjected Mum. 'That does sound like fun.'

'Yes, well, life isn't necessarily about fun, is it?' continued Dad as Mum returned her attention to the rind of the pork chop. 'At your stage in life it should be about education and learning. Which university are you intending to apply for?'

'I haven't really thought about it. What university did you go to, Mr Matthews? Maybe I should go to that one.'

'Well, it wasn't one that offered bushcraft on the syllabus, so I doubt you'd be interested.'

'Harriet and I have spoken about maybe opening a coffee shop.'

'Oh really,' replied Dad with a smirk. 'And how do you intend to finance this ridiculous project?'

'My parents said they would help me with the cash. They are very kind and supportive like that. This pork chop is lovely, Mrs Matthews. You don't have any gravy, do you?'

'No, we don't,' barked Dad.

When Graham had gone, I asked my dad what he thought of him.

'I think he's perfect for you,' was his reply.

I didn't say it, but I absolutely agreed.

As our relationship carried on, it became less intense. Graham started to prioritize his friends over me, and I had to fit in around them. He never made any real attempts to integrate me into his gang, and whenever we went out with his friends, he seemed a completely different person; loud, inattentive, flirty, and desperate to be the centre of attention. It felt like he didn't really want me there, so in the end I avoided joining him when his friends would be around. Sometimes, it was a bit like he was living separate lives as two different people.

When it was just the two of us, I was treated to the version of Graham that worked for me. We would mostly meet up at his house, about two evenings a week, sometimes at the weekend, too, and sit in the front room of his parents' house listening to music and watching DVDs. He always wanted sex, and I was fine with that, but as soon as we'd finished I always sensed that he wanted me to leave.

During the last conversation we ever had, he told me, 'Listen, Harriet, at the end of the day, I've got family and I've got friends. And you? You've got nothing apart from me. I don't need the pressure.'

It hurt, you know, because it was true. I was broken-hearted. First cut is the deepest and all that.

Fast forward and it's weird that, with Matt and myself, the tables have been turned. Matt is happy for me to be the centre of his world and it's me that feels the pressure of his dependency.

I feel a sudden rush of nausea. I press my free wrist into my eye socket for relief. I hear the man shuffle in his seat again, which sends a fresh tremor of fear through me. I open my eyes for no longer than a blink. The room is still pitch black. I guess it must be approaching midnight.

He is scrolling through his phone and I see a snapshot of his face illuminated by the phone screen. He presents as a perfectly normal, educated, middle-class bloke. My work friend Millie always says they are the most dangerous.

Fuck. I wonder how everyone is getting on at work? We have a huge prosecution coming up and I can't let them down.

13

CONKERS

My first evening in Satsuma Heights felt very strange, and it was heartbreaking that Harriet was not there with me. After all, this was more her dream than mine. There was a big empty space at the other end of the dark chocolate sofa that I just couldn't ignore. I tried to make myself busy by unpacking all the cardboard boxes and guessing where Harriet would like things to be put, but stopped after around five boxes when I was hit by the feeling that the task was pointless. Harriet wasn't coming back. At best, I would receive a message telling me where and when to drop her things off. I might as well leave her stuff in the boxes ready to deliver on request.

After I had unpacked all the essentials, I set the streaming services I needed on the TV and fannied about looking for something to watch. I can usually find something on Nutflix (Harriet's 'joke'), but my mood made me unreceptive to any of its offerings.

I remembered that Kiara had given me an additional key when I moved in that morning. It was to open the door to the storage room by the lift on my floor. She said it was where I could find spare fire extinguishers, fuses, light bulbs and so on. I decided to go and take a look just out of curiosity.

It was a small, windowless room – say, ten foot by eight foot, and there was shelving to one side filled with maintenance stuff like plungers, toolboxes, torches and the like. On the wall at the far end was a framed print of a duck in a hurry carrying a briefcase under its wing. Humorous and inspirational; add to basket. Beneath the print was a small veneered wooden table and plastic chair. I removed the dust sheet that covered whatever was on its surface and revealed a laptop and a separate monitor. As I did so, the storeroom door opened behind me and in walked Laurence.

'Hello, Matt Giles, I see you found your little office.' He closed the door behind him. 'I think it's really neat, don't you? I do, without a shadow of a doubt. I love that print on the wall. Something very inspiring about it. That dude is definitely "movin' on" with his biz-e-ness.'

'What do you mean by "office"?' I asked.

'Let me show you.'

He turned on the laptop and both screens came to life. The laptop screen was split into four equal sections, three of them showing apartment interiors and the other just a black void.

'What am I looking at here?' I asked.

'You are looking at the three other flats on this floor. I have cameras deeply embedded within the sprinkler units above the front doors. Isn't that just remarkable and somewhat thrilling? All the really interesting things in life happen behind closed doors.'

'Fuck' was all I could offer.

'Fuck indeed, and forever and ever Amen' was his response.

'What's the blank square?' I asked.

'That's your flat,' he replied. 'Your predecessor insisted that I terminate that feed and I was happy to oblige. I'm not a monster, you know.'

The angle of the camera was identical in each shot, giving a restricted view of the lounge area only. The sole sound coming from the screen was the faint muttering of a television. Laurence clicked on the feed from flat 5C and the full-size image appeared on the monitor screen. The image was crisp and clean and showed a very large man sat on the sofa in a vest and pants eating a hot dog whilst he watched the TV. I couldn't take my eyes off him. A frisson of excitement passed through me. I was temporarily hooked. I could picture myself watching that screen, eating a hot dog of my own and enjoying every minute of the task.

'So, as you can see, Matt, we don't need to worry about closed doors. In fact, they are to our advantage. Like I say, all the best stuff happens behind them.'

'So, who's the big bloke and why is he of such interest to you?' I asked.

'I'm sure you'll find out his name in due course. As to what he means to me, that is something you don't need to know, both for my protection and yours. Do you understand? I hope you do.'

I came to my senses.

'I'm sorry, Laurence, but surely this isn't legal. I can't get involved with something like this.'

For the first time, I saw a slight crack in his slickness – just a nervous twitch at the side of his mouth, no more than that.

'This is my building and I have every right to know what is going on inside it. The legality or otherwise of the cameras is something of a grey area, but to cover any possible doubts, I have taken certain sensible precautions such as ensuring that none of the feeds are recordable and the IP address is untraceable. The tenancy agreements include a clause that gives permission for the owner to record video in all communal areas. My lawyers have assured me that the language is sufficiently ambiguous to cover me. I'm not worried. Are you? You shouldn't be. If I'm not worried, then that is quite the assurance. I have far more to lose than you.'

'Are you asking me to monitor these cameras as part of my duties?'

'No, not at all. It's up to you. Just think of it as a tool that's available to assist you in your observations should you deem it necessary. I have feeds in the penthouse, but I'm not here for a couple of weeks – maybe slightly longer if things develop in a certain direction.'

'There is no way that Harriet would go along with this.'

'Who is Harriet?'

'My partner.'

'You have a partner? Kiara seemed to think that might not be the case.'

'Well, she is wrong. Harriet and I have been together for over three years. I assumed it would be okay with you if she moved in with me?'

'Of course, so long as she is kept in the dark about the store cupboard.'

'I won't be using the store cupboard. Does that mean our agreement is over?'

'Not at all. You've signed your tenancy and, like I say, this room is an option, not a requirement. The previous guy used it for a while and then got bored but, then again, he only lasted a month.'

'Laurence, I'm not going to monitor these screens.'

'That's what they all say. So, why has Harriet not moved in already?'

'She's away at the moment and everything has moved so quickly that I thought I would keep the move as a surprise. She loved this place when we first viewed it so I know she'll be over the moon.'

'Good lad. Ladies love a surprise, probably more than men. Do you agree? I know I do.'

He switched off the laptop and turned to face me directly.

'Tell me, Matt, what is your relationship with your neighbour Carol?'

How on earth did he even know of the existence of Carol?

'She's my neighbour – nothing more, nothing less.'

'Kiara had a little chat with her the other day outside your home and was left with the impression that she might be your lover. She's very perceptive; it's one of her main skill sets.'

'Absolutely not. I'm afraid Kiara is very wrong about that.'

'She is rarely wrong, Mr Giles, but we don't need to debate that right now. Let's hope your Harriet isn't similarly mistaken.'

There was something in his manner that suggested he knew something I didn't concerning Carol and Harriet. I tried to push him a little.

'So what exactly did Carol say to Kiara?'

'You should ask Carol. That would be the correct course of action. Right, I believe we are finished here. Off you go and promise me you will start making those connections with your neighbours. Prove to me that I was right to place my trust in you.'

I offered up a nervous smile and left him inside the store cupboard.

14

HARRIET

I open, then immediately shut, one eye. I see the silhouette of the stranger sat no more than five feet from me, still scrolling on his phone. Panic returns and punches me in the stomach.

What does he want? What are his intentions? I begin to wish he would make a move, put me out of my misery. I'm too frozen with dread to make any move of my own.

Where am I? The room is warm and has an expensive smell to it. I can hear traffic nearby and sirens in the distance. I'm guessing I'm still in London.

Keep your eyes shut, steady with the breathing. Pretend to be asleep. Disassociate.

So, where was I?

That's right, I was telling you about my first boyfriend, Graham.

I only had one other boyfriend prior to the arrival of Matt. He was called Nick.

We met for the first time about six years ago at a food and music festival in Hyde Park, Leeds, where I was working as a

·

legal executive with the local council. I was sat alone on my green tartan picnic rug wearing extremely oversized pink-framed sunglasses and my 'Meat is Murder' T-shirt whilst eating a sausage roll. My two friends had gone off on a wander, leaving me to guard their stuff. Nick sat down beside me and immediately demanded that I take off the sunglasses and let him 'have a go on them'. I handed them over.

They suited him. He wore his dark brown hair in a thick quiff with short back and sides, and he was wearing that famous Nirvana T-shirt with the crooked smiley face and a pair of scruffy, faded electric-blue jeans. On his feet he had dark red brothel creepers. He looked like a wanker but, you know, one of those wankers that you can't help but fancy. He was tall – too tall for it to go unmentioned.

'They suit you,' I said. 'I think tall blokes can pull off a touch of pink.'

'Yeah, I agree. On a small man, pink just makes them look like their life is a struggle and I mean, come on, what's the point of being a shadow when you can shine even when the sun isn't out?'

Yes, he really was a wanker. He spoke with an affected London drawl, like Mick Jagger. I discovered that he lived in London but was up in Leeds helping out a mate who was operating a food van for the festival goers. They were selling hot pork and stuffing rolls and deep-fried frozen chips. He asked me if I wanted a free roll, as that was very much something he could secure for me. I asked him why he had chosen to bother me.

'I've been watching you,' he replied. (*Creepy* . . .) 'And you look bored, like you're waiting for something to happen, so here I am, answering your call.'

'Can I have my sunglasses back, please?'

'No, not until you tell me your name, address and National Insurance number.'

'No chance.'

'Well, what about a drink with me after I clock off from the van?'

'I'm willing to do that if I'm still here.'

'Good decision. I'll keep the glasses till I see you.'

As he bounded off, wiggling his arse, I got the feeling I had just lost ownership of those sunglasses, and I was right.

We met up for that drink and we started to see each other most weekends, sometimes in Leeds but mostly in London. Six months later, I packed all my belongings into his VW Beetle and moved in with him, having secured myself a job as an executive officer with the Crown Prosecution Service.

On that drive to London, Nick had a new air freshener in the shape of a black bowler hat hanging from his rearview mirror, and I leaned forward to sniff it. It gave off the faint smell of orange.

'Why would the manufacturers associate oranges with a bowler hat?' I asked. 'I can't think of any link between citrus and the shape of a bowler hat.'

'Does there have to be one?' he replied. 'Does it have to look like an orange to have an orangey smell?'

'No, but maybe if it was an orange hat that would help sell the link to the sniffer.'

'And you would find that reassuring?'

'No, I couldn't give a fuck really, but I'd like to know if you bought it because it looked like a hat or because it smelt of orange?'

'I suppose I was drawn to its hattiness first and then just checked that it wasn't a smell I hated.'

'What smells do you hate?'

'Onions, Parmesan, watery bacon,' he reeled off confidently.

'No need for you to check the smell then, really. It's never going to be one of those flavours.'

'Yeah, I guess you're right,' he admitted.

'I like the idea of a hat that smells of onions,' I announced.

I lived with Nick in his one-bedroom flat in East Dulwich, an ex-council flat in a four-storey 1960s block. We were on the third floor, served by a piss-tainted lift that had the words 'WELCOME TO ROCK BOTTOM' graffitied on one of its walls.

Nick was easy-going and undemanding. I concentrated on work. My breakthrough case, where I proved I could cut the mustard, was the prosecution of a large ring of petrol station owners in west London who were operating a stolen credit card scam. Basically, the cashiers had a bunch of stolen cards behind the counter and when a customer paid in cash, they would pocket the money and cover themselves by charging an identical amount on one of the stolen cards. The total ran into the hundreds of thousands of pounds. Sounds a straightforward case, but it was a complicated prosecution. The trial lasted seven weeks and involved reams and reams of credit card records that were next to impossible for the jury to make sense of. The prosecuting barrister wanted to withdraw the case halfway through but I put myself on the line and managed to persuade my boss to insist we continue. We won the case. I was the hero. I had arrived.

Nick liked to go to the pub and I would join him on a weekend or whenever work hadn't been too exhausting. He was a loud and confident bloke – a show-off, truth be known. I was happy enough to be his partner, but it never felt permanent. Whenever I glanced over at him entertaining his inevitably quirky friends at the bar, I did wonder if it would be better to be just one of his friends and receive all the joy without any of the obligations.

He didn't have a job as such, but had enough connections to get by. He would work as a barman, a labourer, a courier, a tour guide, waiter, shop assistant, painter and decorator – any work that he could persuade one of his mates to give him. His dream was to own a record shop. He wanted that to be my dream too, but I always knew that Nick was not someone likely to give you a good return on your investment.

Whenever he mentioned his retail plans, I would listen without comment. He seemed to have the idea that I was flush with cash, and occasionally would show me an empty shop he had enquired about and tell me that, with my wages, we could easily afford to rent it and buy enough stock to get started. Come the crunch, I was honest and always told him to exclude my salary from his shop idea.

He drank a lot and, increasingly, did so during the day. Often

I would return from work to find him fast asleep on the sofa with the TV blaring out and the curtains drawn tight. He wasn't looking after himself, the quiff had lost its perkiness and his friends were beginning to contact him less and less with offers of work. I think it was when he started drinking wine rather than beer that his decline really kicked in. His drunkenness changed from friendly and childish to belligerent and antagonistic. I started to avoid going to the pub with him and began to work late in the hope that he would be out by the time I got home.

He returned to the flat one Sunday afternoon with a mate and began bringing box after box of old vinyl records up in the lift. The boxes soon filled the living room, the hallway and half the kitchen.

'What the fuck are this lot?' I asked.

'It's stock, darling. It's goods for sale. It's our future. It's the start of a journey I was destined to make.'

He moved in to give me a hug, but I pushed him away.

'And how much did this all cost?'

'A lot less than I'm going to sell it for and that's a cold hard certainty.'

'It must have cost hundreds if not thousands of pounds, Nick. How did you pay for it?'

'I used your card, darling. It was too good an opportunity to miss out on. We should celebrate, open a bottle of wine, have a dance in our knickers.'

He was laughing and gurning and swaying slightly in the non-existent breeze. He was drunk.

'How much were they, Nick?'

'A few thousand pounds, but what cost happiness and ambition?'

'HOW FUCKING DARE YOU!' I shouted as I walked out of the flat and stood on the walkway in protest and disgust. He didn't follow me.

I wanted to pack up my stuff and leave immediately but I had nowhere to go. My life revolved around Nick and his mates. Why had I put so much of myself into yet another shiny shitshow?

Nick had an orangey smell, but he wasn't an orange. I have to acknowledge that, with Matt, you get what you smell.

I hear the man get off his chair and start moving around the room.

Keep your eyes shut, keep still, don't make a sound.

15

HOT DOG

A couple of hours after my chat with Laurence, at about 9 p.m., I found I could no longer resist the itch that was insisting I go and have a quick peep at the monitors and check what the hot-dog man was up to. I'm only human. I promised myself it would be a one-time-only visit and if I saw anything I felt uncomfortable with I would leave immediately. When I entered the store cupboard, there was a note on the office desk.

Hi Matt,
Let's get going.
User: Lest_p1t@gmail.com
Pass: Oh1Oh2Oh3!
Let's give you a head start:
Flat 5B: Justin Hamper
Flat 5C: William Hoover
Flat 5D: Vacant at the moment. Watch this space.
Speak soon,
Laurence

I logged on and the monitor came to life.

The top-left quadrant of the screen showed the interior of flat 5B, and I dragged the image full-screen onto the monitor. The layout was similar to my flat but was clearly several square feet larger. I guessed this was a two-bedroomed unit. The camera showed the lounge area. On the far left side of the screen you could see the kitchen island, but not the whole of the kitchen. The view of the camera was fixed, as far as I could tell. The flat faced south and the lights of London provided a warm glow across the room. There was also a small amount of light coming from what I assumed to be the appliances in the kitchen. The lounge was clutter-free and slightly sterile, and there was a large, expensive-looking painting or print on the wall to the right above the television. It appeared to depict a heron acting nonchalantly in an abandoned dock. Opposite the TV was an orange L-shaped leather sofa with a large, square, black coffee table in front of it. Under the coffee table was a round woollen rug with orange circles on a cream background. Other than that, nothing stood out. It could have been a show home.

A man sporting bare feet entered the lounge and sat himself down on the sofa. He was wearing tight grey lounge pants and a slightly lighter grey T-shirt and held a glass of red wine in one hand. Justin Hamper, I assumed. He was tall, athletic, and wore his thick dark brown hair in an uneven side parting. I guessed his age to be mid-thirties and his working life a success. A banker was an obvious guess, but the ambience of the apartment suggested something more creative. I plumped for architect with the expectation of being proved wrong.

He topped his wine glass up and balanced a laptop on his massive thighs. He scratched his tanned foot, sneezed, then wiped the screen with the hem of his T-shirt. I watched as he took a large gulp of wine, posed to his phone and took a selfie. I watched as he itched the top surface of his thigh beneath the laptop, put one finger in his ear and jigged it around furiously for five seconds, then twiddled the corner of his right eyebrow. I watched as he took another gulp of wine, then picked up his phone and scrolled, pausing at one moment to pull a hair from his nostril. I watched as he adjusted himself on the sofa and spilt a few drops of wine on the exterior side aspect of his right thigh.

'Fuck!' he blurted.

It was the first human speech I had heard through the computer and it gave me a start. I don't know why, but I had assumed that there wouldn't be sound on the feed. It made the scene feel all the more intimate, and my watching more intrusive. I felt a gentle waft of shame flick around the store cupboard. I turned away from the screen and did an internet search for the name Justin Hamper on my phone. And there he was. His LinkedIn profile read:

Justin is a senior instructor and has been teaching Iyengar and Ashtanga yoga since 2015. He is both a teacher and a therapist and uses yoga to exercise both the body and the mind. Justin believes that through yoga he can create a sense of joy, space, ease and clarity of purpose for his clients . . .

Blah blah blah.

I selected his contact details from the menu, clicked through the links and booked myself a two-session introductory course starting the next day. This felt like a positive step – something achieved, some residential intelligence commenced. Back in his lounge, Hamper was now stood in front of the floor-to-ceiling windows directly opposite the camera. His back was towards me and he was clenching and unclenching his bum cheeks as he took in the view. The yoga thing made perfect sense; his cheeks were as tight and firm as a couple of conkers in cling-film. I coughed a few times. It didn't draw his attention.

In the corner of my eye, I noticed some screen activity in Flat 5C. It was hot-dog man, lowering himself into the huge easy chair positioned directly in front of his TV. Yes, there he was again: William Hoover, looking magnificent in the full glare of the TV. I guessed his age at around fifty, and he was wearing a light blue short-sleeved polyester shirt, which he unbuttoned as soon as he sat down to liberate his belly. His face was round and friendly, with nice symmetry and a good safe distance between his eyes. His skin was smooth and pale, but had a healthy pink tinge. His dark brown hair was thinning badly and, although not a comb-over, there was plenty of space between the strands of hair. Relative to his body, his head was on the small side, though it bulked up under his jaw, giving the fleeting impression that he was wearing a surgical collar.

Through the computer, I heard the ringing of a doorbell, loud and clear and crispy. Hot Dog slowly eased himself out of the chair and made his way to his front door. It was a take-away pizza delivery. Hot Dog thanked the courier and gave him a tip from the pocket of his dark blue tracksuit pants. He made his way back to the chair with a noticeable increase in his speed. After sitting back down, he opened up the box, using his ample belly as a table, and a broad smile appeared on his face. I watched in awe as he demolished the twelve-inch pizza in less than three minutes. I was watching a happy man. Maybe living alone was the key to contentment, I thought. You can be yourself when no one else is around. On the other hand, as a snapshot of his life, it felt desperately sad.

I did a search of Hot Dog's name on my phone, but nothing came up that matched the man in front of me. In any event, I assumed the internet would be largely irrelevant to my task, as undoubtedly Kiara would have searched all the available information on Laurence's behalf. Hot Dog produced a bottle of beer from somewhere within the chair's folds and settled himself down to watch TV.

It was hard to make a guess at what he did for a living. Away from the context of a luxury block of flats, I think I would have him down as a lorry driver, or perhaps a warehouse foreman. Inside this building, however, I was tempted by the thought that he was either a cuddly, eccentric barrister or perhaps a university academic. I assumed he was single. In fact, he seemed to be flouting his independence directly through my screen. He had designed this life around himself and nobody else.

He eventually got up from his throne and turned off the TV. As he left my view, the lights were turned off in the lounge and kitchen. I heard the sounds of him preparing for bed and his flat fell silent not long after.

I glanced at the clock on the computer and was gobsmacked to see that I had been watching the screen for over an hour. The time had flown by. I must have enjoyed it. I was going to have to take care that I didn't become addicted to this voyeurism, and made a promise to myself that this would be my one and only session in front of the screens.

The remaining vacant apartment, 5D, was in more or less total darkness. There was a tiny pool of light in the far-right corner, probably from a standby light, and another strip of light along the bottom of the blinds opposite the camera. The blinds were thick, dense and forbidding.

Out of the blue, just as I was about to turn off the computer, I heard a cat meow. It wasn't the noise itself that gave me a start, but rather the realization it induced that I had left Goodmonson behind in the rush of the move. I panicked and considered phoning Carol to check on him, but it was too late in the night. I would sort it first thing in the morning.

Nothing to worry about. He'll be fine, I told myself. Barbour was a cat lover and would see that no harm came to him.

When I went to bed, I found it difficult to find sleep in the unfamiliar surroundings. The mattress was hard and unforgiving and rain was pelting against my bedroom window. Central London was noisy, with people shouting on the street and ambulances and sirens coming and going from the nearby Guy's Hospital.

I kept thinking about Goodmonson and how confused and

lonely he must be feeling. I could have shed a tear for my precious little boy. I wondered if Harriet had felt this way at any point over these past few days. I hoped so, which I knew was wrong of me.

That night I dreamt of sleeping atop a giant soft-skinned hot dog whilst snow was falling outside. Monson was scratching at the window with a tiny pair of handcuffs around his paws.

16

THIS AND THAT

The next day, I telephoned Carol at 8 a.m., fully aware that she would be at her sentry post in the bay window of her house. She picked up her phone immediately.

'Hello, darling. What do you want? Are you missing me already?'

'Yeah, I just had to hear your voice, Carol. I'm totally lost without you.'

'Oh, darling, you say that in jest but I think it's probably true. Are you phoning to check if Harriet's made an appearance?'

'Has she?'

'No, of course not. Stop obsessing, Matt. Look after yourself or you might perish.'

'I'm trying. Listen, I left Goodmonson behind yesterday. Have you seen him?'

'Oh, you idiot. So what do you want me to do about it? That cat hates me; I won't be able to round him up.'

'But have you seen him? I know you'll be watching the street and he's usually out and about in the morning.'

'No, I haven't.'

'Well, would you go round to the house and apologize to the man and pick him up for me? I'll come over later and collect him off you.'

'Fuck's sake, Matt, he was a total arse with me the other day. I was going to do a cold shoulder and try to turn the whole street against him. Now you're asking me to make a first move when it's *him* who should come to *me* to apologize and beg forgiveness.'

'Please, Carol, I'm really worried about Monson, and Barbour seems the type of person who might report me to the RSPCA or something.'

'Well, I can't do it until he comes back from work. He left about five minutes ago. Now, have you heard anything from Harriet?' she asked.

'No, not yet.'

'Well, be as strong as you can be, darling. Whatever the outcome, you will be okay.'

'Not without my cat.'

'Yes, I get it, I'll phone you as soon as I've spoken to him. See you later.'

'Oh, one more thing, Carol.'

'What is it now? I'm trying to keep an eye on the street here.'

'Do you remember the other day, outside your house, you had a quick chat with the smartly dressed lady with the blonde hair?'

'Yes, vaguely.'

'Well, she works for the man who has rented me the new flat and you seem to have left her with the impression that you and I are having an affair.'

'How ridiculous. I don't know what could have given her such an idea. All I did was point out to her that the street parking was permit only. She didn't even apologize. Not my type at all – very fucking splashy.'

'And that was all that was said?'

'As far as I recall. See you later.'

Feeling reassured about Monson's prospects, I made myself some beans on toast but left half on the plate. I still had no appetite. I considered having a bath in the Hilliard, but instead decided to write a note for my new neighbours:

Hi, my name is Matt Giles. I'm your new neighbour in Flat 5A. I will be your point of contact for any emergencies, complaints, issues etc. . . . Looking forward to meeting you when the chance arises.

I slipped a copy of the note under each of the doors as I made my way down to the lobby. Kiara had told me to introduce myself to the day porter when she handed over the keys to me yesterday. He would give me a list of useful contacts to use in the event of any maintenance problems. His name was Derek.

'As far as Derek is aware,' she explained, 'you are a trusted friend of my client who will be taking over the duties of the previous occupant of Flat 5A. We have told him to give you all the assistance you might need. I think you will find him to be a good connection and a useful source of information.'

Derek was sat behind his impressive counter opposite the front doors of the building. He didn't have a uniform as such, but wore a smart grey suit with a white shirt and dark blue woollen tie. He was well into his sixties with a bald head and a cheeky pencil moustache. On a younger man, the tash would have made him look a spiv, but on Derek it gifted him a distinguished lilt and suggested he might have a tale or two up his sleeve.

I introduced myself and he confirmed that he was expecting me. He gave me a brown envelope that contained a master key card that he explained must only be used in the case of a genuine emergency or with the express permission of 'Mr Laurence'. Every use of the card was digitally logged, so I was to think very hard before ever using it. I tried to turn the conversation towards the friendly.

'That's a nice grey suit. You happy with what it achieves for you?'

'It's comfortable and that's all that matters to me,' he replied.

'Sounds about right. So, how long have you been working here?' I asked.

'Since the building opened nearly a year ago.'

'And do you enjoy it?'

'It pays the rent and I'm thankful for that.'

The lobby lift opened and out wandered Hot Dog.

'Morning, Derek,' he boomed without looking our way. 'Nice day for a bit of this and that,' he added as he walked by.

'It really is, Mr Hoover, and you're the man to make the most of it,' replied Derek as Hot Dog left the building.

'Who's that fella?' I asked.

'Mr Hoover,' Derek answered. 'He's been here a couple of months. Nice enough guy once you get to know him but, between you and me, you don't want to get on his bad side, especially if he's been on a session at the Horseshoe.'

'Thanks for the tip. What does he do for a living?'

'Whenever I've asked him that question he just says "this and that". He spends most days holed up in the Horseshoe, so if by "this and that" he means boozing and snacking, then I suppose that's about right. What about you? What's your line of work?'

'I'm between jobs at the moment. Looking for a change of direction.'

'Aren't we all,' he replied.

I was about to tell him that I was a sales executive in the bathroom furniture game but felt a sudden shame in making that admission. Perhaps it was the rarefied surroundings that made me hesitate. I plumped for a nonsense diversion.

'I was thinking of setting up an eco-friendly trumpeting school.'

Derek gave out a little parp of a giggle.

'I wish you luck with that much-needed initiative,' he said.

I felt a connection had been made, so, rather than blow it, I stepped away and strolled over to the Horseshoe to see if I could keep the momentum and seed a connection with Hot Dog, too.

17

DARTS

The Horseshoe was a stand-alone, wedge-shaped Victorian pub that shared its paved forecourt with Satsuma Heights. It was three storeys high, had a dark green tile and brick exterior and a row of about ten picnic-style tables outside. The windows and door were dark green and the awning that provided some rain cover for the picnic tables was the same colour. A handwritten sign on the door said 'Bar Staff Wanted: Apply Within'.

Inside, the décor was heavily focused on bare wood and the seating was divided up by fixed wooden screens with fancily engraved glass panels. It was very much a pub that cuddled you and encouraged a long, relaxing boozing session. There was even a dartboard at the far end of the room, and that's something you have to respect in these times of instant gratification. It took me until I was thirty-eight years old to hit my first one hundred and eighty, but lord, it was worth the wait.

I ordered a pint of shandy and took a seat three tables along from where Hot Dog was sitting. We were both facing the bar with our backs to the window. Hot Dog was on the Guinness and was munching crisps from the two open bags on his table.

It was around midday and the pub was quiet. A couple of blokes sat at the bar and four or five other people were dotted around passing their time. The tiny speakers spying down from the ceiling were playing crooning songs from the 1950s and 60s – Frank Sinatra, Bobby Darin, that sort of thing. It was pleasant enough.

I had nearly finished my pint when Hot Dog got out of his seat, ordered another Guinness at the bar and strolled over to the dartboard. He pulled a set of darts out of his jacket pocket and began to play. He was pretty good. This was my chance, I thought, so I went over and stood nearby. I waited until he was between shots before speaking.

'Hi there, you fancy a game?' I asked.

'What's your problem, mate?' he replied without taking his eyes off the dartboard.

I was completely thrown off-course by this hint of aggression. 'Sorry, just wondered if you . . .'

He turned around to face me and placed a heavy hand on my shoulder. 'I'm trying to play a game here. Can you not just fuck off back to your shandy?'

'Yeah, sorry, mate,' I replied, holding my palms up towards him in a gesture of submission.

'And don't "mate" me. Do you not know who I am?'

'No, sorry . . . Listen, I didn't . . .'

'I'm Bill fucking Hoover.'

I didn't have a clue how to respond to this hint of notoriety and so quickly decided to abandon the mission.

'Sorry again, Bill,' I said apologetically. 'I'm Matt Giles, by the way. I've just moved into the flat opposite you. I slipped a note under your door this morning.'

I held out my hand for him to shake. He ignored the invite, so I turned and started to walk away.

'Are you any good?' he shouted after me, stopping me in my tracks. 'I don't want to waste my time on a pipsqueak.'

His voice was loud and Northern, probably Yorkshire but maybe more Manchester − I'm shit at knowing the difference.

'Yeah, I'm not too bad,' I replied, turning back to face him. 'If I'm not up to your standard then we can pack it in after the first game.'

'You don't look very darty. You look more of a jigsaw man.'

I smiled in agreement, figuring that was the best way of reassuring him that he was the boss in this little drama.

'Go on then,' he continued. 'I'll give you a game. Do you want to play for cash? Put your money where your boast came from?'

'Don't mind putting a fiver on it,' I replied.

He took a few steps towards me. Shit, he was massive. I realized it might not be a good idea to try and win the game.

'What about best of three for twenty quid?' he asked.

'Go on then, let's do it,' I replied, thinking, either way, it would be twenty quid well spent on working the connection. 'I haven't got my darts with me, though. Can I use yours?'

'No fucking chance, lad, these are Bill Hoover's darts. Ask at the bar − they've got a set you can use.'

I went to the bar and the barman produced a battered set of darts with Union Jack flights.

'Careful with him, mate,' he whispered as he handed them over to me.

I walked the thin line between letting him win whilst at the same time giving him a decent game. After he won the first leg, I gave him a polite 'Well done'.

In response, he pointed the tip of his dart at me and said in very plain Northern: 'Shut the fuck up during the game.'

I won the next leg. He smiled, and asked if I wanted to up the stake to fifty quid. I dared to decline and he laughed at me. The last leg came down to which of us could hit a double first. There was no way I was going to risk winning, so I made sure that my darts were wayward. Eventually he hit double five and the game was his. He shook my hand then held his out to receive his prize. I gave him the twenty quid and when he put it in his wallet, I noticed that he only had a five-pound note in there. He couldn't have paid me anyway. This was a man with darts confidence, I thought.

'I've enjoyed that, Jigsaw. Let me get you a drink from my winnings.' I sat down and he joined me at the table with two pints of Guinness in his hands. 'Get that down your neck – next round is yours.'

We sat chatting for another couple of hours. The drinks kept coming and he wasn't about to let me refuse them. His phone started to ring every ten minutes or so but remained steadfastly in his pocket. I took this as a sign that he might be enjoying my presence.

The drink loosened him up, and he turned out to be great company. I made a mental note of any useful information he gave so it would be mine to pass on to Laurence if I felt it to fall within the scope of residential intelligence. So far, I had gathered the following:

1. He was from Yorkshire.

2. He lost a testicle in the late 90s when a dog attacked him in a laundrette. (He maintained that the remaining one was 'an absolute brute'.)

3. He lived alone. He had been married but she left him four years ago when she had an affair with a dry cleaner. ('Never been happier,' he declared, and I believed him.)

4. For a living he did 'this and that'. (When I asked, he said he preferred 'that', then lifted up his pint of Guinness and added, 'But I'm fine with this.')

5. He said he had never met Laurence – a claim that I knew to be untrue. (Laurence had told me the opposite during my interview.)

6. He used to do a bit of burglary when he was younger. His speciality was disabling burglar alarms by injecting cavity foam into the old-fashioned wall-mounted siren boxes. (He claimed he once broke into Rod Stewart's house and stole a box of wigs. He still had a couple of them and offered to show them to me if I was interested.)

7. He hated the internet, Formula One, seeded breads, tight trousers, students, the police, small dogs, strimmers, wine drinkers, nosey fuckers, high-gloss paint, hummus, solar panels, Bluetooth, politicians and, most of all, conifer trees.

That's about all I got. He had given me very little information about himself or his present circumstances. I wondered if
this was deliberate. More likely it was because I avoided asking
him too many direct questions. I didn't want to come over as
a 'nosey fucker' and raise any suspicions. He showed little interest
in me, though did ask if I had been bothered by the sound of
his TV. When I said I hadn't, he replied, 'We should get on just
fine then.'

Eventually he answered one of his incoming calls and ended
the brief conversation with 'I'll see you in a minute'. Not long
after, the driver who had brought me to Satsuma Heights came
into the pub and walked straight to the toilets. Hot Dog got
up and followed him. Less than a minute later, the driver
emerged and walked straight out of the pub. Hot Dog came
out a few moments after and sat back down with me.

'I'll get the next round if you'll fetch them,' he said as he
opened his wallet. It was now bulging with cash.

I stumbled back into my flat around 3 p.m. I had really
enjoyed my afternoon boozing session with Hot Dog. It was
years since I had sat down in a pub with another fella and just
passed some lazy time together. Maybe deep down I craved
some male company more than I cared to admit.

So, Hot Dog was a drug dealer. Laurence was going to be
plenty impressed with me. This job was a breeze and they had
definitely chosen the right bloke, I thought, as I lay on the sofa
and drifted off, the drink having temporarily unburdened me
of my Harriet anxiety. I was woken up a couple of hours later
by the sound of my phone ringing. It was Carol.

'So, you won't believe this, darling,' she declared.

'Oh, hi, Carol. Won't believe what?'

'He won't give him back. I've just been over there and he refused to hand him over. Says he's his cat now.'

'What? Are you having me on?'

'No, of course not. He told me straight to my face that the cat belonged to him and that in any event, it was none of my business. We need to fuck him up, don't you think, darling?'

'Okay, I'll be right over.'

I found Monson's carrier amongst the packing boxes and headed out of the flat.

18

HARRIET

There is movement in the room. I open my eyes no more than a millimetre or so. He is stood with his back to me in front of an open door. He is talking to someone very quietly, as if he doesn't want to take the chance of me hearing. I should scream and alert the visitor. I try to summon the breath to do so but it won't come. My throat is still locked with fear. He turns back towards me. I shut my eyes. The arm that's bound to the radiator is aching. I can't keep still for much longer. I hear the door shut and the room return to silence. I think he is standing beside my chair but I can't be sure.

Block him out. Search for some calm within my little story.

After Nick, I moved into a shared house arrangement with a work colleague called Bradley Iles. It was a three-bedroom end-of-terrace Victorian house in Hither Green. I had my own bedroom and en-suite bathroom in the loft conversion. Bradley lived there with his wife Sarah and their daughter Catherine. I didn't mix with them much; I was grateful for the favour and felt the best thing I could do in return was to be invisible. It was a lonely time, but I was enjoying my work.

I had progressed enough to be only handling important Crown Court cases; fraud, money laundering and the like were my speciality. I wanted to 'win' every case, and a great sense of achievement would rush through me whenever a defendant was found guilty. I always thought I was the linchpin, even if it was the prosecution barrister that took all the plaudits. Whenever we 'won' a big case, the whole office would go out for a drink together and slap each other's backs all night. I lived for these evenings; they were the joyful little punctuations in my otherwise plodding timeline. I was a happy lass.

Then I met Matt, and life shifted.

Bradley was hosting a party at the house. Matt was a friend of his and Sarah's, and that's where we met.

He was plain-looking, I thought, certainly not as striking as the green puffa jacket he was wearing, with brown eyes and short dark hair. His face was round and pleasant, though, and he had an open smile. I was hating the party, and from his hunched stance staring at the flowers in the borders, I guessed that he was too. I said hello to him to pass some time until I could politely retire to my room.

Matt always says that I called him 'Willy fucking Wonka' when he expressed his love of alliums. I don't think that's true. I think that's what he wished I'd said. I've always thought that when he was young, he must have had an invisible friend that always laughed at his jokes and always replied with a quip of equal quality. He does it now with his cat Goodmonson. I expect he's told you that I don't like his cat. It's not true, but I am a bit jealous of it.

Matt was easy to talk to and he didn't seem interested in me just because I was a single woman. He sold bathrooms and seemed passionate about his work. He didn't talk about much else other than his job when we first met. He was a great listener; I don't think he interrupted me once that first night. I must have bored him stiff but he didn't show it. Before he left, he invited me to come and have a look at the furniture on display at his bathroom showroom in Dulwich.

I took up the offer the following Saturday, arriving at his showroom just before closing time. He had been on my mind all week. I had chosen my arrival time carefully in the hope that he would invite me for a coffee or something after work, and to his credit he did. We crossed the road outside the show-room and were the first customers of the evening at the Raj Pavilion Curry House.

He was a different man from the moment we entered the restaurant – no longer so cautious or reserved in his demeanour. He had brought his 'A' game, non-threatening first-date persona with him. I was happy to be on the receiving end.

'Have you ever been in an Indian restaurant before?' he asked as he pulled out my chair for me.

'Yes, Matt, hundreds of them,' I replied.

'Have you ever sat opposite a man in an Indian restaurant?' he asked as he sat down opposite me and placed his chin on his hands like a benevolent professor.

'Yes, Matt, many times, and even, on occasion, adjacent to a man.'

'That is an excellent detail but, tell me, have you ever picked up a menu from the table in an Indian restaurant and perused it with great intensity?'

'Yes, Matt, usually when the conversation isn't flowing too smoothly.'

'Another excellent detail but, tell me, have you ever re-arranged the cutlery on the table in an Indian restaurant so that the knife and fork are perfectly aligned?'

'No, Matt.'

'Ah, at last I have found a flaw in your cover story, but you were good, very good, and I award you a thousand delightful stars for your efforts.'

I laughed fully, and appreciated the joy that spread across Matt's face at his success. I would have loved to collect up those delightful stars and put them in my handbag to be released again on some dreary day in the future.

How long have I been in this room? Ten minutes? Two hours? Two days?

I keep drifting off. It's hard to pin down the minutes as they pass. It's still pitch dark. My left leg is going to sleep. I can feel a throbbing pain at the back of my head. I need to adjust my position. I let out a soft moan as I try and shift my weight. My eyes are still shut, but I sense the stranger approach. He places something into the crook of my arm and walks away. I take a glance and see a plastic bottle of water just inches from my face. I'm desperate to take a drink but I don't. I close my eyes once again. Tight shut.

Back to the restaurant.

Matt eventually calmed down, and we ordered our food and both drank ice-cold pints of golden continental lager. I gave him a précis of my life to date, while he smiled and laughed and sympathised as required, always appearing interested in what I was saying. I was wearing a blouse with the buttons open to a slightly low level, and I never once caught him taking a glance.

When I asked about his history, he gave me very little detail. He had been to university and hated it and then plumped for sales and marketing as a career.

'Why did you choose sales?' I asked. 'You seem a bit on the shy side. Which, I should add, is fine by me. I've usually been let down by the "people persons" that I've known.'

'That's the thing. I am basically shy – always have been – but when it comes to delivering a sales pitch or even a cold call at some factory or office, I'm kind of able to drop that baggage and become a different person. My voice even changes a bit and I adopt unusual stances and gestures. It's a performance, I suppose. I'm not selling myself; I'm selling shower heads or sinks, and I find that very liberating.'

'So was that nonsense when we sat down at the table a performance? Was that Matt the salesman?'

'Yeah, a bit. He always creeps in when I'm under pressure. What did you think of him?'

'Okay, but I couldn't eat a whole one.'

He'd had one serious girlfriend called Beth. They were together for about seven years. He met her when he was working for a company that manufactured kitchens and sold them on to wholesalers, property developers and retailers. He reckoned he was at the forefront of the 'Kitchen Island Shitstorm' and that his company was the first to introduce concealed electricity outlets into the concept. Beth was one of the designers at the company head office and the only person he made any real connection with apart from Goodmonson, who he found sat meowing under his car in the car park one day after work. 'It was love at first sight,' he declared.

Beth and him shared a flat in Bromley for five years or so. She left him for another man who worked for the same kitchen company.

'Were you devastated?' I asked.

'Yeah, totally and absolutely and without relief.'

'Do you torture yourself still, wondering why it happened?'

'No, not at all. He had a very fast car, very tight jeans, a gang of beautiful friends and magnificent craftsman's hands. If that was the package she was after then of course it was wrong for us to be together. I got to keep Goodmonson, though, so it wasn't a total waste of time.'

We went back to his flat that evening. We drank beer and listened to music all night, taking turns to pick which albums we played. We fell asleep on the sofa together. He didn't try to make a move on me. Was he the wonderful brother I had never had, or was he the partner I had been seeking for many a long year? As you know, it turned out to be the latter.

I wish he was here with me now.

No, I don't – that's an awful thing to say.

19

DISHCLOTH

I arrived back in Hither Green around 7 p.m. to find Carol stood in her front bay window anticipating my arrival. I went to open her front gate but she banged on the window with a stern look on her face and pointed her finger to indicate I should go straight round to my old house before bothering her. When I stood in front of the familiar front door, I automatically reached inside my coat pocket to fetch the key. Realizing my error, I knocked on the door with a friendly, playful little trill, then took a few steps down from the door, fearful of his oral gas.

'Oh, it's you,' he said on opening the door. 'I'm surprised you even dare show your face. You didn't do any of the cleaning I asked and I'll doubtless be cleaning up your filth for the rest of the week.'

'Well, I tried my best,' I said. 'You have very high standards.'

'Yes, I do. A lot higher than yours, anyway. I'll be invoicing the agents for the time I spend cleaning and doubtless they will deduct that from your deposit.'

'Doubtless. So, anyway, I just wanted to apologize for leaving my cat behind. He just got forgotten in the mayhem of moving. I hope he hasn't caused you any trouble.'

'If you are referring to the stray cat that was here when I viewed the property, then he's been no trouble at all. In fact, I'm sure you will be pleased to know I've decided to adopt him. He's a lucky boy.'

'But he's my cat. I've had him for over ten years, you can't just steal him.'

'What do you mean "steal him"? How dare you? You told me yourself that he wasn't your cat.'

'That was just because the agent was here and pets aren't allowed. Come on, you know he's my cat. He'll be missing me. Can you fetch him for me please?'

'No, I can't, and if you don't go away, I will call the police.'

With that, he slammed the door in my face. The motion of the door sent a brief breeze of coffin vapour my way. I knocked on the door more aggressively this time and gave the bottom of it a sharp kick.

'Stop that,' he shouted from the other side of the door. 'I'm calling the police right now.'

'Good,' I shouted. 'I'll wait here until they come.'

I stood on the pavement outside the house for ten minutes or so, occasionally calling out Monson's name. At one point he appeared briefly at the front window and stared directly at me before leaping down out of sight. The thought of losing both Monson and Harriet was too awful to contemplate. It struck me how passive I was being in both situations and I wanted that to change.

Carol was watching me from her window and beckoned me to come inside. Once I was through her door, I told her what had happened.

'Cheeky bastard,' she said. 'It's you that should be phoning the bloody police. I can back you up when they come. I knew he was a wrong-un the moment I met him. Do you know what? I've a good mind to put a brick through his front window. With a bottle of mouthwash attached to it.'

'Calm down, Carol. I'm sure we can sort it out with the police when they arrive.'

But an hour later and there was no sign of the police. It was now dark, and I started to think about whether a snatch and grab would be possible. I remembered I had taken the tape off the cat flap in the back door. Perhaps if I got into the back garden via the back alley, I could entice him out. Or, even better, he might already be having a wander and I could just pick him up. Carol thought it was a good idea but insisted I wear a black bobble hat and a large black cape-style overcoat of hers for the mission.

We walked to the end of the terrace and then back down the little alley that served all the houses on the row. When we got to the back of my old house, I started to call Monson, but he didn't appear. I climbed over the fence, leaving Carol to wait in the alley.

'Good luck, darling,' she whispered.

'Thank you. I didn't think the cape would fit me but it feels great.'

'No, "good luck", not "good look".'

'Oh, right, soz, see you in a minute.'

The back door was about forty feet in front of me across the lawn. I could see Barbour walking about through the back kitchen window. There was no cover to hide behind, so I took it a step at a time, checking after each step that he hadn't seen me. I got to the shed and dipped behind it. Safe for a moment or two, I called Monson as loudly as I dared. He didn't appear. I was now only about ten feet from the back door. I could no longer see Barbour through the windows and noticed a light go on in the upstairs bathroom. This was my chance. I rushed over to the back door, got on my belly, gently pulled the cat flap towards me and called Monson. After a few calls, his nose appeared at the other side of the flap opening.

'Alright, boss,' he said, playing it cool and not indicating in any way that he was happy to see me.

'I've come to fetch you. Come on, get out, quick,' I urged him, but he didn't make a move forward. 'Hurry up, he'll be back down any minute,' I said.

Monson didn't shift, just took a step back, sat down and swished his tail across the floor behind him.

I made the familiar clucking sound toward him that I always used to indicate I might have a tasty treat in my hand for him.

'Come on, Monson . . . *cluck cluck cluck.*'

'Are we going to a motorcycle event or not?' he asked.

'Yes, okay, I promise. Come on, we need to get out of here. Get a move on.'

Monson got back on all fours and his head and shoulders appeared through the cat door. As I got up off my belly, ready to grab Monson and make my escape, he was suddenly and violently pulled back into the house by his rear end and the flap banged shut.

'Thief, you bloody thief!' Barbour shouted from behind the door. 'The police are on their way and you'll get what's coming to you!'

He carried on shouting as I legged it back over the fence and into the alley. Carol was waiting there and, on seeing the panic on my face, joined me in a breathless sprint back to her house.

We sat on her sofa waiting for the inevitable knock on the door from the police. Carol made me a veggie sausage sandwich and offered me a bottle of beer, which I refused.

'You look dreadful, darling,' said Carol as I relaxed back on the sofa. 'Like a discarded dishcloth.'

'That sounds about right,' I replied. 'Abandoned and slightly damp, just waiting for the mould to take hold.'

'I suppose you're allowed a bit of self-pity, but it doesn't look good on you, darling. Why don't you phone Harriet right now and turn the tables your way. Put her on the spot and ask her what the fuck is going on?'

'Would you phone her?' I replied. 'She won't pick up for me.'

I gave Carol Harriet's number and she rang. It must have gone straight to voicemail and Carol couldn't resist leaving a message.

'Hi, Harriet, it's Carol here. Listen, I'm sat with Matt and he's beside himself with worry. I really think you should phone him and put him out of his misery. You at least owe him that.

You shouldn't be punishing him like this. He deserves an explanation so he can get on with his life. Am I right? Don't be a selfish cow.'

'Did you have to end it like that?' I asked.

'Yeah, because that's exactly what she is, and I know *you're* not going to tell her.'

'I don't think the tone of your message was very helpful.'

'Oh, stop panicking, darling, I ended the call before I spoke, I just wanted you to hear the truth.'

A few hours passed and we guessed the police weren't coming. Carol suggested that I spend the night in her spare bedroom and it was so late that I agreed.

Laid in bed, I thought of nothing but Harriet and Monson and the possibility of losing them both. I slept on and off. At some point in the night I heard a noise outside my door and opened my eyes slightly to see what it was. I froze when I saw it was Carol stood in the doorway, staring right at me. I closed my eyes and pretended to be asleep. In the morning, my door was shut fast.

20

PIE AND PEAS

Carol had made me pancakes for breakfast – thick, American-style ones with maple syrup and blueberries. She told me that Barbour had already left for work, so the house would be empty if I fancied another attempt to rescue Monson. Before leaving, I asked her not to phone Harriet again, and she agreed. She gave me a hug on the doorstep and told me to take care and stay in touch. If there was anything she could do to help, she said, then I just needed to ask.

I went back down the alley and climbed over the fence. The cat flap had been taped shut and a wooden cupboard placed in front of it. I pressed my face against the back window to peer inside and Monson was not in his usual spot on the sofa. I called his name but he didn't appear. What was I meant to do? Call the police myself? Go and see a solicitor? Break down the door and grab him? I had absolutely no idea. Harriet would have known what to do.

I took the train back to London Bridge. Just as we pulled out of Lewisham, a lady plonked herself down on the seat opposite me. It was the waitress from the café in the park. She was wearing a long black puffa coat and a baseball cap with the NASA logo on its front.

'I thought it was you,' she said. 'I saw you on the platform and thought, *Oh, look, it's that creepy guy. Hope he doesn't see me.*' Her smile indicated she was being light-hearted.

'But you decided to come and sit with the creepy guy,' I replied.

'Yeah, I'm only joking. You're all right, I reckon. You've got a friendly vibe.'

'Aren't they the ones you should be worried about? The ones who come over all meek and friendly?'

'Maybe, but I can tell it's not an act with you. You're not pervy friendly, just friendly friendly. There's a big difference.'

This wasn't the first time I'd heard myself described as such. My mum used to call me a pushover, which was much the same thing, and I'd lost count of the number of women who were happy to be my friend but nothing more than that. I'd never been sexy or intriguing and even this young lady had picked up on that. Harriet sometimes used to say I was like 'the boy next door' but without the latent appeal.

'Where are you off to?' she added. 'A strip club?'

'Yeah, I know this place where you get ten strippers and a pie and peas lunch for eight quid,' I joked.

'Bargain,' she replied. 'Tits and peas for under a tenner: dreamland. So where are you really going?'

'My new flat. We've moved out of Hither Green.'

'Oh yeah? When you say "we", do you mean with that

woman from the café? You done a runner from your girlfriend that you told me you loved?'

'Why on earth would you say that?'

'Oh, come off it. It was obvious that you fancied the pants off her. You even got super defensive on her behalf when she turned all patronizing and shitty with me.'

'Carol is a friend, nothing more than that.'

'So you say.'

'Yes, I *do* say. Are you still broken up with your boyfriend?'

'Yeah,' she replied, taking a sneaky puff on her vape from the side of her mouth. 'I've stopped trying to contact him, which is a start.'

'You still want him back?'

'Yeah, but I need him to want it too, and that's out of my hands.'

'You've got that right,' I replied. 'I like your puffa coat.'

'I didn't really want a coat as long as this, but it keeps my backside under wraps and that works for me,' she said.

'I've never understood this thing with girls and their arses,' I replied.

'I've never understood this thing with blokes and their tits and peas.'

I asked her why she was heading into town and she told me it was for an interview for a waitressing job in a posh hotel. She wanted to make a new start. Before I got off at London Bridge, I mentioned to her that the Horseshoe Inn was looking for staff and it seemed a nice place to work. It was right next to the station and she could be on a train home within minutes. I gave her the address and she thanked me.

Back in my flat, I received an email from Laurence. It simply read:

Anything?

I replied by telling him of my suspicion that Hot Dog might be a drug dealer. I figured that a landlord had the right to know that information.

I got his reply almost by return.

Good work. It took the last person nearly a week to find that out. Promising start. I think this is going to work out well.

    Laurence

21

HARRIET

'Why don't you take a sip of water, Harriet?' says the stranger.

My body twitches with fear at hearing his voice interrupt the silence. I don't respond; keep my eyes shut. *He knows my name.* I can't decide whether it's a positive or negative development. *How does he know me?* My first thought is that he must be someone I've successfully prosecuted and he wants his revenge. That was something that happened in my line of work. More likely, he had just searched my wallet and found my name.

'Take a sip, Harriet. You should keep hydrated.'

I don't respond.

'Playing dead, are we? No matter. I've got all the time in the world.'

Silence.

I begin to tremble. He must be able to see the little twitches and spasms. He coughs. My shoulders shake with the shock of the sudden noise.

Take myself out of the room. Eyes tight shut. Back to my story.

Matt and I moved into our house just under two years ago. We had both been renters all our adult life, so hadn't gathered much furnishing moss, yet we still managed to fill it with a mismatch of possessions and trinkets that we had both accumulated over the years. Some of the things that Matt brought with him stand out as indicators of the type of man I had committed myself to for an unspecified amount of the future.

- A brown duvet cover with a frighteningly realistic owl motif in the centre
- A framed, signed photograph of the drummer from Culture Club
- A full-size resin replica of the HMV dog with one of its ears missing (Matt's cat Monson pushed it off a shelf)
- An old, beige, enamelled ironing board that could only be raised up to about two or three feet off the ground (he told me he would kneel while doing his ironing)
- An orange leatherette bean bag missing so much of its filling that you had to sit on it with caution to avoid direct impact with the floor
- One blue work suit and four identical off-white shirts (he would wear Monday's shirt again on Friday)
- A large, 48-inch flatscreen TV (without its remote)
- A set of orange plastic plates and bowls unsuitable for dishwasher cleaning (it melts them)
- An electric hand whisk with a power cord so short the sight of it broke my heart

- An oar (I never asked)
- A small sealed box with 'SEDIMENT' written on the top (I asked; he couldn't remember)

Everything else was forgettable.

The first person to visit us in our new home was a neighbour called Carol. She strolled into the front room as I was unpacking a box of ornaments and introduced herself. She had brought a welcome gift of a home-cooked bean stew in a Tupperware bowl.

She looked a few years older than me but was in fantastic nick. Her backside was on full display in her tight leggings and was impressively taut. She was wearing a short zip-up running top and white and orange trainers, though she hadn't been exercising. She smelt of Coco Chanel and her hair was pulled back and tied in a perfect short ponytail.

'Oh, look at those trinkets!' she gushed. 'How cute are they? Absolutely adorable. Here, let me help you unpack them, darling.'

I declined her help but she insisted, then stopped helping the moment Matt came downstairs.

'Matt,' I said, 'this is Carol, our new neighbour. Maybe you should offer her a cup of tea?'

'Hi, Carol, I'm Matt. How do you do?' He offered her his hand to shake but she went straight in for a hug.

'It's so exciting when new people move in. I can't wait to get to know you,' she said with a saucy grin on her face that briefly sickened me.

'Would you like a cup of tea, new neighbour?' Matt asked in his flirty voice.

'Only if it's too much trouble,' replied Carol, laughing largely through her nose and widening her eyes as she snorted. 'Don't worry, darling,' she continued, 'you'll get used to me. I'm, how do you say, rude as fuck but generally hilarious to boot.'

Her nostrils flared slightly to alter the tone of her laugh-grunt as she followed Matt over to the sink, where he began filling the kettle. She had lost interest in me. She told Matt that she was the chairperson of the Neighbourhood Watch, represented the area on the local police consultation panel and was on the board of governors at the nearby school. She had all the contacts a person could ever need to tap into – 'If you know me, you know everyone who matters' was her claim.

We soon learnt that she was a single mum whose eldest was about to leave school and head off to university. She had two daughters, both of whom had excelled at school and were much loved by one and all. She was worried how her youngest would get on at boarding school as she was achingly pretty and bound to attract the wrong kind of attention.

Monson entered the room and gave her the once-over.

'Oh, you have a cat?' she asked.

'Yes,' I replied, 'I'm not that keen, but it comes with Matt as part of the package.'

'Oh, *I love cats!*' she screeched. 'Come here, little fella . . . *tsk tsk tsk.*'

Monson turned his back on her and walked out of the front door that she had left open. I admired him for that and said, in a light and friendly tone, 'Don't worry about him – he's *very* choosy.'

She sat herself down on the sofa and told us all about the parking problems in the street, the disruptive neighbours at No. 7, the time a young boy got mauled by a devil dog and how her imbecile husband had left her for a woman of zero substance. She spoke directly to Matt and rarely turned her gaze my way. I could tell from the off that she was one of those women who preferred the company of men. I didn't take to her at all and believe me, I'm a pretty easy-going girl.

When she eventually left, after telling me again how much she adored my little trinkets and inviting us round for lunch the following Sunday, I shut the door behind her and gave an exaggerated sigh of relief.

'Fucking hell. What a shitstorm,' I said. 'I thought she'd never leave.'

'I thought she seemed nice. Good to have a friendly neighbour, and she likes cats. Maybe she can look after Monson if we go away.'

'I saw you looking at her arse when she left.'

'No, I didn't.'

'Yes, you did.'

'No, I didn't,' he insisted. It wasn't very convincing – a touch too serious in its delivery, I thought.

That following Sunday, I was feeling knackered and just

couldn't face going round to Carol's for lunch. Matt went on his own armed with a bottle of wine and the empty Tupperware bowl. (I threw the stew in the bin. It smelt like cave droppings.) When he returned, two hours later, he was half cut and went straight to sleep on the sofa, where Monson joined him. As he slept, I noticed a couple of long brown hairs on the shoulder of his jumper. I plucked them off and placed them on the dining table for future reference.

'Sorry, I must have nodded off,' he mumbled apologetically when he eventually woke.

'How was it?' I asked.

'It was okay. She's really interesting. Used to be an air stewardess on first-class flights. Met all sorts of celebrities. She once had Elton John on board and he ate his meal without using his hands – you know, just face down into the plate, like it was a trough. She married a super-rich property developer and took him to the cleaners in the divorce. Doesn't ever have to work again. She's got a flat in central London and a holiday home in Palm Springs.'

I took the hairs off the table and took them over to him.

'What were these doing on your jumper?' I asked as I dropped them into his lap.

He looked at them incredulously and gave a shrug from his shoulders. 'Must be Carol's. She's a bit of a hugger. What do you expect me to do – push her away and flounce out like I'm Doctor Who?'

'You need to watch her,' I said. 'I know her type. She'll come after you if she smells the chance.'

'Yeah, I know, she's a live wire. I'm not stupid.'
He gave me a hug and at the time I felt reassured.

I open one eye, just a sliver, for half a second. I see the silhouette of the stranger still sat to my left. The bottle of water falls from the crook of my arm onto the floor. I shut my eyes even tighter. I feel a gentle nudge on my cheek. I think it is a cat.

22

YOGA

I was disappointed that my revelation about Hot Dog's drug dealing didn't have the impact with Laurence I had hoped, but felt encouraged by his response all the same. It was time to get ready for my yoga class with Justin Hamper, of Flat 5B fame. I found an old pair of tracksuit bottoms that had lost their drawstring but gripped okay when folded over at the waist. I combined these with a Henry the Hoover T-shirt and my light-outdoor-use slippers. The Hamper worked out of a studio attached to the rear of St Mary's Church, about half a mile away on Kipling Street. I decided to walk.

'You didn't come back last night, Mr Giles,' said Derek as I passed his desk. 'Everything okay?'

'Yeah, just work stuff,' I replied vaguely.

'Playing with your trumpet?'

'Yeah, something like that.'

As I walked to the church, I was once again visited with anxiety and fears over Harriet and doubts about my passive approach to the situation. I couldn't shift them from my head, so decided to phone her at work again on the off chance she had returned. The receptionist informed me that Harriet was not in the office today. I asked to be put through to her colleague Will, but he was also unavailable.

I checked our joint bank account on my phone and there had been no activity. No big deal in itself, as she had her own separate accounts, but it did cause the thought to flash through my mind that this could be a missing persons situation. Maybe I should inform the police? I soon came to the conclusion that, given the note she left, it would be pointless; I'd never be taken seriously.

St Mary's Church was a depressing sight, long since closed for worship and a favourite haunt for the homeless. The walls and buttresses were a patchwork of moss and ivy, and the large rose window above the entrance was boarded over with plywood. A set of padlocked metal doors protected the inner doors from intruders, while a low brick wall and iron railings defined the boundary. The railings had become entwined with brambles and desperate, traffic-tainted weeds, and there was one of those signs (now blistered and fading) that declared the building was protected by some security company or other which had evidently long since abandoned its duties.

To get to the Hamper's studio, you had to walk down a narrow pathway at the side of the church and then through an iron gate to follow a track that divided the graveyard. This led you to an arch-shaped wooden entrance door at the back of the church. A small, laminated, handwritten paper sign was pinned to the door: 'FOR YOGA PLEASE RING THE BELL'.

I did as I was asked and, moments later, the door opened to reveal Justin Hamper.

We shook hands and exchanged greetings before walking through a dark and damp vestibule into the windowless yoga studio with whitewashed stone walls. There was a large square of turquoise carpet on the grey laminated wood-effect floor, with two red yoga mats on top of that, ready to receive their prey. Up against the right hand wall, there was a dark wooden sideboard with a statue of the Buddha on top. The room was very brightly lit.

The Hamper was wearing something akin to grey ladies' leggings and a baggy, bleached white T-shirt. They affected a casual Robinson Crusoe vibe but at the same time glowed with expensiveness. His tanned feet were an identical matching pair, with the nails of each big toe painted sky blue.

He lit the fuse of a joss stick on the sideboard and invited me to sit down on the turquoise carpet for a chat.

'So, Matt, are you comfortable in this space? Does it make you feel receptive and open? Inspired, even, by the beautiful light?'

His voice was churchy and easily interpreted as patronizing.

'It's a wonderful room,' I replied. 'If I'm not mistaken, the lights are LED – really crisp, good choice, especially for a bathroom or kitchen.'

'You're so right, Matt. Is the bathroom somewhere that you feel safe? Would you like to think of this space as a bathroom? It's important that you feel relaxed and comfortable.'

'If you want me to, then I can do that.'

'But do *you* want to?'

'No. I'm fine just thinking of it as is.'

'That's great, Matt. Tell me about your journey to get here today.'

'It was easy. I'm just down the road in Satsuma Heights by London Bridge.'

He let out a long nasal groan and followed it up with a sequence of about ten very fast blinks. He maintained a crooked smile throughout this display, suggesting it was his version of a sarcastic laugh.

'No,' he said. 'I mean in your life, Matt. Have you made the progress that you expected or hoped for?'

'Never really thought about that. I try to avoid goals and ambitions, just go with the flow of things,' I replied honestly.

'That's fine, Matt, it's a trough that many feed from. But why are you here? What has brought you to this moment?'

'I need to start exercising – need to lose a few pounds. I've been doing office work most of my life and I reckon my body needs springing back to life.' I found myself agreeing with what had been intended as a fabrication.

'And I recognize that, Matt, I really do. It's very apparent. But what about your brain? Does that need springing back to life?'

'I don't think so. I'm still quite sharp and focused, a bit like these lights.'

A hint of impatience flashed across the Hamper's face. He clearly didn't want any levity in his church.

'Forget about the lights and please, don't do analogies in

151

here – they never help; they just confuse. Is that all right, Matt? I want this to work, and by that I mean for both of us.'

'Yes, of course, sorry, I didn't mean to be disrespectful.'

'Let me ask you a question, Matt. Would it be possible for you to leave your old habits and behaviours outside this room and try and make a connection back to your real self?'

That was me kicked right out of my comfort zone. The Hamper was clearly working the therapy, spirituality, self-realization grift. This was not an environment where I would be able to tap him for information. More likely, it was me that was going to be under the spotlight.

'I can try,' I answered solemnly. 'I will try my very best.'

'That's very brave of you, Matt, very brave indeed.'

'Thank you. That means a lot.'

'So, Matt – and please try and be honest with your response – here's a simple question: are you happy?'

'I think so. I've definitely been happier at times, but, yeah, I'm not depressed or anything.'

'Then why is there so much pain and distress in your face? Why is your aura so de-energized and flat? You seem troubled, Matt, and you won't be able to suppress the pain much longer. It needs to come out. Talk to me.'

And, for whatever reason – maybe the LED lights, maybe the Hamper's tone, or maybe the churchy environment – I did as he asked.

'I mean, you're right to an extent. You see, my girlfriend seems to have walked out on me, possibly for another man. I can't be sure. I haven't spoken to her since she left. She won't return my calls and she hasn't been at work. And a man has stolen my cat. I miss them both very much but I'm sure it will be fine. I'll get through it. I always do.'

'That's powerful stuff, Matt. How do you feel now you've shared it with a stranger?'

I knew what I was required to say.

'Much better – a real load off my shoulders.'

'Tell me about your girlfriend. Tell me what she means to you.'

'Well, she is, *was*, everything to me. I'm in love with her. We are like one person, you know. We made each other whole. We've even been talking about starting a family together. It sounds corny, but I don't really understand my relationship with the world without her. She was my life. She made me happy.'

'So when you said you were happy earlier, you were lying. That's not very helpful, is it, Matt?'

'I suppose not, but I didn't mean any offence.'

'And I didn't take any, because it was yourself that you were deceiving, not me. Do you get that?'

'Yes, I do.'

'That's superb, Matt, and very brave. So, tell me, did you ever feel lonely within the relationship? Is that something you can be honest about?'

'Maybe now and then, maybe especially these last few months, since I've been out of work. There are things I can't or daren't say to her and things that I would like her to do and never ask and I suppose that makes me feel a kind of loneliness.'

'Do you think she ever felt lonely inside the relationship?'

'Well, certainly not in the physical sense – we are always together and I'm always there for her. I think I frustrate her a lot with my lack of drive and ambition but, like I say, we're a team and she provides that in bucket loads. You would have to ask her, I suppose.'

'Did *you* ever ask her?'

'No, I never did.'

'Did you ever ask her if she was happy?'

'No, I don't think I ever did.'

'Interesting,' said Hamper as he nodded his head wisely for a total of eighteen heartfelt nods.

The Hamper took me through some basic yoga poses, which I managed to achieve without too much fuss. He then gave me a closing speech about how yoga could be the start of my journey of reconnection with the spiritual energy hidden deep within me.

As I was about to leave the studio, he mentioned that he also lived in Satsuma Heights.

'Oh, really, what a coincidence. What floor do you live on?' I asked.

'Fifth floor, facing the park.'

'Me too,' I replied. 'I just moved in a couple of days ago. 5A. I actually put a little note under your door to say hello. You should pop round sometime, have a glass of wine or something.'

'That's very kind, Matt, but I don't drink and I don't like to mix business with pleasure. Talking of business, can you tell that bastard Laurence that the shower head in my flat is broken?'

'Yes, of course, but could you not just tell him yourself?' I asked.

'None of the tenants are allowed to deal directly with him, and nor would they want to. Anyway, your little note said that was your job. So, will you pass on my complaint?'

'Yeah. He's away for the next few weeks, but I can arrange for a repair no problem.'

'You're sure he's away?' he asked with great interest.

'Yes, as far as I know, he left last night.'

'Definitely?'

'That's what he said,' I replied.

I started crying as soon as I left the place and didn't stop until I got back inside my flat. I had never asked Harriet if she was happy and now it was too late. For the first time in all this, I accepted that she had left me and wasn't coming back.

23

PEPERAMI

That evening I talked myself into a visit to the store cupboard for a surveillance session. It was exactly the diversion that my mind needed. Hot Dog was in his usual position sat in front of the TV, only occasionally rising to fetch a snack from the kitchen or use the toilet. At 9:09 p.m. he took a phone call. I could only hear his side of the conversation.

'What.'

'No chance.'

'Fuck off.'

'I fucking dare you.'

'No, fuck you.'

'Why?'

'When?'

'Fuck off.'

That was it. He was watching a show where members of the public went through a pretend SAS training course. He occasionally laughed at their antics, but more often shouted 'wanker' at the screen when one of the participants failed their challenge.

I switched the feed to the Hamper's flat. The lounge was empty and as tidy as ever. A laptop on the seat of the sofa was the only thing that stood out as having being introduced to the scene. Classical music was playing quietly in the distance. The circular orange and cream rug under the coffee table caught my eye. I liked it – very 1960s. It gave the room a quirk.

I decided I should try and introduce a quirk into my lounge. Maybe a 1950s jukebox or a long cushion in the shape of a parsnip, that sort of shit.

After a couple of minutes, a young lad, around ten years old, entered the lounge and sat down on the sofa. He was wearing pyjamas and happily eating from a large tub of ice cream. He picked up the TV remote and selected a channel to watch. It was hard to see the TV screen from the oblique angle of the camera, but whatever it was he was watching was giving him great delight. I suddenly coughed. The boy turned his head towards the kitchen area as Hamper entered and jumped onto the sofa beside the boy. Hamper poured himself a large glass of wine and then, as he adjusted himself on the sofa, spilt a few drops of wine onto the inner surface of his slightly raised left thigh.

'Fuck,' he said, and the boy laughed at him hysterically.

'Dad, you swore!'

'Fuck, I did, didn't I?' replied Hamper, causing them both to break into another fit of laughter.

Once they had calmed, Hamper announced that it was time for bed. He scooped the boy up and tickled him all the way out of shot.

When he returned to the lounge, Hamper sat down on the sofa and held his head in his hands. He then let out a visible sigh, collapsed back into the cushions and stared intensely at the ceiling. After a minute he got up, shoulders slumped, and poured himself another glass of wine from the bottle on the coffee table. He took three large gulps, stepped over to the window, and stared at the skyline beyond.

He seemed suddenly deflated and lost, in stark contrast to his demeanour when in the company of his son. By the trembling of his shoulders, I guessed he could well be crying. He took another gulp from his glass of wine. God knows what hole he was trying to fill with the drink. Perhaps that was what Laurence was challenging me to find out. This solitary figure felt very far removed from the guru I had encountered earlier that day. He seemed my absolute lonely equal.

I wondered whether I should mention the boy to Laurence, but decided he would almost certainly be privy to his presence already. The drinking, though – maybe that was something I should inform him of. You know, to cover my back.

I pinged off an email to Laurence.

Hi Laurence,
   Did you know that Mr Hamper in 5B appears to have a bit of a problem with the booze? I'm sure you did, just wanted to pass it on.
   Matt

I received a reply almost by return.

Hi Matt,

    That's vaguely interesting, but please try to operate a filter regarding what information you pass on. We all like a drink, don't we? I know I do.

    Laurence

I'd obviously messed up a bit, but he didn't seem angry. I was glad I hadn't bothered him with mention of the boy.

As I closed the store cupboard door behind me and turned around, I was confronted with the bulk of Hot Dog walking down the corridor towards me. He was wearing a vast pair of red boxer shorts and a dirty vest that was sticking to some ointment on his belly. He smelt hot and medicinal.

'Good evening, Jigsaw. What the fuck are you up to at this time of night? All looks a bit surreptitious to me.'

'Oh, ha ha, yes, it must do. I was just fetching something from the storeroom,' I said unconvincingly.

'So, where is it then, this thing you were fetching?'

'I couldn't find it.'

'Would you like me to give you a hand looking for it? I've got a good eye in a search.'

'No, that's okay. It can wait till the morning.'

'What did you need so urgently that you're poking around out here after midnight? I can't personally imagine what that might be.'

What could I pretend I had been looking for? Bleach? Mousetraps? Some type of oil? What would even make sense at this time of night?

'A medical kit, for some painkillers. I've got a throbbing headache – can't sleep. Simple as that.'

'I'm very sad to hear that, Jigsaw, my heart bleeds for you. Can I have a look in the storeroom, please? I've a great affinity with storage areas. I think it's because my dad used to lock me in the cupboard under the stairs if I was playing up when the wrestling was on the TV.'

I felt the hairs standing up on the back of my neck and a tingling of fear spread around my body.

'I can't do that,' I said.

'Yes you fucking can, you've got the key in your hand. Stop farting about and give us a look.'

'Honestly, Bill, I'm not allowed to let anyone into any of the restricted areas. Laurence has got cameras in every corridor; he could be watching now. If he sees me letting you in, then that's it for me. He'll boot me out of here.'

'I don't want you to lose your job, Jigsaw, but tell me: why do I never see anyone else using this storeroom? What's the big secret?'

'There isn't one. It's just a storeroom, a very average one at that.'

'I sense you've got a bit of a panic on, Jigsaw. You're a sneaky little bugger and do you know what, I like you for that. I'll be keeping my eyes on you.'

Then he slapped me, medium hard on my left cheek.

'What the fuck?' I said, holding my cheek and sensing the heat rising within it.

'Best cure for a head pain,' he replied. 'Forces the brain to concentrate on a different ache. Goodnight, Jigsaw, sleep tight.'

He ruffled the top of my head before walking away and returning to his apartment. Was he onto me, or was it just a chance encounter? I think the slap was intended as some sort of warning not to mess with him. That, if he wanted to, he could crush me into a fine powder and sprinkle me on one of his evening pizzas.

Back in my flat, I decided to make myself a snack. There was little on offer. I was out of bread so couldn't default to toast and all that was in the fridge was a Peperami salami and a half-eaten bag of rehydrated dates. I checked the freezer and the previous occupier had left behind a small bag of frozen peas. I thinly chopped the Peperami, sliced the dates and put them in a bowl with a couple of handfuls of frozen peas and a teaspoon of water. After a couple of minutes in the microwave, the peas looked cooked, so I took the makeshift soup out and tried a spoonful. It wasn't that bad. It didn't cheer me up.

24

HARRIET

He's boiling a kettle.

'Would you like a cup of tea, Harriet? I've got some sand-wiches if you're hungry.'

I shift my body slightly to relieve my muscles and to turn my face away from him. I keep my eyes tight shut. I hear him approach.

'I know you're awake. You've got to eat and drink, Harriet. We could be here for some time. No point in making yourself ill, don't you agree?'

'I'm okay, thanks,' I whisper, eyes still shut.

'Ah, there you are,' he says. 'Lovely to hear from you. Just tell me when you're ready for a chat. You must have so many questions. No rush. Like I say, we've got all the time in the world.'

He sounds friendly. The kettle clicks off as the water comes to the boil.

I don't want to look at him. I'm frozen with fear at what the next stage of this encounter might be.

Go back to your story. It's far safer there.

Things turned irretrievable between Carol and myself a couple of months ago, when I agreed to take a holiday in the house that she owned in Palm Springs. For the first three days, Carol would be staying in the house with us. It was Matt's idea. He'd seen it as a way to celebrate the first couple of weeks of his redundancy. The house was beautiful and we were staying for free; all we had to pay was the cost of two cheap flights from Gatwick.

It was a three-bedroom, mid-century home nestled at the base of the San Jacinto mountains, probably worth well over a million pounds, and she had taken ownership of it as part of her divorce settlement. The garden was immaculate, with palm trees and succulents adorning the perimeter, while cicadas provided a tropical soundtrack. Tiny hummingbirds hovered here and there in search of nectar, and it also had a glorious swimming pool, complete with diving board and plunge pool. It should have been paradise, but with Carol there, I found it hell on earth.

For the three days we overlapped with Carol, I was suffering from jet lag on top of the exhaustion caused by working for three solid months without a single day off. All I wanted to do was sit by the pool and drink cocktails until sunset and then sit down for a session of American TV before rolling into bed. Carol, however, wanted to show us the full Palm Springs experience.

On our first evening there, she had booked us a table at

some flashy restaurant in the mountains. I went along out of obligation and I suppose a bit of gratitude for the free vacation. She talked, and boasted, non-stop, and took every opportunity available to make me feel small and unsophisticated.

'You really should wear sun block in the evening with your pale skin. Am I right?'

'You should really wait until the soup is served before eating your bread; it's the same here in America as at home.'

'Matt could do with some new clothes. I should take him out shopping when you get back.'

'The problem with working for the civil service is that there isn't really any incentive to excel. Am I right?'

'You would have been much better off with a shawl rather than a cardigan. It can look very touristy.'

'I know a marvellous plastic surgeon in Harley Street. I'm sure he could do some contouring on your knees.'

Matt didn't seem to notice and appeared to be thoroughly enjoying himself. I hadn't seen him so animated or chatty for months. He kept talking about ridiculous business ideas he was formulating (one of them involved importing copper taps; another was an online nut and seed subscription service), and Carol encouraged him and kept hinting that she might be able to help him with some investment. He was showing off and being inattentive, suddenly morphing into a version of my previous boyfriends.

I decided to have a sulk. It was a bad idea. The success of a sulk depends on how negatively it affects the people around you, and my sulk didn't seem to bother them at all. If anything, they upped the volume on their 'banter' and seemed relieved by the implied permission to ignore me. I went to bed as soon as we returned to the house, blaming my tiredness on the jet lag.

'Oh, darling, how awful,' said Carol. 'I thought you looked a bit peaky tonight. You have a good night's sleep. You certainly look like you need it. Am I right?'

It took me an age to get to sleep because of the noisy air conditioning and the constant cackles of laughter coming from the living room where Matt and Carol drank on late into the night.

I slipped myself out of bed in the morning so as not to wake up Matt and tiptoed around the kitchen, making myself a cup of coffee before quietly opening the patio doors and sitting poolside to enjoy the rise of the early morning desert sun. I put on my straw cowboy hat and lay back on a turquoise lounger by the pool. It was a lovely indulgence and I could almost feel my body creaking and stretching into holiday mode. I would have felt like a movie star if it wasn't for the thatch of pubes crawling out from both sides of my swimsuit gusset and the little pools of sweat forming in the craters beneath my knees. I reassured myself that Carol would be gone in a couple of days and then it would just be Matt and myself.

I must have fallen asleep at some point, as I was woken by the sound of Matt jumping into the pool from the diving board. I was annoyed at having my peace disturbed, so didn't bother to acknowledge his presence. Carol then burst into the scene wearing a fluorescent lime-coloured bikini, orange flip flops and an orange baseball cap. She walked straight over and took her place on the lounger next to mine.

'Morning, darling,' she said. 'I think perhaps you should cover yourself up – it's not a pretty picture.'

I immediately assumed she was referring to my pube explosion and took appropriate offence.

'Well, don't look at me then! It is what it is. I'm on holiday, I couldn't give a fuck.'

'But you're burning up, Harriet. You need to get out of the sun.'

I took off my sunglasses and looked at my body. My thighs, arms and shoulders were shouting for shelter from the heat. It was already ninety degrees and my pale, weak skin just couldn't take it.

'Oh fuck,' I said as I rushed back indoors for relief.

I spent the rest of the morning indoors, covered in beige aftersun cream and occasionally watching through the window as Carol and Matt frolicked in the pool. Matt checked up on me every half-hour or so but the sunburn was increasingly angry and I didn't give him much encouragement. Just before lunchtime, they both came inside and Carol announced that it was time to go for a ride on the mountain cable car.

'Oh, you must come, Harriet, it won't be the same without you,' she declared without a hint of sincerity in her voice.

166

I declined. Matt made a half-arsed pretence of not wanting to go without me but I told him to sod off and let me heal in peace.

After they had gone, I risked a little walk around the pool wearing one of Carol's expensive silk kimonos. I stuck to the shaded side of the garden and my route took me behind the little pool house that contained the boiler and the pool pump. On the ground, I noticed a screwed-up piece of paper that looked out of place amongst the perfectly maintained grounds. I picked it up and unfolded it. Inside was a little handwritten message.

You don't have to ask and I would never tell x

It was Carol's handwriting, and by the condition of the note, it had been written that morning.

I tolerated Carol's presence for the next couple of days and kept a close eye on the two of them whenever they were together. I was furious with her, and even more furious with her perfect body, which she flaunted morning, noon and night.

When she finally left, Matt hugged me tightly.

'Thank God she's gone. Now we can have our holiday,' he said.

When I wasn't thinking about the note, I managed to have a nice time. When I thought about it, my blood boiled and I wanted to scream at the mountains so loudly that an avalanche might come tumbling down on Matt's stupid head. I didn't show him the note, but I kept it so that I could, if necessary, confront Carol with it at a later date.

I feel a water bottle being placed on my lap and a hand give my knee a gentle squeeze. I shiver with fright.

'I'm going to take a little nap, Harriet,' says the stranger. 'You really should have a drink. Wake me if you need anything.'

25

THE LONG SHOE

In the morning, the sun was out again, so I decided to go and explore the area and do some food shopping. I walked round to the rear of Satsuma Heights and entered the little community garden behind the immigration offices. It was about the size of two tennis courts, with hedging and lime trees around the perimeter and raised beds and honey-coloured gravel paths inside.

In the furthest corner from me I spied Hamper and the young boy I'd seen in his flat last night sitting on the most secluded bench in the garden. Despite it being a sunny day, the boy was wearing an anorak with the hood pulled up around his face. He was licking away at an ice cream while Hamper scrolled through his phone.

I walked over and feigned surprise at their presence.

'Oh, hi there,' I flounced. 'Fancy bumping into you. And who is this? Your son?'

'Yes,' replied the Hamper.

I stooped down slightly and addressed the boy.

'What's your name, fella?'

'Callum,' he replied.

The Hamper stood up. 'Come on, Cal, time to get back.' He took his hand and led him away.

I stood and watched them walk away, then took their place on the wooden bench and drank in the beauty of the gardens. Daffodils were blooming, and in the raised borders, shrubs were squeezing out their buds and unfurling their leaves. The magnolia trees in each corner of the garden were in full flower, their pink and white blooms adding the calming power of a pensioner's blouse to the ambience.

Now, if it was down to me, I would plant every square inch with alliums – just pop the bulbs in and wait for the show. Harriet would choose a mix of vegetables and roses. We would compromise and plant alliums in the free spaces between the vegetables. I would fail to put in the care and graft required to maintain the planting. The vegetables would get diseased and the roses would fail to flower. The alliums, though, would flourish and explode into life when the time was right (that's just what they do as long as you leave them be). Harriet would be furious over my neglect and refuse to admire the alliums. I would decline to mention that the roses and the spuds were her idea, not mine.

I took a stroll down Bermondsey Street to buy food in the delicatessen – bread, cheese, ham, olives, that sort of shit. On my way back, I popped into Vinegar Yard, a street food and junk market opposite the station. One of the stalls caught my eye. It had 1950s curtains, some retro chairs and furniture and a wooden art-school mannequin on display. It held the promise of a quirk, which was something I was beginning to desire in my life.

The bloke manning the stall had a long, thick, scruffy beard, the sort that if you lifted it up you might expect to find a couple of ants feeding on a lump of mango. He looked well into his forties, but was probably only in his twenties. Ten years ago, the beard would have been a king quirk, but its feverish uptake up by the hipsters had severely diluted its impact.

'Alright, mate,' he said. 'Ten per cent off marked prices today. You after anything in particular?'

'I'm looking for something quirky. What's the quirkiest thing you've got?' I asked.

He sighed and shook his head slightly. 'Everybody is chasing the quirk these days. Nobody wants the functional or timeless. What about that mannequin? Has that got sufficient quirk for you?'

'Yeah, definitely, but I doubt I'll be able to afford it.'

'It's three hundred quid, mate, absolute bloody bargain. Quirk don't come cheap, you know.'

'Nah, it's too much.'

'Too much quirk or too much money?'

'The latter. What about that bar stool with the pink furry seat?' I asked.

'Fifty quid. Very popular – jam-packed with quirk.'

'I'm not sure. If it's popular, then its time has probably passed.'

'Hold on,' he said, pointing a finger up to the sky. 'I might just have the perfect thing for you.'

He delved under the trestle table that fronted the stall and emerged with a two-and-a-half-foot-long, black leather winkle-picker-style shoe with a brass and onyx ashtray set into the hole where the foot enters the shoe. He held it up with reverence and a glint in his eye.

'You want quirky, mate, then check this out. Could you even handle this amount of quirk?'

It was certainly striking. It forced you to ponder who had made it, why they had made it, and if its manufacture had caused any regret or pain. I could place it on my kitchen island and every visitor would be forced to comment on it and hopefully be intrigued by its owner. That owner could be me; a quirker at last, interesting by default. I wanted the shoe.

'Hmmm. How much you want for it?' I asked in a manner that suggested I wasn't too fussed about it.

'It's marked up at a hundred and twenty-five, but you can have it for a hundred.'

'Shit, that's a lot even for a shoe of that length.'

'Yeah, but it's long on quirk as well – you won't find another one.'

'I'll think about it. Thanks for your help.'

'Don't take too long thinking. Like I say, everybody's chasing the quirk these days.'

I arrived back at Satsuma Heights just as Derek was returning from his lunch break.

'Lovely day, Mr Giles – a trumpeter's delight, I should imagine,' he said.

'Every day is good for the trumpeter, Derek, that's why we do it.'

'You been out for a walk?'

'Yeah, I had a sit in the gardens. I bumped into my neighbour Mr Hamper and his son. He's a quiet young lad. Have you met him?'

'No, I didn't know he had a child.'

'Yeah, they're staying here together. Surely you must have seen him?'

'No, never. How is your trumpeting school coming on?'

'Just need to buy a trumpet to get things off the ground. Tiny steps.'

'Indeed,' he said.

I went back to the flat and made myself a fancy brie and ham open sandwich and a cup of tea. It was around midday and I wanted to avoid my mind being drawn into thoughts of Harriet. Hot Dog would be in the Horseshoe for a bit of his this and that, so I decided to join him. He was good company and, after all, it was my job.

He seemed happy enough to see me and invited me to join him at his table. We chit chatted and then, out of the blue, he asked me:

'Have you ever had a fight? A proper, full-on British fight?'

I told him I had never had a fight, British, European or otherwise.

'I love a fight,' he continued. 'I've had many a fight and I've only ever lost one. It's such a rush, such a high. You can't beat it.'

'What do you mean by a "British" fight?' I asked.

'You know, just fists and holds – no knives or kicking or biting or any of that foreign shit.'

'Do you think you could beat me in a fight?' I asked, just for the cheek and fun of it.

'If we had a fight, it would be a fight that you would lose within seconds. I would knock your block off with one full-on British punch.'

'You never know, I might have some moves. I might be a little demon.'

'Shall we find out?' he asked. 'I'll fight you now if you want, you little fucker.'

He was smiling; I hadn't overstepped the mark.

'No, that's okay,' I said. 'I'll give you a game of darts though.'

We drank and played darts for a couple of hours. I casually asked him if he knew the bloke in 5B, Justin Hamper.

'Not really. I don't like the look of him. Doesn't interest me.'

'Sounds like you got a beef with him.'

'A bit, yeah. First three nights after I moved in, he came round banging on my door yelling for me to turn down my TV. I didn't even bother to get off my chair, just shouted "Fuck off" through the door. On the third night I did open the door and he was stood there in the corridor bouncing from one foot to the other and chewing on the inside of his cheek with a right nasty look in his eye. I think he was wanting a fight but thought better of it when he saw the size of me. I told him I would turn the TV down if he asked me politely like a decent neighbour would. The following evening that is exactly what he did and we haven't bothered each other since then.'

I mentioned the little boy, but Hot Dog denied any knowledge of him. I asked about the mystery flat and he told me he heard the occasional noise coming from in there but had never seen anyone coming in or out. He reckoned it was some posh bloke who probably used it as an occasional stopover when he was in London.

Eventually I took the plunge and tried to press him on what he did for a living. He tried to fob me off with his usual 'this and that' reply, but I kept at him and he eventually gave in.

'Put it this way: if people are in trouble, they come to me and I help them sort things out.'

'What, like a gangster?' I asked.

'No, Jigsaw, like a friend.'

I immediately thought about Monson trapped alone in the house with Barbour.

'Somebody has kidnapped my cat and is keeping him trapped in their house. I can't go to the police because it would be my word against his. Is that something you could help me with?'

'I don't like cats, but thieves are even worse. Tell me the whole situation. I might just be your man.'

26

DRY RISING INLET

When I got home I had a kip and then a long, indulgent bath. I found I could actually float in the tub without any part of my body touching the sides. I thought about the long shoe and my encounter with Justin Hamper and his son Callum. He had cold-shouldered me and led his son away as soon as I attempted to strike up a conversation. It was going to be difficult to pursue a connection with him; he was a hard nut to crack. True to his word, he wasn't the type who mixed business with pleasure, or even, perhaps, sought pleasure at all.

After my bath, I sat down on the sofa with a bowl of olives on my lap and was hit with another bout of yearning for Harriet. I made a mental list of the pros and cons of our relationship. Maybe it would help convince me that life without her would be bearable. It worked out something like this:

PROS

I love her

I depend on her for, well, everything (apart from housework and gardening)

She's beautiful

She's independent

She makes me laugh, a lot

She doesn't rely on quirks

She's strong, sensible and practical, i.e. everything I'm not

She's a striking dancer

She understands electricity

She likes the food I cook

She once told an estate agent to 'go and fuck a dry rising inlet'

She likes an Indian takeaway on the weekend

She's happy to not bother with friends and socializing (God help me if I ever met a girl who wanted to go to dinner parties or concerts or comedy clubs)

We like hiking together summer and winter

We like the same music

We like the same movies and TV (apart from football)

We rarely argue, and if we do I am happy to back down

I miss her (yes, I think that's a pro)

CONS

She doesn't want to be with me

She's an accomplished duvet wrangler

She doesn't like the song 'Alison' by Elvis Costello

I gave up on the cons. I was clutching at straws. It all just boiled down to two simple facts: I loved her, but she didn't want to be with me.

Another con then slipped into my mind: she wasn't that keen on Monson, and that instantly reminded me of his plight. I missed them both.

That evening, to divert myself away from the sad, I failed to resist a session at the screens in the store cupboard. The need for diversion outweighed the guilt of the dubious activity. In the Hamper's lounge, Callum was sat on the sofa eating a bowl of cereal as he watched something on the television. The Hamper was not on camera, so I assumed he was in the bathroom or one of the bedrooms. I switched the main feed to Hot Dog's flat, where I saw he was sat topless on the sofa singing along to the Bruce Springsteen song 'Glory Days'. He was clearly prepping himself for another session in the Horseshoe. I stuck with the feed long enough to see him put on his coat and jumper and exit his flat.

Then, out of the blue, I saw some movement within the darkness of the mystery flat. I dragged the feed onto the monitor screen to examine it more closely. It was impossible to see anything in detail in the absence of any lights being turned on, but there were clearly two people stood side by side in the lounge. Neither had much more definition than ghostly shadows or reflections within a candlelit cave. One of them, a man, judging by his body shape, shoved the other person onto the sofa before walking away out of sight of the camera. The shove could have been playful, but had an aggressive slice to it, I thought. A light was then turned on in the bedroom area for no more than a second or two, allowing me to see that the person on the sofa was a lady.

She had short blonde hair and was wearing a grey work suit. Her face was looking downwards to the floor and her hands were held together behind her back as if they might be tied. Slowly, she dropped her body sideways and pressed her face into the sofa cushions. Then something was placed over the camera lens and the feed went pitch black.

My heart pounded and a sudden flush of heat radiated throughout my body.

It looked like Harriet.

I bolted out into the corridor and banged furiously on the door. There was no response. I shouted Harriet's name and kicked at the base of the door, but nothing stirred. After running back to my flat and grabbing the master key off the kitchen island, I opened the door to the mystery flat, switched on the lights and called out Harriet's name. The sofa was empty; there was nobody in the lounge or the kitchen. I glanced up at the wall above the door. The sprinkler unit was free of anything that might block a camera feed.

I crept, step by step, through the kitchen and into the hallway that led to the bedroom. I hesitated for a moment. I had seen the shadowy figure of a man walk towards the bedroom; he must still be there. My heartbeat continued to pound in my chest and behind my ears. My legs felt weak and slightly numb. I shouted Harriet's name again. No response. The first door I came to was the bathroom. I opened the door slowly and turned on the light. It was empty; just a single orange towel on the towel rail and a bottle of hand wash on the sink. Only the bedroom remained. That was where they must be.

The thought crossed my mind that I should get out of there and seek help, but the knowledge that Harriet might be just a few feet away inside the bedroom spurred me on. I opened the bedroom door and stepped inside. It was empty. The bed was made up and undisturbed. I rushed back through to the lounge and out of the door. I dialled Harriet's number but there was no reply. I took the lift down to the ground floor with some half-baked idea that I should run over to the Horseshoe and report what I had seen to Hot Dog. I hadn't even got as far as the front door before I realized that to let him in on my spying activities would not only blow my cover, but probably lead to a severe beating.

Was it Harriet? Or was I just wishing that to be the case? Had my mind turned deceptive on me in its weakness?

I took myself behind Derek's concierge counter to find that the security camera from my corridor was actively recording. It had a straightforward rewind function, so I wound it back a good ten minutes. The first thing I saw was Hot Dog leaving his flat and getting in the lift, then nothing else happened until I saw myself running from my flat, banging on the door of 5D, returning to my flat, then using the master key to get into flat 5D, before running out again a few minutes later. What was going on? I felt like I was turning wayward, like my brain had suffered a temporary twerping.

I rushed up the stairs back to my corridor and re-entered the mystery flat. It was just as I had left it; empty and undisturbed. I ran into the store cupboard to check the screens. The feed from the mystery flat was back to its normal dark, blank state. Why had I witnessed those few seconds of light? And could it really have been Harriet I'd seen?

When I returned to the mystery flat once more, the blackout blinds concealing the floor-to-ceiling lounge window grabbed my attention. Something about them didn't tie in with image I had seen on my screen of the man, the lady and the sofa. I ran that image through my mind again and clear as day I saw that the window in that footage had been concealed behind a pair of fancy red and silver patterned curtains. Also, on the wall adjacent to the window was a painting of what my fleeting memory told me was a large white daisy.

Then it dawned on me. I had left the lights on in the mystery flat, but the feed on my screen was back to its usual darkness. The mystery flat was not where the incident had occurred. Where on earth had the footage I'd seen come from? Was it a different flat within Satsuma Heights? Was it even from within this building? Was it Harriet? Where is she?

27

HARRIET

He's asleep, I'm sure of it. His breathing is regular and steady.

I open my eyes. It's too dark to get any proper fix on the room. There are a couple of dark squares breaking up the light-coloured wall opposite, probably paintings. Between them is a doorway. It's just a black rectangle; I can't tell if it's open or shut. There is a large low piece of furniture against the wall beyond the stranger, probably a sofa. I can hear the low hum of the central heating system and the occasional clunk from a water pipe somewhere within the building.

I am going to confront him when he wakes. I cannot bear this torment much longer. I suspect my fate has already been decided, so I might as well try to find out what he plans to do with me. I'll wait until he wakes up, though.

In the meantime, back to my story. I'll be quick, and hope I have time to finish it.

When we returned from Palm Springs, my feelings towards Matt had fundamentally changed. He wasn't acting any differently, and if anything was being more attentive than ever, but everything he did and said had started to get on my nerves.

Rather than 'laid back', I began to see him as lazy. Rather than a teammate, he became an opponent. When we chatted, I didn't really listen, and when he made his little jokes, I didn't find them funny any more. I was glad to leave the house for work every morning and started to dread my return. I worked late whenever the work justified it, and that was most days, as I was preparing the biggest and most complicated fraud case I had ever handled.

I didn't hate him; I just felt numb and indifferent to the relationship. Matt didn't seem to notice. I was more or less certain that he wasn't having an affair with Carol, but the nagging doubt was always just around the corner from my next thought. It would hit me as I ordered a coffee in the canteen at work. Then again when I opened my desk drawer to grab a stick of chewing gum, or whenever I saw Matt's name come up on my phone. Most of all, it would hit me every single morning when I passed by Carol's house and she would wave at me from her seat in the bay window. I had started to pretend I was on my phone every time I walked by, but noticed from the corner of my eye that Carol continued to deliver her morning wave. I didn't think they were sleeping together, and I didn't believe that Matt was the type to stray, but Carol's advances towards him had poisoned me. I didn't want to get hurt again. I wanted to protect myself from the awful pain of rejection and deception and the drudgery of recovery.

One morning, about a week before I made my big decision, Carol emerged from her front door just as I was passing.

'Hi, Harriet. You haven't been giving me my morning wave. I haven't upset you or anything, have I, darling? We've hardly spoken since Palm Springs.'

'No, of course not,' I replied, experiencing a sudden urge to bite her right in the middle of her face. 'I'm just distracted with the case I'm working on. It takes every minute of my time; I'm walking around like a zombie. How are you, anyway?'

'Oh, busy busy busy, you know me, darling, everybody wants a bit of the Carol action. You do look a bit drained. You should come over at the weekend for one of my legendary stews, that would perk you up. Am I right?'

'Yes, maybe,' I replied. 'Sorry, got to go, don't want to miss my train.'

'No worries. I'll ask Matt about the weekend when I see him in the park café later.'

I couldn't hide the look of shock on my face. I think my right eye might even have started to twitch and my left knee buckled slightly. 'Oh,' I said, as nonchalantly as I could, 'I didn't know you were meeting Matt. He didn't mention it.'

'Oh, yes, we meet up in the café every morning after our run. I thought you knew! We have such fun. You're so lucky to have him, darling.'

I couldn't bring myself to reply but managed a weak smile and a wave of my hand as I walked away, knowing that Carol was watching me with a great big beaming victory smile on her face. For the rest of that day I was filled with hatred for Carol and for Matt. The both of them could rot into the ground as far as I was concerned.

I had to find out what, if anything, was going on.

There was no point in asking either of them. They would just deny it and I would be left looking like a dumb, jealous fool. I needed some proof to hang my suspicions on and suddenly thought of a way I could get exactly that. My friend Bradley, whose house I was living in when I met Matt, had recently told me that his daughter, Catherine, was working in the park café. I had always got on great with her and we had occasionally messaged each other since I moved out of her family home. I was sure that she would help me out.

I arranged to meet her after work in the Horseshoe Inn, a pub I had been to with Matt near London Bridge Station. She was up in town visiting her boyfriend. We chatted for a while and I bought her a burger and chips. I told her about my problem and she immediately agreed to help. She reckoned she was the ideal person for the job, as she had a downer on men generally and particularly cheaters. (She had some suspicions around her own boyfriend.) I gave her a photo of Matt and a description of Carol. She recognized them straight away. They had recently started coming into the café every morning and she had always assumed they were a couple. She promised to email me a report as soon as she had collected her evidence.

The 'report' arrived in my inbox three days later during my lunch hour, the day before I made my big decision.

Hi Harriet, Catherine here.

This has been such fun! Sorry, I know it's not fun for you . . .

So, yes, they are still meeting up in the café nearly every day (sometimes Matt is there alone). They always sit together and seem very VERY comfortable in each other's company.

She is a right flirt and a rude bitch if you don't mind me saying. I would definitely say that she fancies the pants off him. It's not so obvious with Matt. He sometimes seems a bit embarrassed by her flirty behaviour, probably because he's out in public and gets a bit nervous. That's just speculation but you know what I mean.

I haven't seen them kiss or hold hands but she is forever touching his arm and putting her hand on his shoulder, you know the sort of thing. They always leave together. I did manage to follow them one time but they parted when she got to her house. They didn't kiss goodbye or anything, but I reckon by her body language that she wanted to.

I've got a bad feeling about it, but nothing concrete!

My verdict at the moment would be 70:30 in favour of him cheating on you. He's a man after all and she's clearly putting it on a plate.

I'll keep watching. Don't do anything drastic just yet!

Stay strong.

Catherine x

It didn't really help. If anything, the information just made me more confused and angry. I'd been avoiding it, but it was time to confront Carol.

I left work an hour early and spent the journey home trying to think of the right words to use when I met her. Everything I came up with sounded either too pitiful or too aggressive, so I decided to clear my mind as best I could and just pray that the right words came to me in the moment.

When I knocked on her door, my mouth was dry and my legs felt like wet string. She answered the door breezily with her expensive teeth grinning at me like a seductive chimp. She started a greeting but silenced herself when she read the furious look on my face.

'We need to talk,' I said as I brushed past her and took a standing position beside her marble kitchen island.

'Bit rude, don't you think?' she said as she walked towards me with a glass of late afternoon wine in her hand.

'You think I'm rude, do you?' I replied.

'Yes, as a matter of fact I do. What's the matter with you anyway, darling? I can't be doing with any drama. I was having a nice day.'

I reached for my wallet and took out the note that Carol had written in Palm Springs. 'Sorry to ruin your day, but could you explain this please?'

I handed her the note and she snatched it off me while expelling an overly extended sigh.

Her demeanour didn't change one bit as she read the note. She took a sip of her wine, then crossed her arms defiantly.

'What's to explain? Can you not read or something?'

'Of course I can fucking read. Why did you write it? What's your fucking game?'

I wasn't shouting, but there was real anger in my voice. It was a tone that I hadn't felt the need to use in years.

'Oh, do calm down, darling,' she replied. 'It was just a bit of fun, a bit of flirting in the sunshine. Why do you think I wrote it? Come on, what are you suggesting? Why don't you just say it?'

'Are you having an affair with Matt?'

She snorted out a laugh and then worked herself into a rhythm of hysterical laughter.

'It's not funny, Carol. ANSWER THE QUESTION! ARE YOU HAVING AN AFFAIR WITH MATT?'

I was shouting now.

She stopped laughing and I sensed a little quiver of concern flash across her face.

'Harriet, I am not going to answer that question because it is so totally outrageous. If you think Matt fancies me then you are probably right. I can have any man I want and if I decide to have Matt then I will, but I won't be telling you about it. Have you asked him? I bet you haven't because you don't really believe it yourself. Now, get out of my house and let me drink my wine in peace.'

'That's not an answer to my question.'

'Well, it's the best you're going to get. Please leave.'

I could tell that the conversation was over, but a lump of unquenched anger remained inside me. I strode up to her, took the wine glass out of her hand, drank the contents down in one, then punched her full force on her left temple. As I marched out of her front door, I felt my rage slowly evaporating. A smile of satisfaction crept, uninvited, across my face. I needed to calm my giddiness and digest what I had just done.

I took myself for a walk around the park. As I sat by the lake looking up the bank towards the café where Matt and her would meet, it hit me: I needed to get away from Matt and her and the house and my work. I needed to think, to be quiet and to be by myself. If I didn't, I was in danger of going mad and losing it. I needed a break – a few days, a few weeks, whatever it took to sort my head out. That is what I needed to do and I knew exactly where to go. Matt could wait, work could wait, and everyone could just fuck off.

That evening, I sat on the sofa on my laptop double-checking everything was in order for the big trial starting next week. I messaged my office and told them I wouldn't be in work for a few days. My colleague Will would be able to handle the case just fine. I had prepared it beautifully and to within an inch of its life. Matt didn't seem to notice how quiet and agitated I was and just sat happily watching a football match on the TV. He started making an irritating noise with his fingernails and I snapped at him, then he started talking about croissants and for some reason mentioned how much Carol liked them. I got up, went to bed, and cried myself to sleep.

The stranger's breathing is regular. He's still asleep. I slowly inch my free hand up towards the bottle of water and unscrew the top in tiny increments. As I pull the bottle up to my mouth, some water spills onto my lap. I let out a little yelp of surprise. The stranger's breathing takes a jump. He adjusts his position.

I freeze, hold my breath and close my eyes. I can feel the pulse in my temples and a throbbing on the back of my head. I listen. His breathing returns to its slow and regular sleeping rhythm. I take a drink from the bottle and then another. I can feel its cold journey all the way from my throat to my stomach.

A sudden rush of sadness hits me.

28

LENGTHY REGRETS

Back in my flat, I sat down at the kitchen island with the image of the lady face-down on the sofa still flashing through my mind. The scene played out like a few frames from a snuff movie. The lack of any sound to accompany the images also added to its homemade feel. Was it Harriet? The woman certainly had the same physical frame as her, and the grey suit looked familiar. The white training shoes I didn't recognize. The hair looked right, but maybe a bit scruffier and a tiny bit longer than I remembered when I last saw her. Were her hands tied behind her back, or had I just imagined that?

I went to the store cupboard to see if there was any way that I could replay the footage. It couldn't be done, at least not by someone with my technical abilities. The feed from the mystery flat still looked as it always had; empty, with blackout blinds covering the window. Given what I thought I had seen, I needed to take the matter up with Laurence urgently. I wrote him an email.

Dear Laurence,

I thought I saw something untoward occurring inside flat 5D this evening and used the master key to get inside and check it out. Everything was fine with the flat, but it was clear that it was not the flat that had appeared on my screen, which had showed a man and a woman possibly having a fight or argument. Has there been a technical error? Where exactly is the flat with the arguing couple? Anxious to hear from you ASAP.

Cheers,

Matt

I ran the whole scene through in my head again and timed it at no more than three seconds. The more I ran it, the more my memory seemed to alter it, so that the resemblance to Harriet was lessened. Then I would play it back again and my brain would revise it so that Harriet stared straight up at the camera with an accusing look on her face. It was hard to trust myself. I had to know where the image actually came from and why it had appeared on my screens. Hopefully Laurence would provide the answer and some reassurance. In the meantime, I needed to speak to someone just to divert my panic. I gave Carol a ring. It went straight to answerphone, so I left a message for her to contact me. The only other option was to join Hot Dog in the Horseshoe Inn. It was gone 9 p.m., but I guessed he would still be in there topping up on his this and that.

As I hoped, he was sat at his usual table drinking a fresh pint of Guinness. There were two empty glasses next to him and a couple of empty packets of crisps. He beckoned me over. I was still on the confused side of jittery, but found the prospect of his company reassuring, so I bought myself a pint and joined him.

'Evening, Jigsaw,' he said once I'd sat down opposite him, 'you look like you've seen a ghost. No, scratch that, you look like you *are* a fucking ghost. Have you got the shits or something?'

'That's very perceptive of you, Bill. I have indeed just had a bit of a shock.'

'Do you want to talk about it?'

'No, I'm okay.'

'Thank fuck for that. I'm in too good a mood to listen to other people's bullshit.'

'Oh yeah, why such a good mood?'

'I bought this earlier today and I fucking love it.'

He bent down and picked up a long, pointy black shoe from the floor beside him. It had an onyx ashtray in the hole where the foot should go.

'Look at this beauty!' he said proudly, holding it up to my face as if he were presenting a luxury feline to a judge at a cat show.

'Woah, that is a cracker,' I said, realizing it was the very long shoe that I had declined to purchase earlier that day. 'Very nice indeed.'

'Don't I know it. Tell me, how much length d'you reckon we've got here?'

'Got to be over two foot,' I replied.

'Bought it off a fella who came in here earlier. I spotted the front end of the shoe sticking out of his bag and asked him if he was a juggler or a fucking clown of some sort. He told me he was a market trader and if I liked the lengthy shoe I could have it for fifty quid. I jumped at the chance and here it is.'

He ran his fingers along the top of the shoe from just beneath the laces to the very tip.

'Just look at the duration of that length. You can get lost in it. Wonderful,' he gushed.

'You know what, I had the chance to buy that very shoe this morning for a hundred quid, so I reckon you've got a very long bargain there.'

'Of course I have. I've got an eye for this sort of thing. So, why didn't you buy it when you had the chance?' he asked.

'Just hesitated. I think buying something like that, you need to be spontaneous, you know – go with your gut and just do it. I loved the shoe, loved its length, its presence, but I'm just not a bloke that makes a decision in the moment. I need to dwell on things for a while.'

'That's a shit way to operate. That's why I've got the prize and you're full of regret. Come on, let's change that. Let's do summat impromptu. Let's go and get that cat of yours.'

'Don't you think it's a bit late for—'

'Shut the fuck up,' he interrupted. 'Come on, drink up, let's get going.'

He downed his pint and took his shoe over to the bar for safe-keeping. I hadn't noticed earlier, but the girl serving at the bar was the waitress from the café in the park. It was nice to see her. I walked over to say hello but was intercepted by Hot Dog, who virtually dragged me out of the pub.

We got on the 10:12 p.m. train from London Bridge to Hither Green.

29

SEPARATE!!!

When Hot Dog and I arrived at the house, I saw the lights from Carol's TV flickering against the blinds of her front window. My old house was in total darkness, with no sign of life inside. Hot Dog strode straight up the front steps and knocked on the door. There was no reply. As he walked back down the steps, I saw Monson poke his head up at the window. I gave him a wave and he jumped back out of my sight. It was lovely to see him.

'I've just seen Monson. He's inside,' I whispered excitedly.

'Well, let's get in there and fetch him. What's the easiest way in?'

'You going to break in? I don't know that I want to sign up for that.'

'There's no alternative, Jigsaw. From what you've said, he isn't going to give the cat up voluntarily. We're in a shit–or–bust situation here.'

'Fuck it, let's do it,' I replied with a great big spoonful of adrenalin slipping down my throat and into my stomach.

We walked to the end of the terrace and entered the alley that ran behind the houses. My old house looked as empty from the back as it did from the front. No curtains were drawn and the only light came from the appliances in the kitchen. I climbed the fence and told Hot Dog to wait until I checked the coast was clear. As I made my way over the lawn to the rear door, I noticed that the little shed had been moved about six feet nearer to the house, and there was a patch of flat, compacted mud where the shed had previously been. Maybe Harriet had returned to the house and been gassed to death by Barbour before being buried beneath the mud where once there had been a shed.

At the back door, I discovered there was no longer a cat flap, and the opening had been sealed shut with a large square of wood. I went over to the rear kitchen window and peered inside. I shouted Monson's name as loud as I dared and he popped up onto the work surface to stare at me through the window.

'Hi, Monson, how are you doing?' I asked, only a short distance from a tear arriving in my eye.

'Like you give a shit,' he replied.

'Of course I do.'

'Is the motorcycle event sorted?

'Yeah, I've got a few options I want to run past you.'

Out of the corner of my eye, I saw Hot Dog running towards the back door. He rammed into it with his shoulder and bounced back off into a heap on the floor. The piercing sound of the house alarm invaded the night. Barbour must have had dead bolts and a sensor installed to the back door. What a bastard he was. I ran to the centre of the lawn and heard Hot Dog shout 'Separate!' as he ran past me and over the fence. I followed him over and then ran in the opposite direction down the alley. When I emerged into the street, I walked casually to Carol's front door and rang the bell. She let me in, gave me a welcoming hug, and sat me down on the sofa.

'I was worried about you, darling. I got your message and you sounded somewhat distressed. I've been ringing you all night but you don't pick up. Your choice, your loss.'

'Sorry, Carol, I've left my phone back in the flat. It was nothing that urgent. I just fancied a chat.'

'Is that alarm something to do with you?'

'Yes, I tried to break in to rescue Monson.'

'Good for you, but you failed of course.'

'Yep, and now he's going to be on even higher alert.'

'Don't you worry yourself, darling. I'll get him for you as soon as I can be bothered. I'm an accomplished thief, you know – haven't got a shred of conscience. I was just waiting for you to ask, but as always you force my hand with your uselessness.'

'I didn't have you down as a thief. That's probably the reason I didn't ask you to get involved.'

'I'm one of the best, darling – mainly garden centres and bookshops, but charity shops are good too.'

'Why on earth would you shoplift, Carol? You've got money coming out of your ears.'

'The thrill of it, I suppose. If you've never walked out of a shop with a pack of best back bacon down your trousers, then you wouldn't understand. Some say it's a substitute for sex, but then again, isn't everything. Am I right?'

'I'm not willing to talk about sex, Carol. I have absolutely nothing to say on that subject, as I've told you a million times before.'

'You're in denial, darling. I bet you think about me every night, especially now you haven't got Harriet as a diversion. I presume she still hasn't been in touch?'

'No, I keep messaging her but I think she's turned her phone off. I'm getting used to the idea that she's gone, but I would love to know if she's okay. Just so, you know, I can stop worrying.'

'She's okay, believe me. Probably having the time of her life. Typical of her to leave you hanging like this. Such a selfish cow.'

'I thought I saw her tonight.'

'What do you mean, you "thought" you saw her? You either did or you didn't.'

'On my computer screen.'

'Oh, so not in actual real life, where the rest of us live. Have you been searching her Facebook and all that nonsense?'

I wanted to tell her about the screens in my flat and the short clip of the blonde pixie-haired lady that appeared, but I just couldn't think of a comfortable place to start. I decided to leave it and just agreed with Carol's suggestion that I had been looking at Harriet's social media. As far as I knew, Harriet didn't have a Facebook account or the like, but it put an end to what could have been a difficult conversation.

'How long have you known me, Matt?' she asked.

'About two years, I suppose.'

'And have I ever given you a bad piece of advice?'

'No, you are generally spot on when it comes to advice and I know it makes you very happy to give it out.'

'Don't get splashy with me, darling, it's not worth the comeback you'll get. My advice remains that you should forget about Harriet and start a rebuild. You're just delaying an inevitable process. I'll look after you, and that cat needs you fully fit, not all anxious and, if you don't mind me saying, needy.'

I really liked Carol. Harriet and her did not see eye to eye, but she'd always been a solid, dependable neighbour and friend. When she said she would look after me, I believed her.

'If you had recovered your cat, how would you have got him home?' she asked.

'I don't know. Under my coat, or I could have nicked a bag from the house. It was a spur-of-the-moment thing. I was in the pub and the bloke I was with persuaded me to give it a go. Probably the drink that juiced me up.'

'What bloke?'

I told Carol about Hot Dog and she congratulated me on making a new connection. She liked the sound of him and told me I should invest in this new friendship. It would 'progress my healing', she said. I asked her if she had had any contact with her new neighbour, Mr Barbour.

'None whatsoever. That man doesn't interest me, and let's not forget he's a fucking thief,' she replied.

'Just like you,' I said, with a finger point. 'And how do you plan to get Monson? Have you even got a plan?' I asked.

'Yes, but I think it's best if you don't know what it is.'

After another beer and some chit chat, the alarm at my old house stopped sounding. The lights were back on and presumably Barbour had returned. The police hadn't made an appearance. Carol asked if I was going home or if I wanted to stay for the night. I was conscious that Hot Dog might be at the station waiting for me but it was so comfortable and comforting sitting within this familiar little bubble that I decided to stay.

I went to bed alone and reflected on the fact that I had not only potentially lost Harriet and Monson, but had also missed the opportunity of owning a long shoe. Probably an all-time low, even by my high standards of lowness.

When I woke up early in the morning, Carol was asleep on the easy chair in the corner of the bedroom. A light whistling was coming from the corner of her mouth and she was clutching a blanket tightly under her chin. I crept out without disturbing her and made my way back to Satsuma Heights.

30

SEDIMENT

I arrived back at Satsuma Heights at 8:15 a.m. The black Mercedes that had picked me up from my old house was parked in the reserved bay at the front of the building. Derek greeted me from behind his desk.

'Good morning, Mr Giles. Another busy night?'

'Yeah, I was out trying to rescue a cat.'

'Did this cat want to be rescued?'

'Difficult to say.'

'And did you succeed?'

'No, I failed miserably.'

'Mr Laurence is in the building,' announced Derek. 'He was asking after you with a hint of urgency. You should contact him straight away.'

'Will do. Derek, can I ask you something?'

'Not if it's about cat rescues. I know nothing about them other than that they often involve a ladder.'

'No, it's about the security screens behind your desk. Do you ever get glitches? You know, see things on the screen that you can't explain or bits of footage appearing out of the blue as if some wires have got crossed?'

'Listen, Mr Giles, if you spend too much time staring at these screens, your mind can go off in a direction of its own. It's happened to me often enough and I'm a very resilient individual. Just this morning when I looked up from the screens, I could have sworn I saw Mr Hoover walk past carrying the longest shoe your mind could ever conjure up. I don't think that actually happened. Just screen sickness.'

'But what about on the actual screens? Do you ever see snippets of footage that must have come from outside the building or just flashed up from God knows where?'

'It can occasionally happen, but the image is gone nearly as soon as it appears so I tend to just put it down to a glitch inside my head rather than in the system. Nobody understands what electricity actually is, never mind how it manages to transport images via cabling, and I don't think I've got the brains or the inclination to be the first to explain those mysteries.'

'I get you,' I replied, trying to hide my disappointment in his vagueries. 'And by the way, my rescue didn't involve a ladder. It was a low rescue – you know, floor level or thereabouts.'

'My favourite rescue scenario,' he replied before turning his attention back to the security screens.

When I stepped into my flat, Laurence was already in there, sat on the sofa, examining a little wooden box of mine with the word 'SEDIMENT' written on its lid. He was wearing a black turtleneck jumper, black woollen trousers and black training shoes that didn't appear to have any laces. The gold watch on his wrist looked like it weighed more than a fox's head. He didn't get up when I entered.

'Good morning, Mr Giles. So pleased to see you have arrived at your workplace. Derek tells me you weren't here last night, so obviously I'm curious as to why not. I think you would be curious if the shoe was on the other foot, as it were. Do you agree? I think that you must.'

'I was with Mr Hoover. You know, investing in the connection. I think I'm making—'

'What is inside this box?' he interrupted. 'It would appear to be glued shut, which means it intrigues me.'

'I've no idea. It was something my mum kept from my school days. I presume it was a school project or something. I've always imagined it's a soil sample or maybe some sand and stuff off a beach.'

'So you've had it for decades and you've never been tempted to open it? I don't know that I could do that. It would eat me up not knowing. Does it not eat you up?'

'It's kind of become a thing to *not* open it. Like, that's become the actual point of it – a little box of mystery in my life. I think I'll know when the day comes for it to be opened.'

'I hear you, Matt, I really do, but I don't understand. Shall we open it now?'

'No thanks, it's not the right time.'

He tossed the box onto the sofa next to him, wiped some imaginary dust off his jumper and clasped his hands together under his chin.

'This visit is very inconvenient for me. As I told you

previously, I did not intend to be anywhere near this building for the next few weeks. I was, however, intrigued by your message. So, tell me about last night. Tell me about it now.'

I sat down at the far end of the sofa and explained to Laurence what had happened. I told him about the girl on the screen and how, because of the blonde pixie haircut, I thought it might be Harriet.

'And you are sure that the room that was on the screen immediately before you ran out of the store cupboard was not flat 5D?'

'Well, it was definitely not the flat 5D opposite me. The flat I entered has the blackout blinds and the one on the screen had fancy red and silver curtains. I left the lights on in there but the feed from the flat on my screen was still dark.'

'And how do you explain that?' he asked.

'Well, Derek reckons he sometimes gets strange little bursts of footage on his desk screens and he also suggested that just staring at the screens can play tricks on your mind.'

'And what do you think?'

'He might be right. I just got panicky because in the actual moment I thought it was Harriet I'd seen. I'm not so sure now. The image is kind of etched in my mind but the more I see it, the less I can form a face to the girl. It's the haircut that really triggered me, but when I think about it there are thousands of girls that have that hairstyle.'

'So did you phone Harriet to check that she was okay and not in any distress? Have you done that? That is what any responsible person would do, don't you agree?'

'Yes, of course, but the truth is, Laurence . . . ' I hesitated momentarily, slightly nervous of revealing too much to him in case it somehow jeopardized our arrangement. 'Harriet and I are separated at the moment. She's taking some time away from me and isn't answering any of my calls, so I haven't been able to get that reassurance.'

Laurence got up from the sofa and walked over to the kitchen island. He sat on a bar stool with his back facing me.

'Maybe I can give you the reassurance you are seeking. My records show that you used the master key at 8:53 p.m. You will not be aware that I also have a camera in another flat occupied by my assistant Kiara. You remember her, don't you? Absolute diamond, I'm sure you agree. I've checked in with her and she tells me she returned home last night at exactly 8:53. The camera in her flat is activated the moment she enters; if she wants her privacy then she simply obscures the lens with a little cover that I provide for that very purpose. From what you have described, I would suggest that for those few moments of her arrival, the feed briefly switched to her flat. A glitch that I will, of course, immediately address. She tells me she wasn't distressed in any way, just exhausted, and that she was alone and not with a gentleman, as you suggested. Are you reassured? I hope you are.'

As if on cue, there was a knock on my front door and in walked Kiara, wearing a grey work suit and white training shoes. Her hairstyle was very similar to Harriet's, a bit scruffier and longer, but very much in the same pot. She definitely could have been the lady I saw on the screen.

'Your car is waiting, Mr Laurence,' she said. 'Oh, hello, Mr Giles. I think maybe you need to get yourself more organized. This place is a mess. That won't help you progress in life. Sorry to have interrupted you.'

Kiara turned as if to leave. I stopped her in her tracks.

'Kiara, is it true that Laurence has a camera in your flat?'

Kiara turned around and looked towards Laurence. It seemed she was seeking his unspoken permission to answer. Although I didn't see his response, he must have indicated in the positive.

'Yes, that is true, and I am very grateful for its presence. It makes me feel safe. I think that maybe one day it might even save my life. It's a terrible world we live in, Mr Giles.'

'And do you have a big painting of a daisy in your flat?'

She looked towards Laurence again for permission to answer.

'Yes, I do, thank you so very much for asking.'

Kiara left the flat and Laurence gave me a winning smile.

'She does look very similar to Harriet,' I said.

'I wouldn't know,' he replied. 'Tell me about this man you mistakenly thought you saw. Kiara has never lied to me and I doubt she ever will.'

'He was just a shadow really, but I'm sure he was there. When the camera lens was covered up, Kiara was sat on the sofa, so somebody else must have been in the room.'

'Hmmm,' he responded. 'Maybe I need to do some more digging.'

'Have you got a camera in *my* flat?' I asked.

'Of course not. I told you that the first day we met. I have no interest in your life beyond the information you gather for me.'

He got up off the stool and walked towards the front door.

'Will you be sending me a report about your evening with Mr Hoover, or was it uneventful and dreary?'

'I don't think I have anything to report, but I am meeting Mr Hamper this—'

'Maybe you are not trying hard enough,' he interrupted, turning to face me. 'Perhaps you weren't the right man for the job after all. I do hope that's not the case.'

He left the flat. I wasn't totally convinced by his explanation of the mystery feed or by Kiara's little performance. I knew she was either hiding something or just downright lying, as I had definitely seen two people on the footage, and one of them was clearly a man.

I decided to pretend to be reassured for the time being and treated myself to a shower. As I dried myself, I caught the unwelcome sight of my upper back in the bathroom mirror. The hair on my shoulders was out of control. If she was here, Harriet would have insisted on using her hair-melting cream to obliterate the forestry. I would have squirmed like a child as she applied it and accused her of being a dermal thief and a witch.

I wondered what she was looking at at this very moment. A wall? A frozen food display? A leaflet offering lawn revitalization? A leaking downpipe? Another man's shoulders? The thought of another man hurt me hard in my heart and guts and made me feel momentarily vengeful. If she was with someone new, as Carol suspected, then I bet he had a fucking quirk. Every bloke seemed to be utilizing a quirk these days. It really was time I got on board.

It was 10:45 a.m. and time for me to leave the flat and attend my second introductory yoga lesson with the Hamper. As I passed by, I pressed my ear to the door of the mystery flat. There was no sound coming from inside.

31

HARRIET

It's still pitch black. I can tell from the stranger's breathing that he's asleep. Feels like a good sign. If he's able to sleep, then maybe his intentions aren't too grave. I quietly search my pockets for my phone. I don't have it. I tug at the strap around my wrists but there's no give. A part of me wants to rouse him so that I can start some sort of dialogue, but I can't bring myself to do it. I'll let him sleep.

Back to my story. Hopefully there's time to finish it before he wakes.

The morning after I made my decision to take a break from Matt, Carol, work and everything, I got out of bed, making sure not to wake Matt. I filled a small suitcase with sensible clothes and toiletries and grabbed an anorak from the coat hooks in the hall. I left a little note for Matt in the post basket, explaining that I didn't know when I would be returning and requesting that he didn't attempt to get in touch with me.

Our car was a 2014 beige Skoda Octavia Estate. Matt would pretend to miss it, but the truth is he hardly ever drove it – too busy walking around the park and having coffee and croissants with Carol. I hated the car – its colour, the lumpy seats, and the lingering smell of dog that just wouldn't shift. Matt had insisted on buying it because he loved its 'anonymity'. Typical of him to choose lack of style over substance. I was fine with him wanting to be anonymous, but did it really have to come at the expense of my comfort?

I was on my way to the Lake District, where my parents owned a small boathouse on the banks of Lake Ullswater. They rarely used it these days apart from the occasional visit to check it over for repairs or leaks and the like, and I knew where they kept a spare key hidden. The place was totally off grid – no TV, no phone signal, all its electricity provided by a small red diesel generator housed in a lean-to shed at the rear of the property.

I had stopped at a service station somewhere near Nottingham and checked my phone. Matt had sent me a wavy hand emoji. I returned the compliment and immediately regretted doing so. I needed to be strong here and just focus on myself. I also had a few messages from Will at work gently enquiring as to my whereabouts. I didn't reply. I wasn't in the mood for explaining myself to anyone. Doubtless Will would be concerned about the fraud case due in court the following Wednesday, but he had no need to worry. The file was in perfect order, all beautifully prepared by the dependable Harriet.

I could tell already that my phone was going to be like a very persistent stalker. I would be glad when I was at the boathouse and it could no longer be a cause of distress. For now, I turned it off and put it in the car boot. It had been a restless night and a long drive, so I found a quiet corner of the car park, covered myself with my coat, and forced myself into a deep sleep.

I woke up with a huge crease across my face from using my hand as a pillow. I looked old and worn out, like a dried apricot. The car park surroundings reflected my mood: rubbish trapped in the branches of the supposedly ornamental shrubs; an overweight bloke in a saggy tracksuit scratching his backside; two pensioners sat silently in their car eating homemade sandwiches; potholes in the tarmac filled with muddy, oily water; and a child screaming after spilling her ice-cold blue drink on the floor.

A few months ago, Matt and I had finally agreed that it was time that we tried for a baby. My clock was running down and I suspect that Matt loved the idea of being a stay-at-home dad. We both wanted to have a boy (though of course we both nodded profusely when I said a girl would be nice too). He wanted a son because of football and tools and, later on in life, pubs. I wanted one because I thought I could mould the first decent bloke to inhabit the parish. If this was to be the end of our relationship, I would definitely mourn the end of this little dream. I had no idea if I was making the right decision by up and leaving, but at least I was doing something to oil the wheels of change in an as-yet-undecided direction. It certainly felt like the beginning of the end of Matt and Harriet.

There was a sudden tapping on the door window. It was a man in some sort of official-looking uniform asking me to wind down the window. I quickly obliged and gave him a pleasant smile. He had a big round face and a thick, dark moustache. His double chin was smooth and taut and I instantly admired his decision not to cover it over with a beard.

'You've been here over two hours, love. If you don't leave now I'm afraid you'll have to pay a parking fee,' he said as he pulled his parking notice machine from his satchel.

'Sorry, officer, I'll leave right now. Didn't realize I'd been here that long.'

He stared at me quizzically and pointed his pen at my face.

'You alright, love? Your face looks a bit skew-whiff, like you've been slapped or something.'

'No, of course not,' I replied. 'I've just been asleep.'

'Blimey, that must have been a deep kip. Like I say, you look like you've been slapped in the face.'

'Christ's sake! I haven't been slapped. Who could have slapped me? I'm in here on my own.'

'The slapper could have vacated the vehicle. I'm not saying he did but . . .'

'Why do you say "he"? Women can be slappers too.'

'So are you saying that a woman slapped you?'

'No, I haven't been slapped, I've been asleep, and either way it's not really a parking matter, is it?'

'If a slapping incident has occurred in my car park, then I think I'm duty bound to enquire.'

'And that is what you have done,' I replied as I wound up the window and drove away, remembering the epic punch that I had delivered to Carol's foundation-saturated cheek. I was doing the right thing.

I stopped at Penrith to buy some groceries and booze at the

supermarket, using my own debit card rather than the one for our joint account. I didn't want Matt knowing where I was. I intended this to be my last contact with civilization for a while. I arrived at the boathouse around 4 p.m.

By the time I had fired up the generator, collected logs from the woodpile and generally brought the place back to life, the sun was setting behind the mountains. I took a chair onto the small patio overlooking the lake and opened a bottle of wine. There was hardly a breeze in the air and the surface of the lake was calm and inviting. The only sound was the water gently lapping against the little stone pier that jutted out from the boathouse. I stripped down to my underwear, descended the steps to the pier, and dived into the water. As I floated on my back, looking over to the empty boathouse, I fleetingly wished that Matt was there with me.

That evening I went to bed early and tried to read a book, but couldn't concentrate. Images from my time with Matt kept entering my thoughts and refused to dissolve until they had played out to their conclusion.

Not long after we had met, he had taken me to Hastings for a day by the seaside. It was windy, wet and miserable, but he insisted that we play a game of crazy golf. Every time he hit the golf ball, he'd raise one of his legs and make an exaggerated parp noise with his mouth, then turn his head towards me and declare, in a very posh, stilted voice, 'It's nothing, darling, don't even worry about it.'

When we went to the supermarket, he would always insist that I pushed the trolley. Whenever I left it unattended, he would sneak in an item that we couldn't possibly need: a packet of nappies, a multipack of yeast tablets, a pack of firelighters, a 36DD bra. Usually I would spot the rogue item and tell him to put it back, but sometimes one would remain in the trolley until we were placing them on the checkout. I would hold it up to him with a sour look on my face and he would reply, 'That's one-nil to the man with the golden face. I'll put that back for you, shall I, madam?' Then he'd flounce off like Sherlock Holmes to return the item to the shelf.

Whenever we went to see a movie at the cinema, at the very moment the film ended, he would hold the popcorn carton above him and shake the remaining contents over his head to create a popcorn waterfall. 'Our work here is done,' he would announce, before quickly rising up from his seat and leaving the auditorium at great pace.

Stupid little moments, but it was within them that our bonds had formed.

My first few days at the boathouse I spent reading, cooking, walking and sleeping; anything to stop me from thinking about Matt and work. Just trying to find a state of mind that would allow me to make the correct decisions about my future.

The Saturday was difficult. I had started to worry about my absence from work. It was a bad time to let them down. The money-laundering case was a seriously complicated prosecution and, despite my efforts to convince myself otherwise, my presence would definitely be missed. It was going to cause panic in the office and give Will a sleepless night or two. I made the decision to return home on Tuesday, the day before the trial. This eased my conscience enough to begin enjoying the surroundings again. I took a walk around the lake and treated myself to lunch in the pub beside Pooley Bridge. It was pleasant, but a bit too loud for me. Did they not realize what I was going through?

In the afternoon, I sat on the little pebble beach by the boathouse and spent a couple of hours building a fire pit out of large stones and pebbles. Using a shelf from the boathouse oven, I transformed the pit into an outdoor grill and cooked a veggie burger and some broccoli above the flames. Matt would have been proud of me.

By Tuesday my mood had evened out enough to properly contemplate my future. We were about to move house, and if Matt got himself a new job, which I was confident he would, we could afford a decent place, hopefully a lot nearer to my work. Carol would no longer be our neighbour and that was an important factor in my musings. Up until that holiday in Palm Springs, I had never once suspected that Matt might cheat on me. It was one of the reasons I fell for him – the absence of a wayward glint in his eye. He always seemed happy in my company and a bit standoffish and shy with other ladies. He just wasn't the Romeo type. It wasn't in his genes.

Carol was the problem; she had brought him out of his shell and into her web. I've known women like her all my life and they can be ruthless with their manipulations. Maybe Matt was the victim here and not me; maybe getting her out of his life was all that was needed. I knew I could forgive and forget because I had done it many times in the past.

At lunchtime, I made up a flask of tea and a ham and Dairylea sandwich and took the small rowing boat out onto the lake to enjoy a floating picnic. My father used to fish from the boat when I was young and the small steel anchor was still on board. I rowed to the north-east end of the lake, where the boat was surrounded and dwarfed by the mountains, and placed the oars inside to just let it drift with the motion of the water. Apart from the drone of the occasional speedboat, there was nothing to be heard. I inhaled a great big greedy breath of the Lakeland air and remembered a day last summer when Matt and I had holidayed together at the boathouse.

The weather had been glorious, and we were sunbathing on the jetty. I was laid on a towel wearing a red two-piece bikini. Matt was stood up throwing pebbles into the lake. He was wearing a pair of old shrunken grey underpants that were far too tight for him and forced his pot belly to overhang the waistband. His back was hairy around his shoulders but his upper arms were hair-free. If his arms had been hairy, we could never have worked. I had always fancied him, especially when he was messing around in the outdoor sunshine.

It was early afternoon and the sun was high in the sky over the mountains. We were sharing a bottle of cheap champagne that Matt had been awarded for being salesman of the month over a year ago.

'Do you still fancy me?' I asked, taking a sip of the plonk.

'Do bears shop in Aldi?' he replied.

'Answer the question, Matt.'

'Yes, I do. More than ever, actually. Would you be so kind as to take your top off?'

'No chance.'

'What about a quick flash? You know, in recognition of my monthly sales.'

I obliged with a quick tug down of my top. He responded by making the sound of a fog horn, rubbing his eyes in disbelief and diving head first off the jetty into the lake.

I laughed as he slowly made his way back to the jetty, stumbling with every other step on the greasy rocks, shouting '*Mother!*' every time he slipped. He sat beside me on the jetty with his arms around his raised knees and began to shiver. I wrapped my towel around his shoulders and as I did so he stole a kiss on my lips.

'Why the kiss?' I asked.

'Sorry, just felt like it,' he said, looking anxious, as if expecting disapproval for his little gesture.

'No, I'm sorry, that was a stupid question.' I put an arm around him and returned the kiss.

We both laid back on the boards and soaked up the sun's rays. I closed my eyes and counted the waves as I heard them lap against the jetty.

'Do you want me to put some sun cream on you? You know how quickly you start to burn,' he asked out of the silence.

'No, I'm fine thanks,' I replied without opening my eyes. I could sense that something was on his mind.

'I've got a feeling that work might be about to give me the boot,' he said.

'Does that bother you?' I asked.

'Not if it doesn't bother you.'

'Fine by me,' I replied. 'So long as you get another job pronto. We need two wages coming in. Anyway, I thought you said you had lost your passion for the bathroom furniture game, and were starting to hate the place? To be honest, it's about time you moved on to something better. Might make you happier.'

'It's not the place I hate, it's just the fact of actually having to work. What about we just live here together, off grid, and make quilts or pepperpots to sell to tourists?'

'You would miss the TV too much,' I replied.

'No, I wouldn't, I'd be too busy foraging for pepperpot materials. Hey, hold on, what do you mean, "Might make you happier"? Do I seem unhappy? I think I'm happy. You know what I always say, "If you're happy, then I am too".'

I opened my eyes and sat up on my elbows. 'That's not true, though, is it? You've just said that you hate your work, and that's a big chunk of your time.'

'Yeah, but that's just life, isn't it? Nobody enjoys work.'

'I do,' I replied. 'In fact, I fucking love it.'

'I know you do, and it makes you happy, so that's a win for both of us.'

'No, it's just a win for *me*,' I said.

The conversation paused for a moment. Matt was always uncomfortable inside any serious talk about our relationship. I knew he would try to deflect the conversation by making a joke, and sure enough, that is what he did.

'Do you not believe in the pepperpot project?' he asked. 'I could call it Pepperarmies and design each pot as a different soldier so that they become collectable. Jesus, we could create generational wealth on the back of these pots. Wouldn't be surprised if there was a bidding war between Costco and Home Bargains to stock them.'

I lay back down and closed my eyes. 'You're always acting the clown, Matt, and as we all know, clowns aren't happy people.'

'Not all clowns. That Ronald McDonald seems like he's *lovin' it.*'

'But he's not real – and I doubt he has a girlfriend.'

'I don't know about that. He's fucking tall and plenty of ladies go for a bloke who's impossible to tap on the head.'

'Matt, the only thing you seem to value is making people, specifically me, laugh. It must be exhausting.'

'No, I find it very rewarding actually.'

'Trauma. They say jokers are jokers to help them deal with trauma.'

'Well, if that's true, then it's a perfectly harmless way of coping. Better than going on the pills or falling apart.'

We were silent for a while. I turned myself over so my back faced the sun.

'Did any of your previous fellas make you laugh?' he asked.

'Yeah, sometimes, but they weren't obsessed.'

'You know why I do it, don't you?' he asked.

'No, why?' I answered, genuinely curious.

'Because I never want you to leave me,' he replied.

That was sad. I reached out a hand and gave his arm a squeeze.

'I'm sensing you don't like the name Pepperarmies,' he said.

'It's a strong name, but it's never going to happen,' I replied.

Looking back, he hadn't asked me if I was happy. I think he assumed that if I wasn't, I would up and leave him. That's what he believed he would do in those circumstances. Then again, maybe he was just scared of the answer he might get.

Truth is, most of the time, I was very happy to be the centre of his world. No other person had ever gifted me that indulgence or made such a monumental effort to serve my needs. Perhaps it was time for me to return the favour and see where that might lead us. I had a sudden craving for him to be here, by my side, right that moment, so I could inform him of that intention and ask him to pitch his pepperpot dream to me one more time.

I rowed back to the boathouse and hurriedly tidied up and packed my things into the car. I drove for over five hours non-stop all the way to Hither Green, arriving back in the dark at about 9 p.m. There were no lights on in our house and I was disappointed that Matt might not be home to greet me. Still, it would be a nice surprise when he returned (I hoped). I took my phone out of the boot of the car. There were tens of unread messages and emails waiting to be read, mostly from Matt and Will, but my eye was drawn to a text from Catherine, my little spy.

Good news (I hope). Matt is definitely NOT having an affair with that awful woman. I've been trying to

My phone went blank as the battery gave up. It was the news I had been desperate to hear. I felt a rush of relief and a pang of guilt for doubting him. I owed him an epic apology.

I didn't want to take Matt by surprise, so I knocked on the door rather than use my key. Nothing stirred, so I stooped down to have a look through the letter box. I was hit with an unfamiliar smell – quite unpleasant, as if somebody was grilling sick. I assumed Matt had left some food out to rot or neglected to empty Monson's litter tray. I took the front door key out of my pocket and placed it into the lock. Just as the key was turning, I felt something hard hit the back of my head and I fell down onto the doorstep. Lights out.

32

SMELL TO GET WELL

I sat down with Hamper for his seemingly compulsory pre-exercise counselling session. He didn't say hello to me but gave me a curious insincere smile instead. I sensed a bit of tension, but it may have just been my imagination.

'How's Callum?' I asked.

'Thank you for asking, Matt, that's very caring of you, but could we keep the outside world away from this chamber of rumination and growth? Could we do that, Matt?'

'Yes, of course, sorry,' I replied. 'Can I just say the lights seem even crisper today. Have you turned them up or something?'

'Maybe it is your mind that is crisper, Matt? Perhaps you have digested all of what we spoke of at our last reflection session.'

'Hey, maybe you're right. I do feel quite sharp.'

'Has your girlfriend returned, Matt? I know that her leaving was causing you distress.'

'I thought we were leaving the real world outside these four walls?'

'Of course, Matt, but your distress and your pain is in here with us, inside your head, and should be addressed.'

'No, she hasn't returned, and I'm not particularly hopeful that she will,' I replied with more certainty than I intended.

'Did you live together before you moved into Satsuma Heights, Matt?'

'Yes, we did. In a rented house in Hither Green. Harriet probably thinks I'm still living there.'

'Describe it for me, Matt.'

'Well, it's a London brick terraced house on Ayersome Street with a bright red door and a small front garden behind a low wall—'

'No, Matt, I want you to describe the feelings that the house evokes, not the bricks and mortar; they are irrelevant to spiritual progress. It could be a prison for all I care. Did it *feel* like a prison, Matt?'

'No, it didn't. It felt like a home,' I replied, enjoying my certainty on this occasion.

'You seem agitated, Matt, as if you're lacking balance and serenity. May I introduce you to some essential oils that might help you achieve a sense of calm and equilibrium? Would that be something of interest to you, Matt?'

He handed me a small, straw-lined wooden box with four tiny bottles of very essential oils inside.

'Would you like to open a bottle and rub some onto your wrist? Believe me, it can be a very supportive tool.'

I opened one of the bottles and gave it a sniff.

'Good choice, Matt, that's rosemary and myrrh.'

'Not getting much, to be honest. It's a bit meh.'

'No, myrrh.'

'Yeah, just saying it's a bit meh.'

'It's myrrh.'

'Yeah okay, that as well.'

'Stop resisting, Matt. Be vulnerable; dive in; take a chance.'

I poured some of the oil directly onto my wrist. It was much thinner than I had anticipated and a few large blobs fell onto my tracksuit bottoms. I instantly knew the stains would be tricky to remove.

'Oh fuck, I'll never shift that.'

'Please, Matt, do not utter profanities in the presence of the oils. They need an ambience of calm to penetrate your nervous system. They contain both hydrocarbons and phenols and those are not necessarily the most robust compounds to infuse.'

'Is that all I do, just rub the oil in and sniff at it?'

'It is indeed, Matt. Soon the vapours will send a signal to your brain – a very low part of the brain down near the back of your neck, I think – and this signal will cause your brain to release endorphins and other beneficial substances. That is when the calmness and wellbeing kicks in.'

'Smell to get well,' I suggested.

'Yes, Matt, that's a very neat way of putting it,' he replied.

I took some deep breaths. The Hamper tinkled a tiny little pink bell and we started to chat again.

'Why do you miss your girlfriend so much when there are so many other things that you could be yearning for?'

'What sort of things do you mean?' I asked.

'Your childhood, your youth, spirituality, adventure, happiness. There are many things to desire other than companionship.'

'None of those things seem real to me, whereas Harriet was very real and the hurt I'm feeling because of her absence is actually quite crushing. I'm not really in the frame of mind for adventure or yearning over my past.'

'Is that because you are mentally and physically lazy, or perhaps you have low expectations for yourself? Did Harriet ever talk about adventures, or reclaiming some of the exhilaration of the past?'

'Not that I remember.'

'It's often the case, Matt, that those people who neglect their body also neglect their spiritual and mental development.'

'That could well be true of me,' I admitted.

'Would you say that Harriet neglected her body and spirit?'

'No, I wouldn't. Quite the opposite.'

'Then why would she chain herself to someone who does? It's worth thinking about, isn't it, Matt?'

It was time for some yoga. We scrutted about on the mats and got ourselves into various yoga positions. One of them involved me crouching on my hands and knees and then slowly pulling my backside downwards towards my feet. Whilst doing this, I broke wind.

'*That* smell won't get you well,' I joked.

The Hamper ignored my comment before dabbing a drip of essential oil under his nose.

At the end of the session I had worked up quite a sweat, so treated myself to a shower in the cramped studio bathroom. I hadn't observed my beer belly naked and from above in some time. I was only used to seeing it lying flat in the bath or in bed. It was quite a shock. It made me think about what lies beneath a large sea turtle's glorious outer shell. Probably something the turtle wouldn't be particularly proud to show off. We don't all just carry secrets around with us, I thought; sometimes we grow them without knowing. Either way, it's always an effort to cover them up.

When I emerged from the shower, Hamper was waiting for me by the studio entrance door. He handed me the opened box of essential oils.

'The oils are twenty-nine pounds.'

'I'm not sure that I want them to be honest . . . didn't really get the lift and support you promised.'

'You won't immediately feel the benefit; they are not class-A drugs. You need to persevere, invest in yourself a bit more and, what's more, a phial has been opened so they can't be returned.'

I took the hit in the interests of connection-building.

His classes finished for the morning, he invited me to walk with him back to Satsuma Heights. We strode in silence for a few blocks and then he suddenly stopped, turned to me and asked, 'Did you tell Laurence about Callum? Was it you who snitched on me?'

His tone and demeanour had changed completely, and he took a step towards me. He was a guru hard man with a puckered vinegar face and (I imagined) equally taut buttocks.

'I don't know what you're on about,' I replied, panicking at the accusation. 'What do you mean? Where has this come from?'

'Somebody told Laurence that Callum was staying with me these last couple of days and because of that he is throwing me out of the apartment. I have nowhere to go. Are you his little spy? What the fuck are you doing taking my classes? The state of you, you have no interest in physical or personal development. I doubt you even give a flying fuck about your gut health. You're just putting your neck in where it's not wanted. I should fucking spank you.'

I held up my hands in an act of submission.

'You're wrong, Justin, I don't know what to say. Why on earth would I be spying on my neighbours?'

'Because that's what Laurence does. He spies on people or gets a lackey to do the dirty work for him. And you are just the sort of sap that he uses. He ended my marriage by spying on me and now he wants to throw me out on the streets. Just admit it or I'll beat the fucking truth out of you.'

His face was reddened with anger, his jaw locked tight and his neck swollen and pulsing. He seemed ready to pounce. I glanced at the so-very-essential oils box in my hand. Should I strike him with it? Just go for it? He was about the same height as me but in far better nick. He had muscles everywhere; even his hands looked virile and exceptional. If we were to fight British style, no weapons, then it would be a fight I would lose. A crack around his head with the oils box might at least give me the opportunity to do a runner. He hadn't leapt at me yet, though, so I decided to engage with him rather than make a move.

'What do you mean when you say he ended your marriage?'

He stared at me full in the face and started revolving his tongue inside his mouth and chewing on the inside of his cheeks. I braced myself for an imminent attack.

'Because I was married to his daughter and he had me followed and watched and I was caught having it off with one of my students. My wife threw me out and he offered me the flat rent-free so long as I promised to keep out of his daughter's life.'

The adultery didn't surprise me one bit, and the offer from Laurence had a familiar sound to it. Hamper took a small step towards me and started to knead his right hand as if manipulating a stress ball.

'He threatened to use his fancy lawyers to ensure that I never saw Callum again if I didn't agree. All I get is one access visit a month and I'm never allowed to have Callum stay with me at Satsuma Heights. That would just be too much for Laurence to bear, seeing me and my son happy together inside his fucking palace. But I wanted Callum to spend some time with me in my home, like we were actually a normal father and son. Laurence was away and Callum's mother gave me permission to do it. I took a chance and someone has grassed me up and now I'm fucked. He wants me out of the building and onto the streets . . . He's even accusing me of having an affair with his precious mistress Kiara, which is bullshit. Are you behind that rumour as well? Jesus, why am I actually telling you any of this? You're probably recording everything I say.'

His body tensed up even more and he started to shift his weight between his feet as if preparing to unleash a punch. I took a step backwards and held my hands in front of me in a gesture of subservience and surrender.

'Listen, Justin, I'm not recording anything and I'm really sorry about your marriage and your son, but what on earth makes you think I've been watching you? We've only met each other on a couple of occasions.'

I wondered if the residue of incredibly essential oils might travel from my hands to his nostrils and becalm him. I kept my hands where they were and let them waft slightly in the breeze. He pointed a finger at me then grabbed one of my wrists.

'Why did you follow me into the park yesterday? Why was it that the *very first thing you did* was ask if Callum was my son?'

'I was just being friendly. Isn't that what anyone would have asked?' I replied. 'Can you let go of my wrist? It's a bit raw from the oils. I must be allergic.'

To my surprise, he released his grip and allowed his arms to relax by his side. His gaze shifted to somewhere in the distance over my shoulder.

'So tell me this, then: how is it that an unemployed bloke like you is living in a flat he clearly can't afford? What sort of a deal have you made with Laurence? What has he got on you? Or, probably more likely, what have you got on *him*?'

'Honestly, Justin, you're barking up the wrong tree. I just rented the flat through the estate agents and paid the rent up front from my redundancy money. I'm sorry to hear about your son and the flat, but it's none of my doing. Have you asked Derek if he knows anything?'

'No point. He's one of Laurence's foot soldiers.'

'Maybe it was him that told Laurence about your son.'

'No, I don't think so. I was very careful. He always came in the building when he was away from his desk. You might be right, but you're the only one that definitely saw us together.'

'I promise you, Justin, I haven't mentioned anything about your son to Laurence.'

I had, of course, mentioned his son to Derek. That may well have been a mistake.

He sighed, relaxed his shoulders, scratched the back of his head, then put his hand on my right shoulder.

'I'm going to find out the truth, and if I find out it's you, then believe me, you will never experience peace and serenity again. Do you believe me when I say that, Matt?'

'Yes, I do,' I replied.

He walked away, his magnificent buttocks teasing me with their taut aloofness. He had scared me good and proper, but if he really was prone to violence, then I wouldn't be stood there on the pavement, unharmed and injury-free. Maybe the absolutely essential oils had played their part.

33

CONFESSIONS WITH SHANDY

Back in my flat, I decided to do a sweep of the place for any signs of a hidden camera. There was no sprinkler valve above the front door to hide a device, so I examined all the light switches and fittings in the living room and all the knobs and buttons in the kitchen area. I couldn't find anything suspicious, so concluded I was indeed free from surveillance.

My chat with the Hamper had left me feeling a bit low – not so much his implied threat that he would come after me if I proved to be the snitch; more his suggestion that I was holding Harriet back in her life. He was probably right. I was very set in my ways, very comfortable in my habits and very ambivalent about my future. I had failed her.

While I was living with Harriet, I was happy, and if not happy, then at the very least content. Had this been enough for Harriet? I doubted it. She felt further away from my grasp than ever before.

Once again, I was in need of friendly company. I phoned Carol but she didn't pick up. I left a message asking her to ring me at her earliest convenience. My only other option was Hot Dog. I made a visit to the store cupboard to check the screens. He was sat on his sofa watching daytime TV, the remnants of a full English breakfast on the coffee table and the long shoe on the cushion next to him. He looked as if he didn't have a care in the world. I was flushed with a rush of jealousy. In Flat 5B, the Hamper was packing his possessions into boxes while some variety of moon music played in the background. It made for a very sombre scene.

I returned to my flat and sent an email to Laurence informing him that, by the looks of things, the Hamper was moving out.

I received an immediate reply.

Hello Matt,

Thank you for that information. I knew he was going today because I told him to leave. You can put all your efforts into 5C now. No excuses; just do your job.

Laurence

There was a knock on my door; it was Hot Dog, inviting me to join him for a session in the Horseshoe. I immediately agreed. It was time to dig a bit deeper into what was really going on in Satsuma Heights.

There were only a handful of diehard lunchtime punters in the Horseshoe when we arrived. Hot Dog went straight to his usual seat and told me to fetch him a pint of Guinness and two packets of cheese and onion crisps. The waitress from the park café was serving behind the bar. I ordered myself a pint of shandy, hoping that I would be able to pass it off as a pint of bitter when I sat down with Hot Dog. The waitress seemed pleased to see me.

'So you took the job?' I asked.

'Yeah, I did and I love it. Is this your local, then?'

'Yeah, I live in Satsuma Heights just opposite. It's very handy, very local.'

'You living there with your girlfriend?'

'Do you mean Harriet or are you still trying to suggest I'm having an affair?'

'Bit touchy, aren't we? Don't answer if it's a problem.'

'It's not a problem. I'm living on my own at the moment but hoping that Harriet will be joining me soon.'

She had updated her hairstyle so that it presented as a very high Elvis-style quiff. I took the opportunity to change the subject.

'I like your new hair. Suits you.'

'Yeah, quirky innit. Suggests there's more to me than meets the eye.'

'And have you got back with your boyfriend?' I asked.

'No, but just give me time.'

'Is the new hairstyle part of the plan?'

'Absolutely. Will make him feel like he's with a new woman, and that's what all you fellas want, innit.'

'I don't,' I replied. 'But I hope it works for you.'

'I'll keep you informed,' she replied.

I sat down next to Hot Dog and he immediately shook his head at me to indicate some sort of disappointment.

'What's up?' I asked.

'Shandy! A fucking shandy! You expect me to sit down next to a shandy drinker and maintain any pride about myself?'

'It's the middle of the day. I'm keeping it light and breezy. You know, easing into the session.'

'I don't like that approach, not one bit. Makes you sound like a pipsqueak. It's like you're apologizing for having a drink, and that makes me feel guilty – takes the sheen off things just when I was having myself a really nice time. So thanks for that, Jigsaw.'

We talked for a while (he talked, I listened) about how 'proper men' were rapidly disappearing and could now only be found in agricultural communities and slum housing estates. The world was full of pipsqueaks. I agreed in order to maintain the togetherness of the situation. He also waxed lyrical about the long shoe and showed me some photographs he had taken of it in various positions in his flat. He had placed it on his kitchen island (centrally, with toe facing the oven), on his pillow (a selfie with his face beside the pointy end and one hand caressing the laces), on his balcony handrail, pointing towards the tip of the Shard building (he was giving a thumbs up in this photo), and resting vertically in the corner of the room (didn't work; no sense of scale). Each photo reminded me of the terrible error I had made not snapping it up at first sight.

'Where did you disappear to last night after we ran out of the garden?' he asked. 'I waited for you at the station for half an hour in the fucking cold.'

'I ran to a neighbour's house that I'm good friends with, stayed there the night in the end.'

'Oh, I see, and is this neighbour a lady?'

'Yes, but she slept on a comfy chair, not in the bed, if that's what you're thinking.'

'You got the bed? You must be a tricky fucker to have pulled that off.'

'She just chose to sleep on the chair, no trickery involved.'

'I don't believe you,' he said as he raised his pint in the air and added a 'Good on ya.'

'I'm telling the truth,' I said with surprising force.

'Alright, Jigsaw, don't shit yourself. I believe you,' he replied while delivering an ambiguous wink in my direction. 'So, what's your plan with the cat?' he asked.

'My neighbour friend is going to attempt a rescue for me. She's a very resourceful character. I think there's a good chance she might pull it off.'

He laughed at my unfortunate choice of phrase and I chose to laugh along.

'How long have you lived in your flat?' I asked out of the blue and as casually as I could muster.

'Just under a month,' he replied.

'What made you choose to live there?'

'I didn't exactly choose to live there. It was part of a deal I came to with the owner. Very beneficial to both sides, I might add.'

At first I assumed he was tied into some sort of residential surveillance, just like me, but surely Laurence wouldn't need two people for the job? Could he be watching *me*?

'What do you mean by "part of a deal"?' I asked, assuming

the mention of the deal gave me permission to enquire further.

Hot Dog took a long, slow sup on his Guinness, plonked the glass back on his beer mat and wiped some foamy residue off his lips. I wondered if I had overstepped the mark asking this question.

'Tell me, Jigsaw,' he replied. 'What sort of a deal have *you* got going with Mr Laurence la-dee-dah Moody? Nobody gets to stay in those flats without some sort of a deal. Come on, spill the beans or stop with your interrogation.'

That was the first time I had heard the surname 'Moody'. It rang a bell in a tiny church somewhere in the rear of my mind.

I had come to the Horseshoe seeking answers, so I took the plunge and answered him truthfully. In for a penny, as it were. My stomach flipped itself inside out with a lump of qualm.

'He asked me to watch the residents on our corridor and report back to him any activity or conversations that might be of interest to him.'

'And when you say "watch", am I right to assume that he has a camera fitted up in my flat?'

'Yes, I'm afraid so,' I replied with an expression that screamed 'I'm not worth hitting'. 'But only for a couple of weeks or so, and the camera only shoots the lounge end of your apartment. You can hardly see anything.'

'Dirty nosey little Jigsaw.'

His words were angry but his face still read as friendly. I continued with my confession, deploying a hint of the pathetic in my voice.

'The camera feed goes to a monitor in the store cupboard in the corridor. I've hardly watched it, though – all I've seen is you watching TV and eating your grub, maybe scratching a bollock every now and then, but nothing you wouldn't be okay with. I reckon I've only watched for about a couple of hours since I moved in and I promise I won't look at the feed ever again. I'm done with it.'

He laughed and gave my shoulder a quick squeeze with one of his massive hands.

'I knew it. I fucking knew it! I spent a week searching and searching for a camera and couldn't find one. Let me guess, is it in that little white box that controls the electric blinds? I opened it up and didn't have a clue what the fuck I was looking at. Is that where it is?'

'No.'

'Don't tell me, let me guess. Is it in the intercom thingy next to the front door? There's enough bits and pieces in there to hide a little lens.'

'No, it's in the sprinkler nozzle above the front door.'

'No way! I inspected that and compared it to the others and it seemed perfectly legit. I can't even see where it could accommodate a camera. Must be very state of the art.'

I relaxed. I was going to survive this encounter without a beating. He wasn't angry. My stomach settled and the clamminess evaporated from the skin on my back.

'I'm really sorry I agreed to do it, but if I hadn't agreed then I wouldn't have got the flat. Truth is, I—'

'I couldn't give a fuck,' he interrupted. 'If it wasn't you it would be someone else and I've got nothing to hide. He had a bloke watching me before you arrived and they told him I was a drug dealer, so he thinks he's got that against me now.'

'*Are* you a drug dealer?'

'None of your business,' he said forcefully enough to end that line of enquiry.

'Are you going to tell me about *your* deal with Laurence?' I asked.

'If Laurence Moody finds out I've told you, you will be out on your arse before you can reach round to scratch it.'

'Do you know what, I don't think that would really bother me. I only moved here for my girlfriend, Harriet. We've been having problems and I thought "new home, new start", but it doesn't look as if we're together any more. If I lose the flat, I might move somewhere coastal, maybe Hastings or Margate.'

'You get a lot of pipsqueaks hanging around them coastal areas. I wouldn't recommend it,' he responded.

'You're not going to tell him that I've told you about the camera, are you?' I asked.

'There is no chance of that, son, and, as a sign of my good-will, I'll tell you about my arrangement with Moody. It's a very simple deal. In a couple of days he's up in court facing a shit-load of fraud and money-laundering charges. If he is found guilty, then he goes away for years and years. I am a minor but significant witness for the prosecution. The police are looking for me as we speak because I've disappeared off their radar courtesy of Mr Moody's hospitality. In return for my absence, he is paying me one hundred thousand pounds: fifty grand upfront and the rest when I've failed to appear. He's hoping that the trial will collapse without my evidence. Who knows if it will; that's his lookout. It's a good deal. I'm very pleased with it.'

'So he wants you to be watched in case you do a runner or contact the police or something?' I asked.

'You are correct. He's paranoid, tries to cover all eventualities twice over. I suppose I would too if my liberty was at risk.'

'Well, your secret's safe with me. One hundred thousand pounds. Shit, I'd be tempted, too. Do your family and friends know where you are?'

'Haven't got any. You're the only person who knows about the deal, so, if the secret gets out, Moody and I know exactly which door to come a-calling.'

It was a lot for me to take in. I couldn't immediately think of any reason why having this information would put me in any trouble. Truth is, I felt good to be cleansed of any guilt over my dodgy spying activities. I was growing very fond of Mr 'Hot Dog' Hoover.

'So, now we know where each other stands,' said Hot Dog, 'shall we have a game of darts? A game of darts, might I add, that you will lose.'

I agreed, and we played a few games while I drank a few more shandies. Hot Dog left around 2 p.m. to go back to his flat for an afternoon nap.

As soon as he left, the waitress joined me at the table.

'There's something I think I should tell you,' she said as she

241

reached over and stole a crisp from the bag Hot Dog had left behind.

I thought she was going to warn me about Hot Dog's possible drug-dealing activities, but it was something much more shocking.

'You know when we first met at the café?' she asked.

'Yeah, the day of the egg encounter.'

'Well, I was watching you. I'd been watching you for three or four weeks.'

'Why on earth would you be doing that?' I asked.

'Because your girlfriend Harriet asked me to.'

'You know Harriet? Have you seen her or spoken to her recently?' I asked in a sudden panic.

'No, she's proving very hard to get in touch with. I wondered if she'd changed her number or something,' she replied.

34

WET SLIPPERS

I asked the waitress why Harriet had asked her to spy on me. It turned out that she – Catherine – was the daughter of the family Harriet had moved in with after she split up with her previous boyfriend, Nick. Harriet had become suspicious of my relationship with Carol when we had returned from Palm Springs. She didn't like the fact that we were meeting up most mornings in the café in the park. Harriet knew that Catherine was working in the café and had asked her to keep an eye on us.

'No big deal,' she had said. 'Just want you to nose around them and see if you think anything untoward is going on.' Catherine had agreed because she felt she 'would be good at that sort of thing'. Apparently she had been way ahead of her mum when her dad had a brief affair with a lady he met at the BRIT Awards.

'So, what did you tell Harriet? You must have told her nothing was going on because nothing was or is going on. We're just friends. Is that what you told her?'

'Not quite,' she replied, an apologetic look on her face. 'I told her that you were very comfortable in each other's company and that there was a possibility you were more than just friends.'

'But that's not true! How could you say that? What possible reason did I give you to think that?'

'The way you looked at each other, the way you were so quick to apologize for her behaviour, the way you would leave the café together with a naughty sort of friction between you. I didn't tell Harriet that I thought you were having it off, but I did tell her that it looked as if it was on both of your minds.'

'How could you do that?' I replied angrily. 'She's walked out on me and I bet it's because of your interference. There is *nothing* going on between me and Carol.'

'Yeah, but *she* definitely wants it. It's so obvious, and I think you know it too.'

'Well, that's not my fucking fault, is it? That's just the way she is. And why on earth would you even want to get involved?'

'Sisterhood, innit, mate. Suck it up.' She got up out of her seat. 'For what it's worth, I believe you. I reckon you would be with her now if it was true. I spoke to your darts mate earlier and he says you seem to be very much on your own at the moment.'

'Well, why don't you tell that to Harriet?'

'I've texted her my conclusion that you're not on the cheat but she hasn't picked it up. I've tried phoning her but she never answers. If you speak to her, tell her to give me a ring so I can pass on the good news.'

'Maybe *Harriet* is on the cheat, as you say,' I said.

'No chance,' she said decisively.

'Are you still watching me?'

'Yeah, kinda – you'd better behave yourself, mister,' she said as she tapped the side of her nose to indicate some sort of subterfuge. 'Do you want another shandy?'

I didn't answer. I was still annoyed by her revelation. I just walked out and went back to my flat. The need to speak to Harriet was now consuming me. I needed to tell her that her suspicions were way off the mark. Why had she never confronted me about this? I could have easily convinced her of my innocence. I left her another message pleading with her to contact me. Not long afterwards, my phone rang. It was Carol.

'Alright, darling. I've got your stupid cat. You should come and fetch him. You know he doesn't like me and he's desperate to escape, so I've locked him in the bathroom. He'd better not piss on my slippers.'

I wanted to give her a mouthful and tell her that she may well have been the cause of Harriet's departure, but it didn't feel like the right moment. Best to go and fetch Monson and talk to her face to face.

I arrived at her front door at 3 p.m. with Monson's cat carrier in tow, and she went straight in for one of her theatrical hugs. I brushed it aside and strode into the house.

'Is he still in the bathroom?' I asked curtly.

'I expect so,' she replied. 'Unless he's managed to flush himself out through the toilet. Go and check for yourself, and drop the attitude whilst you're at it, darling.'

I went up to the bathroom and there he was: my beautiful, loyal and devoted best friend.

'Hiya, Monson.'

'Oh, it's you, is it? Was it your idea to have her lock me up in here?'

'No.'

'This room is full of some of the hardest surfaces I have ever encountered. Nothing soft to lie on and nowhere to piss.'

'You can have a piss outside before we go.'

'No need. I did one on her slippers. Quite a thick one. Must be all the worry from you abandoning me. Have you got tickets for a motorcycle event yet?'

'Working on it.'

I put Monson in the carrier and went downstairs. Carol had already poured me a cup of coffee and was sat on the sofa ready for a chat.

'So, what's new, pussycat?' said Carol.

'How did you get him?' I asked.

'I was watching the street, like I do, and saw the cat thief packing an overnight case into his car. He was obviously going away for the night. I waited till he was well gone and then used a wrench on the back kitchen window. Very efficient breach if I say so myself, darling. Didn't leave a trace.'

'What about his burglar alarm?'

'It went off for thirty minutes or so but nobody gave a fuck. You hear them around here nearly every night.'

'Well, thank you, much appreciated.'

'Don't mention it. Like I told you, I enjoy a bit of thieving – gets the juices flowing. Am I right?'

'I wouldn't know.'

I sat down on the other end of the sofa and took a deep breath.

'Listen, Carol, I've had some weird news this afternoon. Do you remember that waitress from the café? The one always dressed in black with the pizza tattoo on her leg.'

'Oh, that little cow. Yes, of course, I never forget an enemy. What of her?'

'Well, it turns out Harriet had asked her to keep an eye on the two of us at the café and report back to her on whether something was going on between us.'

'What? You mean sex?'

'Yes, exactly that.'

'How hilarious,' she snorted. 'That's outrageous. What's the matter with her? I didn't have Harriet down as the jealous type. What did the waitress tell her?'

'Well, that's the thing. She told Harriet that she thought something might well be going on and I reckon that's why Harriet has left me.'

'Oh, darling, that's ridiculous. She's left you for another man, I'm sure of it, and that has nothing to do with me. If that's the reason for her leaving then we can clear it all up pronto. I'll give her a ring now.'

Carol dialled Harriet's number.

'Hi, this is Carol. I must say it's becoming a bit tiresome you not answering your phone. I've got Matt here with me' – I

247

grimaced, wondering if that was something Harriet would want to hear – 'and he's telling me some bizarre tale about you believing that he and I are having some sort of affair. It's an absolute nonsense, dear. Give me a ring so we can clear this up and for fuck's sake get in touch with Matt. Don't be a selfish cow. *Namaste.*'

She ended the call and confirmed that she would contact me if and when Harriet returned the call.

'Did you have to say I was here? You know, given that she thinks something is going on?'

'Stop acting like you're guilty.'

She got up and made her way towards the stairs.

'I'd better check what sort of mess that cat has made. Hey, do you want to come upstairs with me?'

She laughed in a way that suggested she actually thought the invite was funny. While she was up there, I popped into the kitchen to find a teaspoon. I opened a few of the more obvious drawers for holding cutlery, and in one of them I noticed a little handwritten note sealed inside a plastic sandwich bag. It couldn't help but catch your eye amongst the wicker place mats and paper serviettes in the drawer.

As soon as I read it, I recognized it as the note Carol had put on my lounger when we were on holiday (with Harriet) in Palm Springs a couple of months ago. It was daft flirty nonsense. I couldn't for the life of me think why Carol would have kept it.

When she came back downstairs, she was holding a pair

of slippers out in front of her and had her mouth and nose covered with the sleeve of her jumper.

'He's pissed on my slippers! Take them out of here and fucking shoot them!'

I grabbed the slippers from her, picked up Monson's carrier and made my way to the front door. I accepted her one-armed hug as I left the house and headed for the station. I popped the slippers on top of a low wall in the hope that they might be photographed, in black and white, by a passing art student.

On the train back to London Bridge, I took stock of my situation using Monson as a sounding board.

'Where do you think Harriet is at the moment?' I asked him.

'Well, the mad lady thinks she's with another fella, and given the state of you, that makes sense to me.'

'Fair enough, but why isn't she answering her phone?'

'Well, I wouldn't answer the phone to you unless I was desperate for something off you. You know, like, for example, tickets to a motorcycle event.'

'Seriously, though, it's just not like her to be so detached.'

'Maybe she doesn't have her phone on her. Maybe someone has stolen her phone.'

'She does have her phone because she sent me that wavy emoji text.'

'I'm sure she'll get in touch when she's ready. In the meantime, just put all your efforts into looking after me.'

I wondered if she might have contacted her office, or at least been in touch, so decided to indulge in another call to her colleague Will. He answered immediately.

'Hello, Will speaking.'

'Oh, hi, Will, it's Matt here, I was just wondering—'

'Do you know when Harriet will be back?' he interrupted with an urgent tone that bordered on the rude.

'I don't know, Will. I was actually phoning to see if she was back at work.'

'No, she is not, and she's really dumped us in the shit. She won't even respond to any of our emails. There's blind panic here at the moment because a huge money-laundering case she was handling goes to trial on Wednesday and nobody else here is on top of it. What's going on, Matt?'

Monson chipped in. 'Just tell him the truth, boss. Stop being a fanny.'

I took his advice.

'Between you and me, Will, she walked out on me last week and I haven't heard from her since. I have no idea where she is. I'm sorry she's left you in the lurch.'

'Are you sure she's okay?' asked Will. 'Are you sure she hasn't been in an accident or had a nervous breakdown or something?'

'I don't know. My best guess is that she's run off with another bloke. Did she have someone at work she was close to who's done a runner as well?'

'Harriet? Having an affair? Are you joking?'

'No, I'm not. It's the only explanation I have at the moment.'

'Look, even if that were true, she would still come into work. You need to speak to her and find out what's happening.'

'I'm trying, Will, I really am.'

'You better had be. Phone me the moment you get hold of her.'

He ended the call.

'You look like you've seen a ghost,' said Monson.

I emailed Laurence and asked him to contact me urgently.

35

BUTTERWORTH DISPLAY

Back in my flat, I settled Monson in and gave him a big plate of ham. He purred as he ate it in great big greedy scoops of his lower jaw. I sent another email to Laurence asking him to contact me and then did an internet search for 'Laurence Moody fraud' on my laptop. The results confirmed that he was the subject of a major prosecution on various fraud and money-laundering charges arising from his property developments. This must be Harriet's big case.

I phoned Will but it went to answerphone. I left a message asking him to contact me as soon as possible.

I looked through a page of images of Laurence and in every one he looked like a highly educated mature male model. One photo showed him topless doing some hoovering in his pent-house at Satsuma Heights. It caught my eye; he was in amazing physical condition. Could this fancy, charming man really be behind Harriet's disappearance? From what Will had told me, taking Harriet away from the prosecution so close to the start of the trial would be an effective way to help sabotage the case.

It was a scary notion, and one that caused my thoughts to bend towards panic. The image of the pixie-haired Harriet lookalike kept flashing through my mind. Perhaps Harriet hadn't left me of her own free will.

I paced up and down the lounge, accidentally kicking Monson, who was running excitedly around the flat like a puppy on a Monster Munch hunt.

'Are you going to go to the police?' he asked. 'Because I will if you kick me again.'

'Yes, maybe,' I replied. 'But I need to think this thing through before I do. I don't want to put Harriet in any danger and I don't want the police to just dismiss me as a madman, which I'm pretty sure is what they will do.'

'A violent one to boot,' said Monson.

'I could even be in danger myself if I don't tread carefully. I would have to tell them about the cameras and Hot Dog and that could stir up all sorts of shit. Fuck, I might even end up in court. I need a thought bath.'

I usually find inspiration inside a tub, but not on this occasion. Not even a Ransom and Hilliard powdered marble tub could calm my nerves. I turned on the hot tap with my toes and forced myself to lie perfectly still, waiting for the maximum bearable heat level to arrive. This process was disturbed when I heard a female voice call my name from within the lounge.

'Hello?' I replied.

'Hello, Mr Giles. It's Kiara from Lansdowne Estates. I think that maybe you are in the bath.'

'Yes, I am, can you give me a minute?' I shouted.

The bathroom door opened and Kiara's smiling face appeared around the door.

'No need to interrupt your bath, Mr Giles. Laurence said you wanted to speak with some degree of urgency, so let's get on with that.'

I instinctively rolled around in the bath so that my rear was facing the ceiling. (Don't ask me why; it just happened.) The hot water kept running into the bath and the heat was becoming unbearable. I couldn't turn around to close the hot tap, though, for fear of facing Kiara front-on.

'Kiara, could you go back into the lounge please and I'll be with you in a minute?'

'Your back could do with a shave. I think that maybe you are letting your standards slip because you are living alone. Would you like me to do it for you?'

The heat of the bath was beginning to scald. I wanted to scream.

'Please could you get out? This is really awkward.'

'As you wish,' she replied with a sigh. 'It seems to me that perhaps your desire to talk is not as urgent as you have implied.'

I heard the door close behind her and jumped out of the bath like a fat plucked goose. The door opened again and I stood frozen for a moment. For some reason I covered up my tits with my hands rather than my butterworths. Kiara didn't flinch an inch.

'Your arse could do with a harvest as well,' she said, and then left the room.

I put on the white towelling dressing gown that was hanging

on the back of the door and went through into the lounge. Kiara was washing her hands at the kitchen island sink.

'Why is it so dark in here? Do you mind if I open the blinds?' she asked.

'Be my guest,' I replied.

She did so, and then sat down on the sofa. Monson immediately jumped up and perched on her lap. I noticed she was wearing the same grey suit and white and orange trainers as the last time I saw her. Seeing her sat down, it occurred to me that she was maybe an inch taller than Harriet, but I couldn't be sure.

'Your cat is nice, but a bit ugly, I think. Also he smells. You should have taken him into the bath with you.'

'He's just been sick – he's probably spread it around himself a bit having a wash.'

'What a beautiful story,' she replied, pushing Monson off her lap and onto the floor. 'So, Mr Giles,' she continued, 'Laurence has asked me to confirm to you that the footage you saw the other night was of the inside of my flat. I am happy to give that confirmation. We are both sorry that it appeared on your screen but I think no harm has been done.'

'That isn't what I want to speak to Laurence about.'

'Laurence is not available at this time, so I think it might save any delay if you tell me what it is that you wish to discuss. If I cannot answer to your satisfaction, then I will talk to Laurence and get back to you with his response.'

'Why don't you just give me his phone number?'

'That will not be possible,' she replied. 'I sit at his right hand. You sit beneath him. It's as simple as that.'

'Do you know all about the cameras in the other flats on this floor?' I asked.

'Yes, I do,' she replied without a hint of hesitation.

'And you know why Mr Hoover is holed up here in 5C?'

'Yes, I do,' she replied, punctuating the moment with a broad, disingenuous smile.

'And do you know that my partner Harriet is the lead case officer for the Crown Prosecution in Laurence's trial that starts on Wednesday?'

'I did not know that,' she replied. The smile was wiped from her face and replaced with an expression suggesting genuine surprise.

I pressed on: 'And did you know that she has disappeared and that no one, not even the CPS, know where she is?'

'I did not know that. Are you suggesting that Laurence has something to do with her disappearance?'

'Yes, I am,' I replied.

'I very much doubt that is true. I think this is something you need to take up with Laurence directly. I will pass on your concerns to him immediately and make sure that he contacts you.'

She got up to leave.

'Why don't you phone him now,' I pushed, 'here, in front of me?'

'That is not something of which Laurence would approve. I think you should be satisfied with my word that I will pass on your concerns. If you will excuse me, I think it is best that I leave now.'

As she reached the door to the flat, she turned back to face me. The smile had returned to her face.

'That's quite a thatch you have down there,' she said, lowering her head to indicate the area of my groin. 'I think maybe you could cultivate some cress in the undergrowth if you were so minded.'

She left the flat. A few minutes later, my phone rang. It was Will.

'Have you spoken to her?' he asked.

'No, but I wanted to ask you the name of the person involved in the fraud case that Harriet is looking after.'

'I'm not allowed to pass that information on. You should know that.'

'Is it Laurence Moody?'

'I can't share any details of the case with members of the public. I could lose my job, as I'm sure Harriet has told you many times.'

'But it's me, Will. I'm not just any old member of the public. You know me – you can trust me.'

He hesitated for a moment or two.

'I can't share that information with anyone outside of work. You know that. You need to concentrate on getting hold of Harriet. Maybe *she* will be willing to trust you. Have you contacted the police? Because if you don't then I fucking will.'

'I'm on it,' I replied and ended the call.

I stared at my phone with the unformed intention of phoning the police, then rejected the idea. My suspicions were fluffy at best and contacting the police could, in one fell swoop, set me on a collision course with Laurence and maybe even Hot Dog. I would wait and see what Laurence had to say. Then it struck me that I might have already put myself in jeopardy by expressing my concerns to Kiara. I left the flat and knocked on Hot Dog's door. He answered.

'Do you fancy going down to the Horseshoe?' I asked.

'Too early. Maybe later.'

'Can't you come now? I really need a chat,' I asked with the face of a man with an urgent diarrhoea query.

'Well, come in. We can chat in here.'

I raised my gaze up to the sprinkler nozzle above his door and shook my head. 'I'd rather we talk in the Horseshoe if that's okay.'

He gave me a Yorkshire wink. 'Oh, I've got you.'

'So can we go now?' I pleaded.

'Okay, Jigsaw, calm down. I'll see you there in half an hour.'

'See you down there,' I replied.

36

A PECULIAR PLATE

I didn't fancy sitting on my own in the Horseshoe, so took a diversionary route through Vinegar Yard. I checked in at the vintage junk stall where I had first seen the long shoe. The same bloke was behind the counter table.

'If you've come for the shoe, then I'm afraid you're too late. Like I told you, everyone is looking for the quirk these days,' he said.

'Yeah, I know the bloke that bought it off you in the pub. He's very happy with it. Says you sold it to him for fifty quid. You wanted a hundred off me.'

'Yeah, well, have you seen the size of him? You've got to judge each customer on an individual basis and assess how far you can push them.'

'So you had me down as a pushover?'

'Yeah, definitely.'

He was right. I remembered when I bought my last car, a beige Skoda Octavia that was well past its prime, with a knackered driver's seat and a deeply agricultural smell about the interior. I was smitten with its absolute lack of flash that made it almost invisible. The dealer could see the desire on my face and sold it to me for three and a half thousand pounds. When I got home, I checked on the garage website and it was actually listed for three thousand. Harriet hated the car. All I could say to her was, 'You can't put a price on anonymity.' She told me that if there was a price on my head she would shoot me in an instant.

'You got anything new that's on the quirky side of life?' I asked. 'And can we say I'm buying it for the other bloke so you don't rip me off?'

'Nothing quirky has come in, but to be honest, pal, I think quirk fever may be on the way out. I think it's probably peaked over this last weekend.'

He rummaged around at the back of his stall and returned holding a small wooden shield with a pair of antlers attached and a Mickey Mouse cartoon clock face in the centre of it.

'What about this? It's what I would call whimsical, and between you and me, that's the way the market is heading, full speed.'

'It's not whimsical, it's just tat. I don't care if quirk is on the way out, quirk is what I want. You must have something.'

He bent down behind his table and emerged with a pale pink dinner plate that had a small human ankle and foot, no more than two centimetres high, in the centre.

I gave it a curious but disappointed once-over.

'You're not impressed, are you?' he said. 'But wait till you see this.'

He placed his finger and thumb around a little L-shaped handle protruding from the edge of the plate and began to turn it. The tiny ankle and foot in the centre began to revolve, and a music-box melody started to play from somewhere inside the plate.

'Haunting, innit? Draws you in like a bastard. It's almost like it stops time and releases you from all your troubles and worries. It's like a meditation tool, but with a whimsical twist.'

'Wow! I like it. I like it a lot. How much?' I asked. 'And remember, it's for the bloke in the pub, not me.'

'In that case, a hundred quid. You can't deny it's the very definition of quirk.'

'I thought you said quirk was on the way out. I'll give you fifty.'

'Yes, but this piece is on the newly favoured whimsical side of quirky. The little foot adds a lot of humour.'

'Isn't it just peculiar?'

'Yes, it has that going for it as well,' he replied.

'The man from the pub says he'll give you seventy.'

'Well, tell him I'd be delighted to accept his offer.'

We shook hands and I paid up.

I was still a bit early for my date with Hot Dog, so took a seat in the community gardens opposite the Horseshoe. I put the musical plate on my lap and gave the handle a turn. Its little tune was irresistible and drew the mind deep into the very moment.

Out of the blue, the tune selected for my consideration the photograph of Laurence hoovering in his penthouse. And that's when it hit me. The curtains behind him and the painting of a daisy on the wall were exactly the same as I had seen in the rogue footage that night in the store cupboard.

Maybe Harriet was actually somewhere inside Satsuma Heights, in Laurence's penthouse.

37

A HAT WOULD BE NICE

As soon as Hot Dog was settled at the table with his Guinness, I started to unload my worries onto him. I told him about Harriet's disappearance, and her failure or refusal to answer her phone, and the fact that she might be the lead CPS officer in Laurence's trial. I told him about the mystery feed that came up on my computer and my suspicions that the lady on the camera might well be Harriet. He asked me if I had spoken to Moody about it and I repeated Laurence's explanation that the feed was from his colleague Kiara's flat. I showed him the photograph of Laurence hoovering in the penthouse and pointed out that the curtains and painting on the wall were identical to those in the feed from the mystery flat.

'So you think Harriet is being held in the penthouse flat?' he asked with a doubting grin.

'I think there is an unbelievably remote chance that she might be. I mean, no, not really is the honest truth, but it's an itch that I need to explore.'

'I suffer a lot from itches. It's usually best to get stuck in and have a good grate on them. You have my sympathy in that respect.'

'Do you think she could be in there?' I asked. 'I mean, those curtains look like a real one-off job to me.'

'No, it sounds fucking ridiculous. No way would Moody get his hands dirty like that, and think about it: if she was in his penthouse, she would have screamed the place down by now.'

'Do you think I should go to the police?'

'Absolutely not. They would probably try to section you.'

'So what should I do?' I pleaded, sounding every inch a pipsqueak.

He took a long treble gulp from his pint of Guinness and rubbed his nose as if it had been recently peppered. 'I reckon you should break into the penthouse. See if she's there. Put your mind at rest.'

I laughed. 'And how do you propose I do that?'

'Easy. You've got a master key, haven't you?'

'Yes, but it doesn't work for the penthouse.'

'Hmm, that's a shame, a big shame. Let me have a think.'

Hot Dog got up out of his seat and I watched him make his way to the toilets. When I turned back to address my pint, I saw Justin Hamper approaching me at quite a pace and with a rabid look in his eyes.

I tensed up in my seat. He arrived at the table and stood looking down at me with his fists tightly clenched by his side. He was making that same chewing motion with his mouth that he had utilized when he confronted me outside the church.

He clearly wanted to fight. I thought of his magnificent buttocks and perfect torso. It was definitely a fight that I would lose.

'I know it was you,' he said through gritted teeth. 'You've robbed me of my son, Kiara, and my home. You need to fucking pay for this.'

'You're wrong, just calm down,' I replied with my hands out in front of me, indicating a request for peace and understanding. 'Like I told you, I haven't ever spoken about your son to Laurence. I have no reason to. Have you spoken to Derek yet?'

'Get up!' he barked.

'No, I won't. Why don't you let me get you a drink and we can talk this through?' I suggested.

'I don't drink.'

'Yes, you do, you're on the wine every night.'

I immediately realized my mistake. He would know that I had been watching him. I wondered for a split second if I had got away with it. I hadn't.

He lunged forward and pulled me out of my seat, spinning me round as he did so and dumping me on the floor, flat on my back. Then he jumped onto me, straddling my stomach, and raised his fist into the air ready to pummel it into my face. As I waited for the blow to land, his face suddenly flew out of my vision as it was kicked, full-on under the chin, by a chunky-soled black boot.

I raised myself up to see Catherine deliver a further stamp to his head as he lay on the floor moaning in pain. Another barperson joined her and they dragged him off the floor before marching him out of the pub.

When they reached the door, Hamper managed to turn his head and shout towards me, 'It's not fucking finished!'

I crawled back onto my seat and breathed heavily in an attempt to calm my panic.

'Thank you,' I said to Catherine as she passed by on her way back to the bar.

'Don't mention it,' she replied. 'Like I said, I'm still keeping my eye on you, innit.'

Soon after, Hot Dog returned from the toilet.

'Fuck it, let's do it tonight,' he announced, completely unaware of what had just occurred. 'I've missed this sort of action and it's not as if you're going to get any sleep thinking that your girlfriend is a few floors above you in distress. I'll knock on your door at eleven. Make sure you're ready.'

When I didn't reply, Hot Dog seemed to notice something was amiss.

'Jesus, Jigsaw, you look very pasty. What's the matter with you? You need to stop worrying. I'm Bill fucking Hoover. The job will be a breeze. But I can't have a pipsqueak by my side when I'm doing a breaking and enter. Make sure you've found your knackers by this evening. I want you ready and fully functioning.'

'So, how do we get into the penthouse without a key?' I asked, rather more loudly than I intended.

'Pipe the fuck down, will you? Listen, I've broken into more homes than you've entered legally. You'll just have to trust me on that.'

'What shall I wear?' I asked.

'Clothes,' he replied.

'Do I need to wear gloves?'

'No. Actually, yeah, you should wear some gloves. And a hat – a hat would be nice. See you at eleven p.m. sharp.'

He ruffled my hair, got up and walked out of the pub, leaving me to contemplate that I had just agreed to commit a burglary. I had never done anything remotely illegal in my entire life. It didn't seem real; it just felt like a game that was getting out of hand.

I thanked Catherine again on my way out. Back in my flat, I sat with Monson on the sofa.

'So you're really going to break into that flat?' he asked.

'Yeah, probably. Well, I don't suppose I'll be doing any breaking but, yeah, I'm up for it. I think.'

'I keep telling you to phone the police, but you won't listen.'

'Laurence will throw me out of this flat if I get the police involved. We would be homeless. Is that what you want?'

'We wouldn't be homeless. You could shack up with that mad woman Carol and I could live with that bloke at the old house. It's a decent menu he serves up there. Not a dry biscuit in sight.'

'I'll take you there now if you want.'

'Nah, I'd like to see how this plays out.'

Monson jumped down from my lap and walked over to the window to have a good stare at the buildings outside.

'Do you miss not having a garden?' I asked.

'Doesn't bother me. There was a lot of trouble out there. It could get very real – a lot of grudges and beefs. I was always living on the edge, waiting for the door to open so I could get back inside.'

He placed his arms out in front of him and lowered his back into an arch to stretch out his spine before jumping back onto my lap.

'I'll tell you what I do miss,' he said.

'What?' I enquired.

'Harriet,' he replied.

I watched some TV but couldn't concentrate. I found a roll of kitchen paper and some cleaning spray marked 'All Purpose' and wiped down the kitchen surfaces and appliances. The spray wasn't as versatile as it claimed and the oven door and all the metal trims came out in a kind of cloudy rash. I started to unpack a few more of the boxes from the move but everything I removed seemed to be linked with a Harriet memory and turned my thoughts towards the gloomy.

I went into the bedroom and lay on the bed. The noise from outside was far more noticeable in here, so I put on my head-phones to block it out. The rim of the headphones dug into my temple if I put my head in its normal napping position, so I gave up on that and went back to the lounge and tried to listen to a podcast about a serial killer in Wisconsin. The presenter's voice was far too upbeat for the subject matter and started to get on my tits. I turned it off and sat myself down at the kitchen island, desperate for a diversion from my dismal thoughts.

I turned on the mixer tap at full pelt to see what that offered me. Very little, it turned out, apart from a wet shirt and a wipe-up job that I didn't have the impetus to carry out. The peculiar plate was on the island, so I drew it towards me and started to operate the handle. The musical box melody broke the silence within the flat and gave me a simple focus to help calm the tension inside me. It was a decent purchase – too expensive, but decent. I continued to turn the handle round and round and round. It was going to be a long wait until 11 p.m. arrived.

38

CAROL

Okay, it's time that you heard from me. I expect that tart Harriet has had her say, so why not me? I'll be brief, because, unless you've had the joy of actually knowing me, you're probably not that interested. You might not like what you hear, but to be honest, I couldn't care less. Are you enjoying life as much as me? I very much doubt it, darlings.

I've lived at my house in Hither Green ever since my divorce ten years ago. It's by far the largest and most important house on the street. My husband was a property developer and I did very nicely indeed out of the financial settlement. He fathered my two beautiful daughters, so I'm grateful for that, but otherwise I remember him as nothing more than a selfish bore. I was never in love with the man, but definitely appreciated the lifestyle he gave me. I tolerated his affairs and his drinking in return for living a life of leisure and, let's face it, indulgence. Opening my legs for him if and when required was a small price to pay and an equally small organ to accommodate.

Now, I know I'm not supposed to say it, but it's true, so I

will: I'm a very good-looking bird; always have been, and don't see that changing anytime soon. I've had a boob job and a bit of lipo on my flanks, but it's just fine-tuning. The face and hair are the most important things and mine are A1, off the charts. It's a fact, and if you don't like hearing it, it's probably because you're a jealous cow or know that you could never attract someone like me. Am I right?

So, my marriage was unhappy but I was happy within it, if you know what I mean. I was a superb mother to my daughters. In times of distress, they would always come to me rather than their nanny, and never to their father – not that he was around that often to provide any support to either them or me. When the youngest left home to join her sister at boarding school in Hampshire, I did become a bit bored and restless. Only to be expected, I suppose. That's when I discovered my new hobby: breaking up other people's marriages. It was easy; men are so weak and most women too gullible and trusting.

Lots of couples like Matt and Harriet have moved into my neighbourhood over the years. Not many of them stay for long; they sell up and move to more desirable areas with nicer shops and better schools. I will never move. I like being a big fish in a dirty, overpopulated pond, and better still, it's the perfect hunting ground: positively teeming with happy couples. I try to target the childless ones, but if the husband is particularly vulnerable, I'm happy to make an exception.

I think I have put paid to three or four marriages these last six or seven years, and caused a good few hiccups in a number of others. A couple of women have seen me coming and blocked me off at the pass and a few husbands have been strong or foolish enough to resist my advances. Actually, I think those are my favourite – the ones that think they can hold out against me. But believe me, they are few and far between. I've been at the very top of this game for a while now.

You might ask what pleasure can possibly be taken in causing all this heartbreak and misery, and my answer is simple: it's the thrill of the chase and the defeat of the foe. It's the oldest pleasure in the book. When I look out of my bay window and see yet another bedraggled man loading his car with his treasured possessions as the woman he loves watches on tearfully, the joy I experience is immeasurable. I stand proud in the certain knowledge that I am far from the saddest bitch on the block.

But I suppose what you really want to hear about is my involvement with Matt and that splashy cow Harriet. I didn't like her the moment I stepped (uninvited of course) into their house and saw her knelt on the floor sorting through her cheap little trinkets and decorations. She didn't even bother to stand up when I entered. *Fuck you, darling*, I thought, and started blowing the charm right up Matt's backside. I was pleased to see that this fresh target wasn't too bad-looking at all. He was a bit on the short side, but nicely presented, with a pleasant, friendly face and a reasonable body. He was clean and well-mannered and I like that in a man; it's usually a sign that they are pliable and compliant. As I left their house, I could feel him drinking in my amazing arse (it's superb; you would really have to see it, or better still have a good knead on it). I could tell already that this one was going to be easy.

I sussed her out immediately: reserved and lacking confidence; common as muck but thought she wasn't. She had a ridiculous bleached blonde masculine haircut that didn't suit her personality one bit. In fact, I suspected it was a substitute for a personality, because she never displayed such a thing whenever I was in her company. Worst of all, she was Northern. For God's sake, why come down here and blight us with your small-minded ways and chips piled high on your shoulders? I liked it best when the woman involved despised me. It intensified their hurt when the deed was done. To my delight, after just a few short weeks of my passive aggression, she deliberately faded herself into the background, giving me more opportunity to work on Matt.

He turned out to be a more difficult prey than I had expected. Yes, he fancied the pants off me (of course), but the stupid boy also turned out to be lonely. That's not a good thing for my game. Firstly, it keeps them furiously loyal to their partner, and secondly, they are more interested in finding a friend than taking a lover. So, that's what I did. I made him believe I was his friend and kept her at a distance. I reasoned that he would cave in eventually and fall in love with me, just like all the others.

And then the opposite happened. *I* fell for *him*.

It came to a gushing crescendo when I invited him and his tart to stay with me in my holiday home in Palm Springs. I've always felt more lustful and energized in the sunshine . . . Bikinis, boxer shorts, tanning oils and cocktails – it all gets the juices flowing. Am I right?

273

Harriet was pretending to be ill, or jet-lagged, so as to spend as much time apart from me as she could. Matt, bless him, fell for her excuses and so left her alone to 'recover'. We had the time of our lives, swimming, joking, drinking and generally fooling about. I made sure to screech and laugh as loud as I could, knowing that each outburst would cut through Harriet like a knife.

One afternoon, I used the age-old trick of asking Matt to oil me up with sun-tan lotion. As he rubbed it onto the back of my thighs, I could sense excitement growing inside him; his breath became shorter and heavier and the motion of his hands was becoming less functional and more sensual. I smiled to myself.

Gotcha! I thought.

Then he abruptly stopped the massage and rushed back into the house without a word of explanation. He re-emerged through the patio doors about ten minutes later wearing a different pair of shorts. He asked me if I wanted another cocktail and I declined. While he was making himself his drink, I wrote a little note of encouragement and placed it on his lounger. It made it quite clear that he could have me if he wanted and that I wouldn't spill the beans to Harriet. I thought this would be the final nail in his coffin.

He read the note as soon as he sat down then turned to me and said, 'Please don't do this, Carol. We're friends, and I love it that way. I could never cheat on Harriet.'

I think that was the actual moment I fell in love with him. Instead of seeing him as a mark, a man to seduce and then discard,

I actually wanted him for myself. This had never happened with any of the other mugs. The game had changed direction. I can still remember the feeling as if it were yesterday. It was not meant to happen and I hated myself for letting it transpire. The only solution was to banish the little Northern tart and have him run directly to me in his desperation. Even if it hadn't worked on Matt, I thought my little note would be the perfect catalyst. So, I crushed it lightly in my hand and discarded it on the floor by the pool house, where it stood out like a sore thumb.

Later that day, when Matt and I returned from a wonderful trip up the mountains in the cable cars, I checked on the note and it was gone. My trap had been set. I could tell by her demeanour that Harriet had swallowed it whole. The poor cow was seething. I just had to sit back and wait for the day when he emerged from their rented house deflated and defeated, straight into my arms. I mean, it probably wouldn't happen quite like that, but forgive me for being a dreamer.

When they got back from their holiday in Palm Springs, Matt commenced a period of unemployment. I would watch from my bay window every morning to catch him leaving for his morning walk to the park, and soon I started to follow him five or so minutes after and then join him in the park café, where he always stopped for a coffee. Soon enough, this became a regular thing, and I had the best of times pulling him deeper and deeper into my clutches. I was sure it wouldn't be long before Harriet would implode. I bet she looked at that note every single day and tortured herself wondering if Matt took up the offer.

It all came to a head last Sunday evening. The water had come to the boil and the egg was cooked. She knocked on my door and, without a word of welcome, strode through into my kitchen all huffy and entitled like the little frump she is. She took the note out of her pocket (she kept it! I KNEW SHE WOULD) and triumphantly presented it to me as she demanded an explanation. I offered her nothing but some platitudes and a classy smile. I think she realized she was defeated because then, without warning, she grabbed the glass of wine out of my hands and punched me hard in my face. I have to give her credit; it was a very good shot. I was fucking furious but managed to keep my calm. She slammed the door behind her and doubtless burst into floods of tears on the street outside. It was a wonderful moment.

The following day, the good news arrived. Matt popped round all gloomy and distraught to tell me that she had up and left him. He showed me a note she had written. It was pathetically overdramatic and needy, 'I might never be back' or something equally splashy. I comforted Matt and began the process of convincing him that he was better off without her. I speculated that she'd probably gone off with another man. I mean, she probably would meet somebody else in the end, so it didn't really matter that my time frame was slightly off. Am I right?

Matt was in the middle of trying to find a new place to live. Although he doesn't know it, I sorted it for him. I figured that if I found him a new home away from Hither Green and near to my flat in central London, it would help grease the wheels of change, encourage him to make a new start with me (the lucky fucker!). I have a lot of contacts in the property world and got in touch with an old conquest of mine by the name of Laurence Moody. He was the developer of a block of flats near London Bridge called Satsuma Heights. I often required little favours from him; after all, he wouldn't want me informing his ex-wife and children about our dalliances. That would cause him all sorts of anguish. I also knew one or two things about his business practices that could make his life extremely uncomfortable if I decided to spill the beans.

I explained my requirements. The rent would have to be more than reasonable as my 'friend' was not currently in employment. Also it needed to happen quickly – that very day was my preference. Laurence played hardball for about a minute or so and then caved in. I think maybe he's still in love with me, the poor sod. He does have good taste, though. I have to hand him that. He mentioned something about giving Matt some menial caretaking duties to carry out so that he got his slice of cake from the deal. Fine by me, I said, so long as Matt is in there within the next forty-eight hours. I was confident that even useless Harriet would stay away for at least three days.

Satsuma Heights was only a short distance from my apartment in Waterloo. I could help him settle in, introduce him to some old friends who could sort his career out and show him the good time that could be had living in central London with a bit of money behind you. I would help fund his lifestyle as part of my seduction. Money can't buy you love, but it can buy you the opportunities you need to grow it. I saw Matt on a couple of occasions over the next few days. I even helped him recover his cat that he had left behind in his old house. It was difficult for me to hear him witter on about Harriet all the time. Just the mention of her name made me furious inside. SHE HAD PUNCHED ME. I promised myself I would return the compliment (with extra cream on top) if I ever got the chance. With my encouragement, Matt was gradually becoming convinced that she was with another man and would never return. I would give it a few days before swooping in on his new life in his new flat.

Late on Tuesday evening, a week after she had left, I was surveying the street from my bay window when I saw Matt's car pull up and Harriet emerge, alone, from inside. She opened the boot to fetch a few bits and pieces and then began to walk towards her house. I felt myself begin to shake with anger just at the sight of her pathetic frame. I ran out onto the street to confront and gleefully inform her that Matt was gone and wanted to be with me. I crept up to her just as she was entering the house and whacked her on the back of the head with the full force of my elegant fist. Her face slammed into the door and she fell backwards, down the front steps, cracking her head on the entrance pathway. She didn't even see me coming. Am I right, Harriet?

I bent down to her crumpled body and told her to get up. She didn't respond, so I grabbed her by the shoulders and gave her a shake. I wanted her to see my face when I told her that Matt had left the house and that she was too late. Her eyes were shut and she was breathing heavily. I slapped her face to rouse her; she moaned pathetically but her eyes didn't open. The fall had knocked her out cold. Her weak Northern eggshell skull had failed to protect her from the impact. At least I couldn't see any bleeding. I couldn't be dealing with that.

I sensed somebody approaching along the pavement, so turned my head towards the front door and stayed low to avoid being seen as they walked on by.

'Hi there, are you okay?' said the stranger, who was standing more or less on top of us by the front gate.

Panicking, I came out with some bullshit, just to buy me some time. This stranger really was very inconvenient.

'She seems to have had an awful fall – I think she's unconscious. I saw her fall down from my bay window. Maybe we should call an ambulance,' I bleated in my most authentic 'lady who actually gives a fuck' tone.

I moved to the side of Harriet as the stranger bent down to examine her face. She was still letting out the occasional simpering, needy moan and her eyes were attempting to blink.

'She doesn't look too good,' said the stranger. 'Is she a friend of yours?'

'No, not really, we're neighbours, that's all. She's Matt's girlfriend.'

'Harriet?' he asked, taking me completely by surprise.

'Do you know her?' I responded.

'Only by name. I'm a friend of Matt's.'

The stranger checked her pulse and examined her face intently. He spoke her name to encourage a response but all she did was emit the occasional juvenile groan. Selfish cow.

'We need to get her to hospital,' he declared. 'I reckon I could get her there quicker in my car than it would take if we called an ambulance.'

'Fine by me,' I replied.

'Will you give me a hand to get her in the back of my car?'

'Really?'

'Yes, really,' he said. 'We don't want her falling again, do we?'

I reluctantly did as he asked. She weighed even less than me, and you know how successfully trim I am. The stranger asked if I wanted to come along to the hospital, but I declined. I gave him my phone number so that he could keep me updated, and asked him to inform Matt of the situation as soon as he got a chance. That would be enough for appearances' sake. I wanted this whole situation to be many miles away from me. The stranger seemed reliable and trustworthy, and he wasn't bad-looking to boot. (Maybe I *should* have gone with him . . .)

After he'd driven off, I needed a drink to calm my nerves, so retired back to my house. It was frustrating that she didn't actually see it was me that delivered the blow, but I supposed it would be handy if the police ever got involved. A job well done was my conclusion. Am I right?

39

NO HAT

Burglary time arrived. My stomach wallowed and fluttered as I contemplated committing this almost certainly pointless criminal act. I had got changed into a black jumper and my grey tracksuit bottoms with the folded-over waistband. I didn't put on any shoes, thinking that my stockinged feet would ensure an element of stealth. Hot Dog knocked on my door at 11 p.m. sharp. I answered the door and was surprised to see him wearing his usual clobber and holding the long shoe in one hand. I don't know why, but I thought he might be wearing some special gear, maybe a balaclava or something with an outdoor flavour.

'Why the long shoe?' I asked.

'It's my lucky totem. I feel more confident with it on board with us.'

We sat together at the kitchen island to discuss the job at hand. The musical foot dinner plate was sitting on the surface next to Monson's cat carrier. I turned the handle on the side of the plate and we listened to its mournful tune in silence.

'How much did you pay for that piece of tat?' he asked.

'Seventy pounds.'

'I would have paid twenty, not a penny more. Take me with you next time; it could save you a few quid.'

I asked him what the plan was and he explained that he had already 'disabled' the cameras behind the concierge desk so that there would be no recording of us moving through the corridors and entering the penthouse suite.

'That's good, Bill, but how do we actually get *into* the penthouse without a master key?'

'Just trust me, Jigsaw,' he replied. 'You ready?'

'Yeah,' I confirmed, putting on a pair of old gardening gloves.

'Where's your hat?'

'I haven't got a fucking hat,' I replied.

'What do you mean you haven't got a hat? Everybody has a hat of some sort.'

'So what are you saying? You going to call it off because I haven't got a hat?'

'It's a question of trust,' he said. 'You told me that you would be wearing a hat and I turn up and find you hatless. It's not right.'

'I've got a bobble hat, but it's lost its bobble. Does that work for you? Does that count as a hat?'

'Do you still have the bobble?'

'Yeah, somewhere. Do you want me to find it and sew it back on?'

'Show me the hat,' he demanded.

I fetched the bobble-less bobble hat and showed it to him.

'Doesn't look right. Your eye gets drawn to where the bobble should be,' he said.

'Do you want me to put it on or not?' I asked with a tetchy curve on the delivery.

'No, I don't. I don't think it cuts it. I hate it, I really hate it.'

He grabbed the bobble-less bobble hat out of my hands, dropped it on the floor, stamped on it and then rubbed it into the floor with his boot.

'Other than that, you look acceptable. Come on, let's go.'

As we left the flat, Hot Dog placed the long shoe on the floor and used its tip to wedge the door open an inch or so.

'I told you it would come in useful,' he said. 'You might need to make a very hasty return if things go tits up.'

That thought worried me, but Hot Dog had created a momentum that couldn't be resisted.

Less than a minute later, we were stood in the penthouse suite corridor. Hot Dog took out a spray can of some variety and aimed it at the camera opposite Laurence's door. It covered the lens (and the wall below it) with a foamy, custardy gunge.

'Bull's eye,' said Hot Dog.

'I thought you pulled the plug on the cameras?' I asked.

'I did, but I wanted to use the spray. You know, just for old times' sake.'

'What now?' I replied.

'Well, let's knock on the door first, just in case he's home,' he said.

'Kiara told me he wasn't here,' I replied.

'Better to be safe than sorry,' he said as he gave the mahogany door a good rap with his fist. There was no reply.

Hot Dog then began to fiddle with his belt buckle and plunged his hand inside the waist of his jeans. I assumed he was searching for some sort of lock pick or universal swipe card sort of thing, but no, he pulled out a short crowbar and held it triumphantly in front of his face.

'That's it? That's your plan? To break it open with a fucking crowbar?'

'Us professionals call it a jemmy, and yeah, why not? There's no cameras, and let's face it, if Laurence did catch me, he's hardly going to go to the coppers, is he? They're the very people he's hiding me from.'

'What about me?'

'*What about me?*' mimicked Hot Dog in the voice of a small child. 'Don't worry, I'll take the blowback if Laurence finds out. Now, stand aside.'

He inserted the thin end of the crowbar between the door and the jamb and administered three or four destructive heaves before the lock gave way and the door opened.

'After you, No Hat,' he insisted, indicating the way in with an outstretched arm.

Once inside, I clocked the curtains and the painting of the daisy, but I could see instantly that this was not the flat from the mystery footage with the girl on the sofa. For one, it was absolutely HUGE – and what's more, there was no sprinkler housing a camera over the door facing the sofa.

'This isn't the place,' I said to Hot Dog. 'I guess Laurence was telling the truth about the camera being in Kiara's flat. Come on, let's get out of here.'

He didn't reply. I noticed his face had drained of all confidence, and he was staring straight over my shoulder with an expression that suggested he might just have seen a partridge shed its feathers in one brutal explosion of protest. He dropped the crowbar onto the floor.

I turned my head round and there was Laurence, wearing a paisley-print silk dressing gown and smiling like he'd just won that lottery where you win a big house in a pleasant part of the country.

'Hello, you two,' he said. 'You must have really made a good connection. Breaking and entering requires a great deal of trust between the participants. So, tell me, to what do I owe this unexpected visit? Let me guess . . . Ahhh, that must be it . . . Matt here wants to check to see if I really do have a camera feed from Kiara's flat. Is that the case? Have I hit a nail on its head? Tell me I'm right. I love it when I'm right.'

'No,' I replied. 'We wanted to check if Harriet was in here. Fuck, that sounds weird, I know, but I saw a photo of you online and you have exactly the same curtains and daisy painting as the flat where I thought I saw Harriet. Sorry, but I didn't believe Kiara when she said she'd agreed to have a camera in her flat. It just didn't make sense. I don't know. To be honest, I'm a bit fucked up. I'm not thinking straight.'

'Why on earth would your girlfriend be in my flat?' he replied, looking convincingly incredulous at the suggestion.

'Because she's heading up the police prosecution against you and it might be very handy for you to keep her under lock and key. But she isn't here and I apologize and we will just leave and I will pay for the damage to the door and I apologize again. I was wrong. Is that okay? So sorry.'

'I don't think that it is, Matt. I had absolutely no idea about your girlfriend's employment. Tell me, what exactly was it that made you think she was here?'

'Like I said, your curtains and the painting are the same as the ones in the footage. I guess I'm getting a bit paranoid about the situation.'

'I think you are. You will find these curtains throughout this development; it was our mutual friend Carol that recommended them to me. She has a keen nose for what will lure in the weak-minded.'

'Carol chose your curtains? She's a friend of yours?'

'Yes, we go way back. She's quite a character, isn't she? Do you agree? I expect you do. She persuaded her husband to arrange the financing on my first big development. We were having a bit of a fling at the time, but hubby found out and it ended. Terrible inconvenience when a hubby "finds out", don't you think? We still keep in touch, though, and I suppose I feel indebted to her – just like you, I expect.'

'Why do you say that?'

'Because it was her that persuaded me to let you live here in Satsuma Heights. Didn't you know? I thought maybe you did. She told me she needed me to make it happen and I felt obliged to comply. She's not one to cross, if you know what I mean. I expect you do. Don't tell her that I've mentioned this, will you? I might have promised to keep her involvement secret. Is that agreed?'

'Yes, of course, but I thought the reason you wanted me here was to carry out the surveillance for you?'

'Well, yes, that was a little bonus for me, having you cover that task for a couple of weeks. Carol vouched for you and I always like to get something for myself out of a favour.'

I desperately wanted a way out of this conversation.

'I'm sorry about breaking in,' I said. 'Really sorry, and like I say, I'll pay for the damage.'

'*Are* you sorry? I'm not sure you are,' he replied. 'And how did you persuade Mr Hoover here to join you in this little escapade?'

Hot Dog chose to answer on my behalf.

'You know me, Laurence, no way am I going to turn down the opportunity of a caper. It's in my blood, and the little pipsqueak seemed desperate. I've got a big heart, you know.'

'Yes,' replied Laurence. 'No doubt swollen up with huge lumps of saturated fats.'

'Are you going to throw me out because of us breaking in to your flat?' I asked.

'I'll have to think about that, and I can't be bothered right now. I have very itchy privates and I was just about to shower, so if you would leave immediately, that would be just great. I'm sure you agree . . . Oh, and thank you for putting me onto the shenanigans between my dear Kiara and Justin Hamper. She came clean and admitted that it was Hamper in the footage you saw. Naughty girl. I've put an end to that, of course. Oh, and if you ever find your girlfriend, put a good word in for me with whoever is in charge of my prosecution. You know, ask them to go easy, perhaps not bring their A-game to the job? I bet she would love living here at the Heights. Do you agree? I'm sure you do.'

Hot Dog picked up his crowbar as we left the flat and returned to the fifth floor via the elevator. He considered it a job well done and assured me that Laurence would not be asking me to leave on account of the fact that I 'knew too much'. On the same note, he told me that if I revealed his whereabouts to Harriet, I would be as good as dead. I believed him. I got out of the lift. He didn't.

I was fully deflated when I sat back down at my kitchen island. So it had been Kiara and Hamper having a secret affair that I'd seen in the footage after all. I had made a fool of myself and, despite Hot Dog's assurances to the contrary, probably ruined my chances of remaining in Satsuma Heights. Worst of all, I was no further forward in finding out where Harriet was, and the peculiar dinner plate was still there on the kitchen island to remind me of how easily I could be taken advantage of. The cat carrier, however, had disappeared from the kitchen island. I called Monson, but he didn't appear. I checked every room and he was nowhere to be found.

There was no way that he could have got through the shoe-wedged door; the door was far too heavy and the gap far too narrow. Somebody must have been inside the flat and taken him away in his carrier. I rushed down to the concierge desk in reception to check the security footage from my corridor. I had forgotten that the system was dead, thanks to Hot Dog.

I returned to my flat via the stairwell, calling Monson's name all the way back to my door. Once inside, I lay on the bed holding back the tears until a restless sleep arrived.

I had a dream where Harriet and Monson were lying on separate air beds in a huge blue swimming pool. Both of them were drinking champagne and smoking cigarettes. I stood frozen in fear on a diving board a hundred metres above the pool and then began to fall slowly towards them. I woke up just before impact.

40

MUDDY SECONDS

I was woken up around midnight by the sound of my phone ringing. It was Carol.

'Hello, darling, I've not woken you up, have I?' she asked.

'Yes, you have, but that doesn't interest either of us. Have you heard from Harriet?'

'Well, no, not exactly, but I have seen her.'

I was suddenly wide awake.

'What do you mean? Where have you seen her? Did you speak to her? Is she alright?' I asked excitedly, and at such great speed I had to catch my breath as I listened to her reply.

'She came back to your old house this evening a couple of hours ago. I saw her from my bay window. I went out to say hello to her but just as I got out of my front door I saw her fall over on the front step. It looked a nasty fall; she fell backwards and banged her head on the paving stones. I ran to her but she was unconscious and then a friend of yours arrived and offered to take her to hospital. He said it would be quicker than waiting for an ambulance.'

'What friend of mine? Did he give you his name? Where did he take her? Fucking hell, Carol, why didn't you phone me immediately? Why didn't you go with her?'

'I didn't see the need, and I'm phoning you now, aren't I? You should calm down, darling, it was just a bang on the head. I asked him to keep you updated and gave him my telephone number so that he could keep me in the loop. I don't remember him saying his name but he definitely knew you. He was coming round to see you; just happened to arrive at a very convenient moment. He hasn't been in touch with me, so obviously I got worried. That's why I'm phoning, to ask if he's been in touch with you.'

'No, he hasn't, and I can't think of any friends that would be popping round to see me. Did he say which hospital he was taking her to?'

'Lewisham, I imagine. That would be the nearest.'

'Have you contacted them to check whether she's there?'

'No, I've contacted you,' she replied.

'What did he look like, this friend of mine?'

'Well, he was about your height, maybe a few inches taller. White, dark brown hair and kind of athletic. He was wearing a black puffa jacket and very tight grey tracksuit bottoms. I don't know what to say, it's all a bit of a blur. That's all I remember. Look, I'm sorry for the delay in contacting you but I'm a bit shook up by it all. You know how fond I am of Harriet, and it's hit me quite hard.'

'Fucking hell, Carol, I need to go.'

'She left her phone on the steps. Don't worry, I'll look after it.'

291

I ended the call. I was partially elated by the thought that she had returned to our old home. It might be that she just wanted some of her stuff or to tell me to my face that we were finished, but, then again, it might be that she was returning to be with me and get on with our life together. I phoned the accident and emergency departments of all the hospitals that she could possibly have been taken to. None of them had any record of her. I needed to speak to Carol again.

'Look, darling, I'm not taking the blame for this,' she announced when I rang her back and asked her to tell me again what happened. 'It's not like I pushed her down the stairs. I was trying to help.'

'I'm not blaming you, Carol. I'm just in a panic. I think you can understand that, can't you? Please try and remember something more about this friend. You said that he knew me. Maybe it's someone from the bathroom showroom or an old acquaintance or something. I don't know. Did he say anything that might help me pin him down?'

'I've told you all I can remember. He wasn't there for more than a minute or so. I'd guess he was about forty years old. His face was pleasant enough, though it looked as if he had taken a punch or a kick to one side of his face. I thought he seemed trustworthy. He didn't have any awful accent or anything. I'm sorry, I can't think of anything else. Oh, his car was dark grey, an estate car I think, but I couldn't tell you what make.'

'Anything else? Anything at all?'

There followed a moment of silence that I hoped represented her thinking hard.

'Oh, hold on, how could I have forgotten? I think he had a cat carrier the same as yours in the back of his car. Does that ring any bells?'

'Anything else?'

'Well, I don't want to seem trivial, and please don't think I'm not taking this seriously, but he did have a magnificent arse – I mean really splashy. Absolutely outstanding.'

'I have to go,' I replied. 'That fucker Hamper's got her.'

'Who?'

I ended the call. It had to be him. The mark on his face from where Catherine had kicked him, the threat he'd made as he was thrown out of the Horseshoe, his access to Satsuma Heights to steal Monson and his irrefutably excellent behind led to no other conclusion.

I went into the store cupboard and checked the camera feeds. As far as I could see, his flat was empty and abandoned. Another conclusion was reached in a muddy few seconds. Hamper would be at the yoga studio. I had to get there, immediately.

41

HARRIET

The lights were suddenly turned on. I opened my eyes. The stranger was stood above me staring directly into my eyes. My body started to shake. I couldn't tell whether this was due to blind fear or the sickness I was feeling in my head and stomach. The lights were making me nauseous.

'Can you turn those lights down please?' I asked.

'I'm sorry, Harriet, but I can't do that. You will soon adjust to the brightness once your head has settled.'

I stared at him and tried to assess what I was dealing with. He looked incredibly normal and unthreatening. More like a good Samaritan than a kidnapper or pervert.

'Where am I?' I asked. 'And how come you know my name?'

'All you need to know is that I'm a friend of Matt's.'

'What do you mean "a friend of Matt's"? I've never seen you before in my life.'

'We only met a few days ago but we've become very close. I'm a yoga teacher and Matt is one of my pupils. We get on like a house on fire; we are helping each other grow towards equilibrium.'

He sat down on a bean bag opposite me, picked up a glass of wine from the floor and drank its contents in one.

'Please just tell me what's going on. Please just let me go home. I want to see Matt. I won't tell anyone about you bringing me here. Please just let me go.'

'That's a good girl, Harriet. Let it all out. Expel your emotions so they can be examined and rejected or accepted.'

I noticed a slight movement beside him on the bean bag. A cat revealed itself and had a quick stretch before settling back down to sleep. It was Goodmonson.

'Why have you got Matt's cat?' I asked.

'Same reason I've got you: to punish Matt. People can be awful, can't they, Harriet? Especially when they have been wronged.'

'I don't know what the fuck you mean.'

'Let me tell you what this is all about. I think you deserve to be told, given that it's none of your doing. In a nutshell, your beloved Matt has been spying on me at my flat in Satsuma Heights. As a result of his spying, I have lost my home and had access to my son severely restricted. What's more, I have been forced to give up my girlfriend Kiara, and all because of Matt. He needs to be punished, and that is why I have stolen his cat. He loves that cat nearly as much as I love my son. Let's call it a tit-for-tat operation. I didn't have the heart to dispose of the moggy, so I thought I'd keep him here with me as a spiritual companion and something of a trophy for my revenge.

'Now, there is one thing that Matt loves exactly as much as I love my son and Kiara combined, and that, Harriet, is you.

When it eventually clocks with him that you are one of the disappeared, his heart will break and we will be even. Please stop fretting, Harriet. It won't help you. I'm not easily moved by tears unless they manifest real emotional progress.'

'You must have the wrong person. Matt wouldn't harm a fly. He would never get involved in spying on people. And he would never do yoga. This has got to be a big mistake. Please, you need to let me go.'

He poured himself another glass of wine and took two massive gulps.

'I won't let you go and the only mistake I've made is being a tad impulsive and perhaps slightly out of symmetry in my actions. But here's the thing, Harriet: I absolutely believe that some sort of divine intervention has played its part in bringing us together. When I stole his cat, I noticed that Matt's old address was on its collar. I knew from my little chats with Matt that you had taken leave from the relationship, so wondered, what with Matt living in Satsuma Heights, whether I would find you there. I took a chance and visited the house this evening and, lo and behold, when I arrived, you were laid out flat on your back on the front doorstep. What are the chances of that, Harriet? It was as if you were gift-wrapped just waiting for my arrival. The work of a higher power, I'm sure of it.'

'What has Matt got to do with Satsuma Heights? What you're saying doesn't make any sense. We live in Hither Green and Matt just spends his days doing housework and watching TV.'

'Matt is living in Satsuma Heights. Did he not tell you? Has he not been in touch? Shit, maybe he's not in love with you as much as I thought. Maybe I've made a mistake.'

'I haven't had my phone with me. And do you really expect me to believe that Matt is living in a place like Satsuma Heights?'

'You will soon enough.'

He stroked Monson, took another mouthful of wine, then adjusted his position so that one of his feet was resting on top of my left knee.

'Oh, now here's a thing that's been on my mind. Matt told me that he never bothered to ask you if you were happy. So, let me ask you that question: are you happy, Harriet?'

'Not at the moment, but I will be the minute you let me go,' I replied, beginning to feel the birth of some anger towards the man.

'What if I never let you go? Do you think you could ever find happiness within these four walls?'

'Don't be fucking daft.'

'Matt told me that you don't really like his cat,' he said as he picked Monson up and placed him on his stomach. 'Would you like me to kill him for you? Would that make you happy?'

'Stop being weird,' I replied.

'Why did you walk out on him? Was it his laziness, or did you just get bored with him? I know it can't be because of another woman; the sap is far too dedicated to you.'

'None of your business. Just let me go. Listen, my head is really hurting. I feel sick. I need to go to hospital.'

He didn't reply – just stared at me with a sly grin on his face as he continued to stroke the cat and drink his wine.

297

'Where would he be without you, Harriet? I don't think he could cope with life on his own. He's such a superficial type; nothing solid about him at all – apart, of course, from his relationship with you. Do you think he would fall apart without you?'

'Well, he seems to be doing okay without me at the moment. Just tell me what you intend to do with me.'

'I haven't decided yet. Well, maybe I have, but I haven't decided whether to tell you. I'm imagining that the not knowing is very troubling to you. I know it's been troubling Matt, not knowing what your intentions are. Perhaps I am bringing the two of you towards an emotional fulcrum by leaving you both in the dark. Do you feel closer to Matt right now, this very moment, sat there with your head throbbing and tears flowing? You have a think about that while you watch me on the mat.'

He stood up, threw Monson onto the bean bag, then commenced a yoga routine on one of the mats laid out on the floor. As he bent and twisted his limbs, he never took his eyes off me. If I turned my head away from him, he would stop what he was doing and demand my attention.

'I told you to watch. You need to get used to doing as you are told. I am not Matt.'

I watched his display, detached and confused. Monson jumped onto my chair and snuggled up against my hip. Once the man completed his routine, he stood up and gave himself a round of applause before wiping himself down with a towel and topping up his glass of wine.

'Matt was shit at yoga, just not a natural athlete like me,' he said, tossing the empty bottle onto his bean bag.

'I'm glad he was shit,' I replied. 'What do you mean about Matt having something to do with you not being able to see your son?'

His face turned to anger in a flash as he leered over me and grabbed a clump of hair at the back of my head.

'Don't fucking mention my son,' he barked, pulling my head sharply backwards and making me scream out in pain.

'I'm sorry. I'm sorry,' I whimpered.

He grabbed Monson off my lap and returned to his bean bag. His eyes were full of hate and I sensed that he was fighting a strong urge to cause me more physical harm.

42

PUT THE CAT DOWN

I put on my green puffa, picked up the long shoe and headed out into the corridor. I knocked on Hot Dog's door to return the shoe and to tell him I believed Harriet was being held at Hamper's yoga studio, but there was no reply, so I got into the lift and made my way out of the building. It was a five-minute walk, but if I ran I reckoned I could be there in a couple of minutes. I broke into a jog. Although suitable for light outdoor use, my slipper shoes were useless when it came to absorbing the impact of my feet on the hard paving stones. I switched to a fast walk/waddle. There was an energy within me that propelled me at a decent lick. My breathing was heavy but regular. My mind was focused. My heart was bursting with the desire to see Harriet.

As I made my way around the back of the church, I stopped to search for something that might be used as a weapon, should the need arise. I fumbled around in the dark, finding various beer cans and bottles, a traffic cone, some old washing line and a blue washing bowl with a plastic crab and a pair of underpants inside it. Against the church wall I spotted a large lump of sandstone with a short piece of wrought-iron railing embedded in it. I bent down and grasped it by the railing but could barely lift it above waist level. It was too heavy. What about the long shoe? The ashtray fixed inside the foot opening was made of onyx and had a decent weight about it. I tried it out with a swipe of my arm and discovered the length of the shoe did give it a hell of a swoosh. It would have to do.

I approached the door to the studio, utilizing a slight crouch and holding the long shoe by its toe in readiness to swing it if Hamper should make a run at me. I took a pause to prepare myself. My breathing was still heavy despite my stillness and was showing no sign of calming. I hadn't thought this through; I should have phoned the police. A quick pat of my pockets revealed this was no longer an option. I had left my phone back in the flat.

I turned the door handle, took a step inside, and shut the door silently behind me. The little vestibule was dark, but from the light seeping around the studio door I could just make out that it was filled with bags and boxes of the Hamper's possessions. On top of one of the boxes was Monson's cat carrier. I thought I caught a whiff of Harriet's perfume but it could have just been some lingering very essential oils in the air. I heard a snippet of the Hamper speaking inside the studio and the sound of a lady trying to suppress her tears. Two more steps and I would be at the open door of the studio. It was time to make my move; I gripped the point of the long shoe even more tightly and took my place in the doorway. Harriet was sitting on a chair facing away from me, one of her arms outstretched awkwardly to her side. Around her wrist was a pink yoga band tethering her to a radiator. Hamper was crouched on a bean bag, cradling Monson against his chest.

The sight of Harriet so bedraggled and vulnerable stopped me in my tracks. Her hair was tangled and matted and her shoulders shivering with fear. At least she was alive. I wanted to rush over to her and hold her in my arms from that moment and forever, but the sight of her in such danger led me to caution. Maybe I could talk my way out of this.

'Hi, folks,' I said.

'What the fuck!' blurted Hamper, leaping up off his perch with Monson still clutched in his arms. 'You come for your cat, have you?'

'Yes, and Harriet.'

'Matt!' shouted Harriet. 'Call the police! He's fucking insane!'

She went as if to get up but was stopped by the band tying her wrist to the radiator.

'I already have,' I replied. 'Listen, Justin, I don't want any trouble—'

'Too late for that,' he interrupted. 'I think we are all in big trouble whether you want it or not.'

'Can you put the cat down and untie Harriet so that we can talk?' I asked.

'Not a chance,' he replied, tightening his grip around Monson and causing him to let out a plaintive meow.

I didn't know how to respond.

'Who even is this bloke?' asked Harriet. 'He says he's your yoga teacher and you've stopped him seeing his kid and his girlfriend and that you're living at Satsuma Heights. What the fuck has been going on, Matt?'

'Well, this will be interesting,' said Hamper. 'What's your answer going to be? I can't wait.'

Hamper sank back down into the bean bag with Monson still pressed into his chest.

'Let the cat go,' I demanded, surprising myself with the authenticity of my tone.

'Or what?' he replied. 'You going to come at me with that thing in your hand? What even is it?'

'It's a shoe, a long shoe.'

'Fucking hell, Harriet,' he said. 'That's how much he thinks of you, coming equipped with a novelty shoe.'

'It's a *long* shoe,' I replied with a hint of pride. 'With a big lump of onyx at one end. If I have to fight you, Justin, it is a fight that you will lose.' I didn't believe in that outcome for a moment, but maybe Hamper would be swayed by my bravado.

He wasn't. He laughed and squeezed down more tightly on Monson's chest. The poor boy was beginning to squirm and caterwaul, obviously in distress. I raised the shoe up to my side and took a step forward. Hamper stood up and in the same movement threw Monson directly at me. Monson bounced off my free arm and ran out of the studio into the vestibule. Before I could take another step, Hamper was on me, crashing me against the doorway and then throwing me on my stomach on the concrete floor. I tried to get up, but the weight of him straddling my back was too much. I huffed and strained but the energy drained out of me as fast as a toilet flush. I became still as he forced my face into the floor with his arm on the back of my neck. It was hard to breathe and I desperately needed air. It was a fight I had lost.

'Get off him!' shouted Harriet.

Hamper released the pressure on my head. I sucked in big gulps of air as he dragged me across the floor and deposited me onto the vacant bean bag. I still had the long shoe in my hand. He crouched above me, hands on knees, breathing heavily from the exertions of his victory.

'Give me the shoe,' he demanded.

'What's your plan here?' I asked as I handed it over to him.

'I want you to suffer for what you have done and that's as far as the plan goes at the moment. I'm making it up as I go along – that's how people like you live your lives, so why not me for once? I went back to Satsuma Heights with the intention of hurting you, but you weren't there. Luckily for me, your cat was, and I know how much he means to you. I took the cat to your old address hoping that Harriet might be at home. If you really want to hurt someone, then you should hurt the ones they love.'

'But someone else is living there now,' I interrupted.

'What the fuck?' said Harriet.

'Oh, that's fun,' continued Hamper. 'I just assumed she had thrown you out to get on with her life without the weight of you around her neck. Seems I got doubly lucky then, because when I arrived she was laid out ready for collection on the doorstep.'

'And my neighbour Carol was by her side, and she can identify you,' I said.

'Carol,' said Harriet. 'I should have known she would be fucking involved – and he didn't just find me. He smacked me on the back of my head with a rock or something.'

'No, I didn't,' said Hamper.

'Yes, you fucking did,' said Harriet, 'and that's what I'll tell the police when they arrive.'

'I'm not so sure they're coming. Let's find out.'

43

HARRIET

When Matt appeared in the doorway, my first instinct was to make sure he was safe, which is why I told him to leave and get the police. In the moment, that was all that mattered to me. But he didn't move. He was holding some sort of clown shoe in his hand and even in my distress I thought how appropriate a prop it was.

He tried his best to be firm and authoritative with my captor but I could tell that he was absolutely shitting himself. It was physically a very uneven match. I hoped he wouldn't try to be a hero. It soon became clear from their conversation that Matt knew this guy. My heart sank. Could he – 'Justin', Matt had called him – have been telling me the truth? There was obviously something going on here to which I was not fully privy. The situation suddenly felt all the more dangerous.

Matt stupidly made a move and Justin responded by throwing the cat at him and then wrestling him down to the ground. He began to force Matt's face into the concrete floor, and then Matt went limp. I could see that he was having trouble breathing. I felt useless. My stomach retched and my heartbeat pounded around my head. I screamed at him to stop. He dragged Matt onto a bean bag and demanded he hand over the clown shoe. He struck Matt on the side of his head with the thick end of it. It made quite a thump and Matt cried out in pain.

'Did you phone the police?' asked Justin calmly.

'Yes,' Matt replied.

'I don't believe you,' said Justin, at which point he swung the shoe, full pelt and heel first, directly onto Matt's right kneecap. Matt curled up with pain, holding one hand out towards the man in an effort to fend off another blow.

'Did you phone the police?' he asked, bending down and spitting the words directly into Matt's face.

'Yes,' said Matt through gritted teeth. 'You should leave.'

'I don't believe you,' Justin said again, this time taking a couple of steps towards me. 'Where shall I hit her, Matt?' he asked, raising the shoe above his head. 'I'm thinking the chin, but maybe you have a preference, and I'm happy to oblige if it's appropriate.'

Matt didn't reply. Justin lifted the shoe even higher and was about to bring it down on my head, so I wrapped my free arm around my face and squeezed my eyes closed.

'I didn't!' shouted Matt just before impact. 'I didn't call the police. Please leave her alone.'

Justin feigned a laugh and lowered the shoe to his side.

'I thought as much,' he said. 'You might be lying to save her the pain, but my guess is that you're not. We're too far in for it to really matter, anyway.'

Matt stared me straight in the face, his expression pleading for forgiveness. I forced a smile onto my face and he returned the gesture.

It felt like an apology. It felt like a goodbye.

44

MATT

Hamper seemed to relax once I'd admitted that I hadn't contacted the police, and I sensed that the immediate threat of violence had passed. My only thought now was how to get Harriet out of this situation unharmed. I had to talk Hamper down. I needed to placate him and convince him that he and I were on the same side. He tossed the long shoe behind him, took off his T-shirt and sat on a yoga mat in the centre of the studio.

'You do realize,' my pitch began, 'that your real problem here is Laurence, not me. And certainly not Harriet.'

'Shut the fuck up. I need to clear my mind, seek clarity, unburden myself from the moment, manifest some precision.'

'No, you don't,' said Harriet, 'you need to let us go.'

'Another word from you,' said Hamper, 'and I will open up that cut on the back of your head and let you bleed out in front of your pointless boyfriend.'

I wanted to divert his attention away from Harriet. Get him talking, try and calm him down, make him realize that I was not to blame for his situation.

'I'm sorry things haven't worked out with Kiara,' I said. 'But I don't understand what I have to do with it ending.'

'It's all your fault! You told Laurence you saw a video of her in her flat with a man – that was me. Laurence is in love with her and he's a very jealous man. He won't let me within a mile of her now. Your spying sealed my fate.'

'I didn't know it was you in the footage. Honestly, I never mentioned your name to Laurence.'

'Well he's interrogated Kiara and now he knows everything – thanks to you. Now, stop your denials. It's affecting my symmetry.'

Hamper removed a phial of the most essential oil from his tracksuit pocket and rubbed some onto his hairless chest. Then he closed his eyes tightly and indulged in some performative deep breathing. When he was finished, he stared intently at Harriet as if some unexpected revelation had been injected into the front of his mind.

'You didn't answer me earlier. There is a reason for that, I think. He never actually asked you if you were happy during your time together, did he?'

She didn't reply.

'Did he?!' shouted Hamper, making both Harriet and me jump.

'I thought I wasn't meant to speak,' said Harriet.

'You can speak when you are spoken to. Answer the question,' barked Hamper.

'That's none of your business,' said Harriet.

'Oh, yes it is. You see, I'm beginning to wonder if he sees

any value in you at all. Maybe there isn't the equivalence I'm looking for here. You know, between my relationship with my son and Kiara and his relationship with you.'

'He didn't have to ask me,' said Harriet. 'If I wasn't happy, I would have left.'

'But you did leave, didn't you?' said Hamper, with a satisfied smirk on his face.

'We all need a bit of space sometimes. It's no big deal.'

'Yes, and there is going to be a lot of space between myself and my son because of him, and that *is* a big deal.'

Hamper turned himself onto his stomach and raised his head and chest off the floor.

'What's this pose called, Matt? It's the first one I taught you.'

'The Cobra, I think.'

'Yes, and the cobra is a snake, isn't it, Matt? How fitting that you remembered its name so quickly.'

He adjusted his pose to the one where you sit with your knees crossed over each other.

'Do you want to say sorry to me, Matt? Is that something you would like to do?'

'Sorry for what, Justin? I'm still not sure what it is you think I've done.'

It was a risky question that I instantly regretted. It was bound to raise his anger levels. I needed to backtrack and qualify.

'I mean, of course I'm sorry about Callum, and I'm sorry about you losing your flat, and if there is anything I can do to help, then I'm here for you. What's happened tonight doesn't change that.'

311

He didn't respond, just stared at me with contempt and began to chew at the inside of his cheek. I sensed violence building up inside him.

'Are you going to tell Harriet about the cameras or shall I?'

A cascade of regret washed through my body. This line of questioning needed to end. If Harriet found out about the surveillance, she would never forgive me. Hamper looked vulnerable sat on the floor with his knees all tied in a knot, so I launched myself on top of him and grabbed him around his neck in an attempt at a chokehold. My arms locked for a moment but he quickly pulled them loose and swung me round so that he was straddling my stomach. He placed both of his hands around my neck and began to squeeze. I reached a hand up towards his neck but he brushed it away and landed a fist flush on my jaw. The fight inside me was gone. I locked my eyes on his as if daring him to extinguish them. My chest started to tighten and convulse. I tasted blood in my mouth and my vision began to blur.

I could hear Harriet screaming, but her words seemed far away, like she was shouting from inside a distant pudding.

Please let this be quick. Please let this be quick.

I wanted to plead with him to spare Harriet but the words would not form in my mouth. Everything went dark. I was no longer in any pain. I was moving upwards inside a huge tunnel of exquisitely trimmed yew hedge. Far above me was the exit, and beyond, a cloudless blue sky. A magnet powered by joy was pulling me upwards. I had never felt so happy or loved before. My life had been worth it just for this moment.

45

HARRIET

Matt made a terrible mistake. Instead of continuing to engage Justin in conversation, he leapt on him and tried to choke him out. He failed miserably. Justin soon turned him over, got on top, and began to strangle him. I screamed for them both to stop, but the screams soon turned to breathless wheezes as fear consumed my body. I could see that Matt had given up the fight and the man had no intention of stopping.

At that moment, Monson bolted into the room and dived behind my bean bag. I heard a roar coming from the vestibule and a giant of a man entered the studio wearing a balaclava. I recoiled from the shock of his entrance, assuming he was part of Justin's plans. I was wrong.

When he heard the commotion, Justin released his grip and raised his head towards the intruder. Before he had time to react, the balaclava man had picked up the long shoe and swung it with perfect pace and accuracy at the side of Justin's face.

He was knocked out stone cold and lay twitching on the floor beside Matt, who was now perfectly still and lifeless. The balaclava man began to walk towards me and I wondered if I was next in line for a dose of his brutality. He bent down and placed his head next to mine.

'You're alright now, Harriet. It's okay, just be quiet.'

Then he untied me and helped me up off the chair. I wanted to drop on the floor and be beside Matt, but he held onto me tightly and walked me outside the studio. I took a glance down at Matt as I passed and the sight of his stillness made me retch.

'Get some fresh air, love,' he said. 'Don't worry, I'll look after him.'

46

MATT

When I came round, I saw the body of Hamper laid on the floor a couple of feet away from me. There was blood on the side of his face. It was hard to tell whether he was still breathing. I turned my head away just as someone bent over me to speak. They were removing a balaclava from their face. It was Hot Dog. I was in the yoga studio, and I was alive.

'You okay, Jigsaw?'

'I don't know, I think so. How the fuck did you know I was here?'

'Me and Laurence had a watch of you on the camera when you went back to your flat.'

'He said there wasn't a camera in my flat.'

'Of course there is.'

'Where is it?'

'What does it even matter? Anyway, we heard you mention on the phone to someone that Hamper had taken Harriet. We knew he was living here so Laurence told me to come and sort it. Sorry I took my time.'

'Is Harriet okay?'

'She seems it. Why don't you step outside and ask her?'

Hot Dog helped me up and we checked that I was steady on my feet. I felt a bit sickly and lightheaded but not enough to stop me getting to Harriet.

'You done good, Jigsaw. There's more to you than meets the eye,' he said. 'Are you sure you're stable?'

'Yeah, I reckon.'

'I've got to get out of here. Laurence phoned the police, so I need to make myself scarce. Don't worry about the cameras; they'll be gone by the time you get back to the Heights.'

I heard police sirens in the near distance and felt a wave of relief knowing that this whole thing would soon be over.

'Good luck,' he said. 'Don't be ashamed of being a pipsqueak. Truth is, I often wish I was one myself.'

I spotted Monson behind the bean bag. I called him and he slowly emerged and came to me. I swept him up, gave him a kiss and then gently placed him in the cat carrier.

'Could you take him back for me?' I asked Hot Dog.

'Sure thing,' he said.

And with that, he gave me a big old bear hug, put on his balaclava, picked up the cat carrier, ran out of the studio and away through the churchyard into the night.

When I got outside, Harriet was leaning against the wall shaking through the cold and the shock of everything. I took her in my arms and hugged her, my guts full of relief and hope. I had no idea what to say, and I sensed she felt the same. Eventually we released our hold and stared into each other's eyes.

'I love you,' I said.

'I know,' she replied.

'Are you happy?' I asked.

'Not at the moment,' she replied.

'Then I'll have to do something about that.'

'You can start by telling me what the fuck has been going on.'

She hugged me again. It was going to be okay. A thousand delighted moths flapped their wings inside me, then nestled in my heart.

47

RANSOM AND HILLIARD

I was lucky. Laurence sorted everything – removed all evidence of the cameras and provided the Hamper with an expensive solicitor. He was at the police station only twenty minutes after we arrived. A deal was reached between them whereby the Hamper would say nothing about the cameras and in return would be given a flat in another of Laurence's developments, where he would be free to have access to his son. The Hamper would plead guilty to assault and get the best legal representation available. He had a clean record and a very good chance of receiving a non-custodial or short prison sentence.*

Harriet simply told the story as it happened. She was hit on the head and woke up in a yoga studio, tied to a radiator by a man she had never seen in her life. She could not say for certain that Hamper was the one who had struck her, but it

---

* He was eventually given an eighteen-month suspended sentence, leaving him free to enjoy his rent-free apartment in Hackney, courtesy of Laurence Moody. His son now stays there with him every other weekend.

seemed the most likely explanation. A stranger in a balaclava had rescued us.

I gave a 'no comment' interview, thereby declining to accuse Hamper of assaulting me.

Harriet and I were released from the station a few hours later. As we walked hand in hand back to Satsuma Heights, she told me that she had been staying at her parents' boat house in the Lake District. She admitted her suspicions regarding Carol and her doubts about whether I was a serious enough person for her to commit to me. Luckily for me, she had decided that I was.

'I realized while I was away,' she said, 'that the one thing you are serious about is making me happy. Now, I know that might have its downside, and you do get on my tits from time to time, but it's a bloody good starting point and a gift I've never had before and am unlikely to be given again.'

She hadn't mentioned her surveillance operation. 'What was the deal with you having me watched by Catherine, the waitress from the park café?'

'How do you know about that?'

'She told me. We're good friends now. She works in the Horseshoe pub next to Satsuma Heights. She's been wanting to give you her final report confirming my innocence but, like everyone else, she hasn't been able to get in touch with you.'

'I'm sorry. Could we just not talk about that?'

'Of course. All's well that ends well – and I've got a bit of a confession to make regarding surveillance as well.'

I told her the whole story from the first contact with

Kiara to my pathetic burglary attempt on Laurence's pent-house. I kept Hot Dog out of the story. I had promised him I would never give his game away, and after he had probably saved our lives last night, I felt I owed it to him to keep that promise.

I had assumed that Laurence Moody was the one being prosecuted in the big deal trial that Harriet had been working on these last months, but it turns out, she had never even heard of him.

She clearly found it all too much to take in at once. I answered all her questions as best as I could, and she didn't let up until we walked into flat 5A.

'You did it all for this?' she asked, faking indifference, but barely able to conceal her excitement.

'No, I did it all for *you*,' I replied as I let Monson out of his carrier and gave him a hug.

'You could have got into serious trouble,' said Harriet.

'Yeah, well, I did, and I reckon it was worth it.'

'Does it have a bath?'

'Yeah, a Ransom and Hilliard.'

'That will do me.'

After we had both taken a dip in the powdered marble tub, we went to bed, exhausted.

I woke up before Harriet, so rolled out of the bed without disturbing her, put on a dressing gown and went to the store cupboard. The computer, laptop and monitors had all gone. The print of the business duck remained on the wall to maintain a touch of quack about the room.

As I walked back to my flat, I noticed that Hot Dog's door was slightly ajar. After knocking with no reply, I shouted his name into the room. Nothing. I took a peek inside and, from the pristine state of the place, it was instantly apparent that he was no longer living there. The flat was empty, and I noticed that the smoke alarm had been removed from above the doorway. I looked around, and saw the only shred of evidence that Hot Dog had ever been here at all: the long shoe, sitting, resplendent, on the coffee table. It had a note attached.

For Jigsaw. Keep quiet and let's never meet
again. P.S. I left a present on your sink.

Back at my kitchen island, I put the long shoe on the surface and saw a small electrical device on the draining board. I assumed it was a camera. Next to it was the head of the swan that topped the sink's mixer taps. It had a hole where one of its eyes should have been. I had to applaud Laurence for his guile. I had been staring at that swan's face every day and hadn't spotted anything untoward.

I checked my phone and saw I'd received an email from Kiara.

Hi Matt Giles,

My client is very impressed with the discretion and loyalty you have displayed concerning last night's events. He would be most pleased if you would continue your tenancy on the same terms but with no obligations regarding employment. There will be a rent review in twelve months, but my client has instructed me not to be too hostile. He does very much appreciate having a reliable presence on site. Any concerns, please address them to me.

Kiara (Lansdowne Estates)

I would discuss the offer with Harriet, but I knew she would be happy to stay and make Satsuma Heights our home. I turned the handle on my peculiar plate and its little tune started to play. Monson jumped up onto my lap.

'You haven't said anything about that motorcycle event,' I said.

'Nah, I've gone off the idea. I just want peace and quiet. You know, a nice, uneventful life.'

'Good lad. Me too.'

'What's this piece of shit, boss?' he asked.

'Just something quirky I bought.'

'You don't need a quirk to be quirky,' he replied.

'That is excellent advice and I shall take it on board.'

I picked up the plate and the long shoe and threw them in the bin.

When Harriet got up, we decided to treat ourselves to breakfast at the Horseshoe Inn. When we arrived, Catherine was behind the bar. Harriet went over to order two coffees and I took a seat at Hot Dog's favourite table. They chatted for a while before Harriet joined me at the table.

'She's still keeping her eye on you,' said Harriet.

'I know, and it doesn't bother me one bit. Did she confirm my not-guilty verdict?'

'She did.'

Catherine came over with the coffees and the breakfast menu.

'No hard feelings, I hope,' she said, offering her fist up for it to be 'bumped'.

It's an unfamiliar ceremony for me and in the panic of the moment I grasped her fist in my hand like I was the paper to her rock.

'Weird,' she said.

'Sorry,' I replied as I withdrew my grip on her fist.

'Your darts mate not coming in today? From what I saw, it was more likely that you were having an affair with him rather than any lady.'

'Not sure,' I said vaguely. 'Told me he was moving away from the area.'

I knew deep down that Hot Dog wouldn't be coming to the Horseshoe ever again and it made me sad. I would miss him.

Catherine left us to peruse our menus.

'So, who's this darts mate?' Harriet asked.

'Just one of the regulars – kept me company whilst you were away. We just played darts and chatted shit. He liked hot dogs and hated strimmers so, you know, I was drawn to him.'

'Sounds interesting. I would have liked to have met him. Have you got any idea who that bloke in the balaclava was, by the way?' she asked, her eyes fixed on the menu. 'He saved our lives, bless him.'

'No idea, probably some homeless bloke that was sleeping in the churchyard and heard your screams.'

'Be nice to thank him.'

'I did last night, before he ran off. I'm sure he would rather just be left alone.'

'You're probably right. I still can't believe you watched those cameras in the other flats.'

'I only looked at the feeds four or five times. I'm only human. I would defy anyone not to take a peek, and it wasn't me that passed on the information about Hamper's son to Laurence. I'm not to blame for what happened.'

'It's still wrong. People are entitled to their privacy. Promise me you won't do anything so stupid again.'

'I promise – absolutely and without my usual hesitation. You decided what you want to eat?' I asked.

'No, not yet, although it will involve bacon.'

She placed the menu on the table and looked at me with a pleasant, mischievous look in her eye.

'When I was at the boathouse,' she said, 'I got to thinking about your idea to live off grid and sell pepperpots to tourists.'

'It was always a strong, if overly peppery proposal, but let's be honest, you'll never leave your job.'

'Maybe I won't, but I won't leave you either.'

'Promise?'

'I do.'

We perused the menu in comfortable silence.

'Hey,' said Harriet, 'did you see that they do soft-boiled eggs with soldiers?'

'Yeah, but not for me, thanks.'

'Why not?' she said, surprised. 'You love a soft-boiled egg.'

'Truth is, I've gone right off them.'

48

CAROL

The police visited me and asked for my version of events. I told them that I hadn't seen anything much. I heard a noise outside and went out to see Harriet lying unconscious on her steps. I did everything I possibly could to make her comfortable. A man arrived and offered to take her to hospital, but I could only give them a vague description. It was dark and, in the panic of everything, nothing really registered. I told them I barely knew Harriet but nevertheless hoped with all my heart that she was okay. I never heard from them again, which was a surprise, as one of the officers clearly had the hots for me.

That tart Harriet moved into Satsuma Heights with Matt. Big mistake. The people-pleasing thing he does is just his way of controlling her. She's such a mug. One hundred per cent she will up and leave again, and I won't be there to pick up the pieces for him.

I hardly think about Matt these days and there's a very good reason for that.

About a month after my revenge attack, I had the most pleasant surprise. The house opposite me had recently sold and I watched from my window as the new couple moved in. The husband was tall, in good shape, and very obviously under the thumb of his partner. Just how I like them. She was overweight, splashy and as common as muck. No match for me. His name is David and we have been getting on like a house on fire. We even go running in the park together. I've invited them over to my house in Palm Springs. Can't wait, darlings.

ACKNOWLEDGEMENTS

Holly Harris for her support, encouragement and pleasantness.

Kat Ailes for her rigorous and compelling editing skills.

Harry Mortimer for his suggestions and detective work.

Lisa Mortimer for her smashing artwork.

Peter Bell for my new teeth.

My alliums weren't up to much this year but I thank them for their efforts.

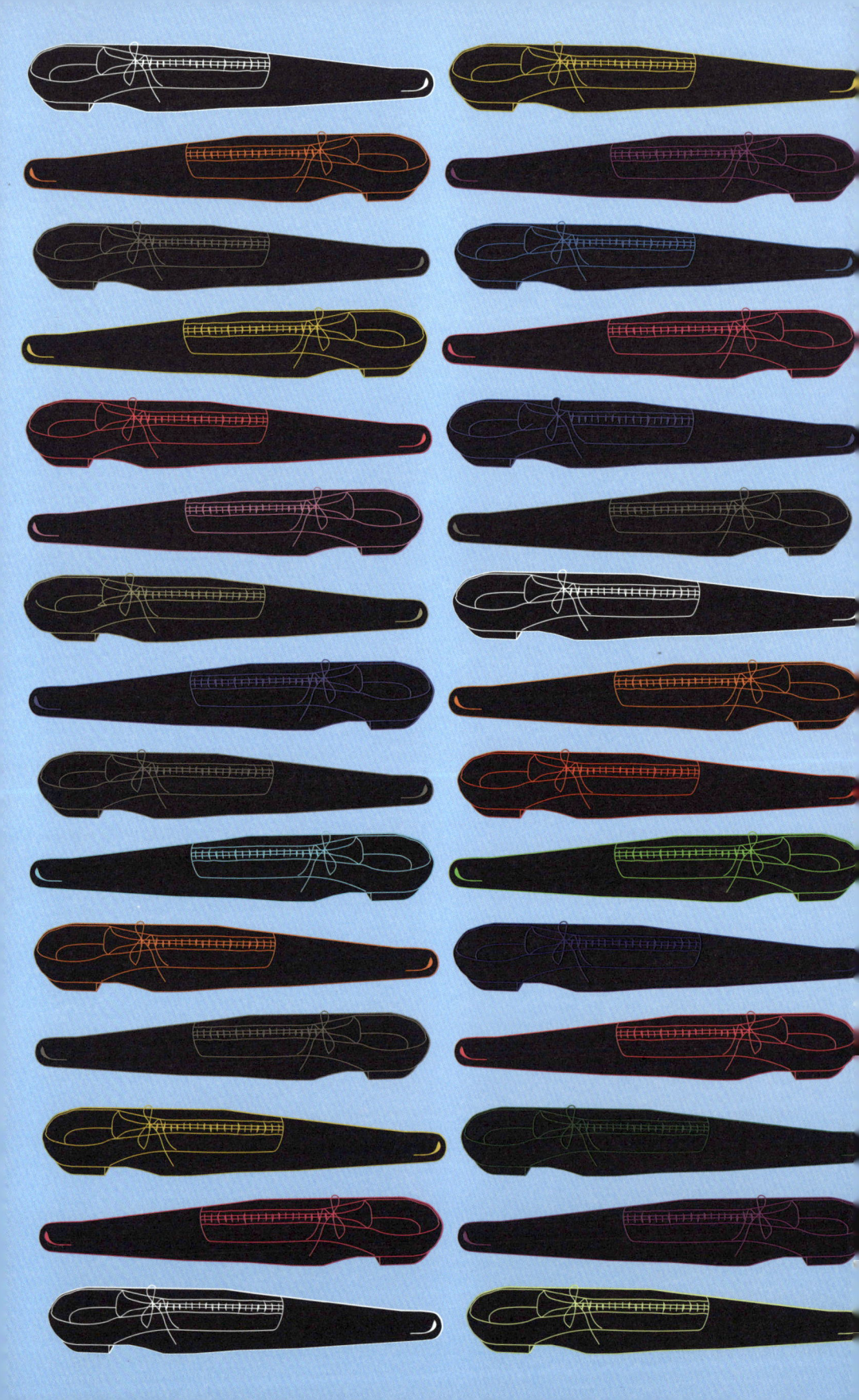